BOOKS BY MAX HENNESSY

The Lion at Sea
a trilogy comprising
The Lion at Sea
The Dangerous Years
Back to Battle

A Cavalry Trilogy
comprising
Soldier of the Queen
Blunted Lance
The Iron Stallions

An RAF Trilogy
comprising
The Bright Blue Sky
The Challenging Heights
Once More the Hawks

The Crimson Wind

MAX HENNESSY

The Crimson Wind

New York ATHENEUM *1985*

Library of Congress Cataloging in Publication Data

Hennessy, Max, —
The crimson wind.

1. Mexico—History—1910–1946—Fiction. I. Title.
PR6058.A6886C7 1985 823'.914 84-45623
ISBN 0-689-11530-X

Manufactured by Fairfield Graphics, Fairfield, Pennsylvania
First American Edition

To my son, Max
who drove with me across Mexico

Author's Note

This book is not meant to be history but fiction based on fact. But, since so much that has been offered as fact on the Mexican Revolution turns out on examination to be largely fiction, anyway, it doesn't seem to matter. Rebel leaders, in particular, seem to have suffered too much from the attention of over-imaginative writers but, as Renato Leduc, the distinguished Mexican journalist who was with Pancho Villa's army, said, a lot that was written about the revolution was a 'sordid, apocryphal and terrifying picture that was invented . . . by the mercenary publicity and information agencies of the capitalist magnates' who stood to lose by the revolution's success.

Part One

1

'You speak Spanish, don't you, Marquis?'

Harley Marquis looked at his editor warily. George Sproat was a large florid-faced man, one of the new twentieth century editors who had eschewed nineteenth century elegance of style, both in himself and in his columns, for bluntness and the sort of language everybody could understand. He moved slowly and spoke slowly, but he didn't think slowly, and when there was something in his mind he needed watching.

'Yes,' Harley said cautiously. 'I do.'

There was something in the wind, he decided, because it was well known in the office of the *Courier* that his Spanish was perfect, for the simple reason that he had grown up speaking it. Why otherwise had he been sent to Spain for the 1905 elections and again in 1908 to cover the troubles in Catalonia? Besides, despite the editorial conference that had preceded his arrival, he'd noticed that nobody had been allowed to delay his entrance, and even the chief sub-editor, who always liked to hang back to further his own career with a few well-chosen words, had been pushed out considerably more hurriedly than he liked.

Sproat paused. 'Wasn't your father something important in Mexico?'

'He was a general in the army. He left Mexico in 1880. In rather a hurry.'

'Why?'

'He backed the wrong side and they have a tendency to

shoot political opponents who lose. Fortunately, he was not without money.'

'Married Florence Harley, Sir Henry Harley's daughter. Am I right?'

'You are.'

'And you're the result. Lázaro Harley Marquis. British by birth if not by instinct.' Sproat made it sound like an insult. 'You were in the army yourself, weren't you? The British army.'

'I resigned in 1902 after the war in South Africa. We didn't see eye to eye.'

Sproat grinned. 'I thought perhaps you'd pinched the mess funds.' He paused. 'You'll know about war then? What did you think of the fighting in South Africa?'

'It was a mess.'

'And the army?'

'A gentleman's club operating a small team of high quality marksmen.'

Sproat's smile came again. 'Ever been to Mexico yourself?'

'No.'

'There's something brewing there.'

'I'm not surprised,' Harley agreed. 'Porfirio Díaz announced as long ago as 1908 that he intended to step down when his seventh term as president ended. In Mexico that usually means the contenders for the job start shooting. Since he's gone back on the statement and got himself re-elected, they've started. However, nobody will worry much. Mexicans regard civil war not as a calamity but as a natural state of affairs.'

Sproat grunted. 'Remember that piece you wrote for me about Mexico?'

Harley remembered it well. He'd given it all he'd got. How the Mexicans had decided in 1810 to throw off the Spanish yoke, had resisted under Juárez an attempt by the French to impose on them as emperor the pathetic Maximilian of Austria, whom – as they did with most people they disagreed with – they'd shot. How, in 1876 with the aid of the army, Díaz had made himself president. It had everything in it and was good – Harley had known it was good – but it had never been published and he was beginning now to see why.

'I liked it,' Sproat said again. 'But what's wrong with

Díaz? Most countries of the world seem to regard him with enthusiasm. After three dozen assorted rulers in the fifty-five years since independence, Mexico needed peace and Díaz gave it them. If nothing else, he's given them stability.'

'Pan o palo,' Harley said.

'What's that?'

'Do as you're told and you get the rewards. Otherwise, the big stick. His supporters made fortunes from the concessions he gave them, so that his generals decided it was more profitable to support him than oppose him. Unfortunately they don't seem to have considered the Indians.'

'Are the Indians important?'

'The Indians think so. Mexico's ninety per cent mixed Indian and white blood – what they call mestizo – with, at the top, a small proportion of pure Spanish and, at the bottom, a small proportion of pure Indian. But if Mexicans aren't all *wholly* Indian they nearly all have Indian blood in them and that means they have a certain amount of thunder in their veins and a great disregard for death, either their own or anybody else's.'

Sproat gestured. 'This is your father talking. What do they want, for God's sake? Mexican bonds are high on the stock exchange. With the Americans, we've provided them with railways, oil wells, textile and canned meat factories, a harbour at Veracruz. Lord Morne alone invested a fortune. So did Lord Cowdray.'

'From which they've picked up several more. And their profits don't stay in Mexico.' Harley smiled. 'It bothers the Mexicans.'

Sproat's gesture this time was irritated. 'Anyway, isn't the trouble already over?'

'I doubt it. When Díaz announced that he wanted to step down, it was for foreign consumption only. Unfortunately, it turned up in the Mexican papers, too, and when he got himself re-elected after all – without doubt fraudulently – the objections increased to the point of rebellion.'

'This chap, Madero, who's making all the fuss.' Sproat looked at a paper on his desk. 'Francisco Indalecio Madero. They seem to think he's Christ come again. What do you know of him?'

Harley shrugged. 'When he objected to Díaz's eighth term,

he was put in gaol. But he escaped to Texas and he's now raising opposition near the Tex-Mex border. He seems finally to have come to the conclusion that the only way to dislodge Díaz from his perch is to *kick* him off.'

Sproat picked up another sheet of paper from his desk and studied it. 'Knowles, our man in Mexico City, doesn't think he'll pull it off. He says the Científicos are well in control. Who are the Científicos?'

'They believe in white domination.'

'A political party?'

'They don't believe in political parties.'

As Sproat picked up a file, Harley saw his name on it: Lázaro Harley Marquis. Marquis a corruption of Márquez, Lázaro for his father, Harley for his mother. Sproat had known everything there was to know about him all the time.

'Married?' he asked.

'You know I'm not.'

Sproat looked up over the file. 'Most people in this office address me as "sir",' he pointed out. 'Why don't you?'

'I said "sir" to too many damn fools in the army. I swore I never would again.'

Sproat's face moved, almost as if he were smiling. 'Is there a girl?'

Harley paused. Isobel Hartnell was angling for him. Her family knew his background but approved of the fact that the foreign blood in his veins was Spanish not Indian and that his father had built up a substantial fortune in England to replace the one he'd had to leave behind in Mexico. He hesitated only a moment.

'No,' he said. 'There's no one.'

'Can you use a camera?' Sproat went on.

'Everybody can use a camera these days.'

Sproat snorted. 'I sometimes think the cameramen this newspaper employs can't,' he growled. 'Ride?'

'I've ridden since I was five.'

'Know much about Mexico?'

'I've listened to my father.'

'Is *he* going to help?'

'He'd like to but he's too old, too married and, after thirty years here, too English.'

'In that case, you'd better go in his place.'

Harley said nothing. Why, he wondered. Was he being promoted? Had he shown some special skill? Sproat put him right.

'There's nobody else,' he said ruminatively. 'Gorman's covering the Balkans. There's going to be trouble there. Eldridge's in North Africa. It only leaves you.'

'I thought the El Paso papers covered Northern Mexico for us. Why can't they now?'

Sproat smiled. 'Because American newspapermen who can't get facts have a tendency to make them up. An El Pasogram has to be seen to be believed. One correspondent says Madero's a saint. Another says he's a fool. I think it's time we knew the truth.'

'Why are we suddenly so interested in Mexico? We never have been before.'

Sproat shrugged. 'There are a lot of people in England with interests in Mexico. Lord Cowdray, for instance.'

Harley began to see daylight. 'And Lord Morne, of course.'

Lord Morne held enough shares in the *Courier* to be listened to with care when he expressed an opinion or made a suggestion. Doubtless, he considered that a knowledge of events in Mexico would help his investments there.

'He says there'll be a civil war,' Sproat pointed out.

'There probably will.'

'In that case we'd like to be first on the job. War's the best story in the world because it's the biggest. We'll insure your life in the usual way. We don't want a crusade, just a few sharp victories. It doesn't matter whose, of course, so long as there *are* some. A few acts of bravery. A touch of horror if you can find it. Readers like horror. And don't forget news is what people want, so that if we're not the first we don't want it.'

'Are you trying to teach me my job?'

Sproat grinned. 'Just reminding you. I did a bit of this myself once, and I know how many correspondents write their reports without going anywhere near the fighting.'

'I'll try to get myself killed.'

'Slightly injured would do.' Sproat was suddenly in a good humour. 'It would read well at the top of your column. But I doubt if you will. I gather the Mexican army's a bit of a circus. Morne was telling me of a 21-gun salute he saw them fire for Díaz. After three bangs they had to stop because the gun went up in a sheet of flame.'

'There's just one point,' Harley reminded him. 'Whose side are we on?'

'Our side,' Sproat said immediately.

'I mean whose side in Mexico.'

Sproat considered. 'As Europeans, we take the side of the Spanish who still form the basis of business and culture there. As British, we naturally favour the aristocratic and the wealthy, which also means the Spanish. As decent clean-living people with a stable administration, we favour the government and the forces of law and order. But – ' he paused, his expression unchanged ' – as a forward-looking journal, believing in the equality of the classes, we favour the oppressed who are in revolt, and as a newspaper which likes a little sensation, we'd like to know more about the people who're shooting the oppressors, so we favour them too.'

It helped a lot.

'I don't want you wasting your time in Mexico City with the politicians,' Sproat went on. 'Knowles can look after that. I want someone where the bullets are flying who knows when to duck. Knowles has always been a lobby man and he wouldn't know a gun if he saw one.' He tossed the file back on to his desk. 'You're booked via New York. You *could* go via Veracruz which is nearer to Mexico City, but I gather there's nothing very fast heading in that direction. So it's got to be New York with a train down to the border. That's where this Madero is, anyway, so you can probably pick up a lot of facts on the way. Arrange for urgent messages to be cabled via New York. Less urgent messages the same way by train and ship. You know what to do. It won't take long and we'll want you back in the spring. There's going to be trouble between Asquith and King Edward.'

Harley smiled. 'I'll need a bit of help,' he pointed out.

Sproat's head jerked up. 'It's only a little war,' he growled.

'It's not a little country. It's nearly as big as Europe.'

Sproat's eyebrows lifted. 'Is it, by God? I hadn't realized. You'll need someone to run errands and look after things then, I suppose. You'd better pick up someone there. Perhaps some American who's out of a job. It'll cost us less.'

2

By the time he reached El Paso, Harley was beginning to think it might have been better after all to go to Veracruz. It was a long way from New York through none too exciting countryside and there wasn't much to do on the train except talk, eat and drink warm beer laced with lemonade. The conductor had a suite with a bath where, for a consideration, it was possible to wash off the dust before retiring to the conductor's compartment to drink his whisky until the train stopped at a convenient halt where Harley could walk back along the track to his carriage. But at least it gave him plenty of time to exchange ideas.

'It's all those oil companies down there,' one of his fellow travellers insisted. 'Standard Oil supports Madero. That English guy, Cowdray, supports Díaz. As for Madero – the guy's a crank. Known when he was young as Loco Franco – Mad Frank. They say he holds seances with his wife to tell him what to do. He's no guy to run a country.'

If nothing else, the delay in reaching the border meant that Harley learned a great deal and, even better, by the time he arrived, events further south had come together a little. The indeterminate hostility to President Díaz had taken the form of an armed rising.

El Paso was a clean bustling town, in places almost Mexican in style. But what had once been a No Man's Land of border saloons, dance halls, brothels and gambling dens, populated by cowboys, filibusterers, smugglers, gunmen, rustlers, train robbers and wild women, was slowly becoming respectable. It now had a sedate psychology, with business blocks taking the place of the shanties of the frontier days. Under the weight of anti-alcohol and purity crusades, the saloons had become quieter and the gambling dives had been driven across the border. In Little Chihuahua, in the lower part of the town, which took its name from the neighbouring state in Mexico, there was a large and well-established Mexican population, which, totally indifferent to the American gospel of progress and hygiene, still followed its lazy Mexican ways of street hawking, spitting, guitar twanging and fiestas.

From his hotel room, Harley could see the International Bridge over the Rio Grande that joined the town to its Mexican neighbour, Ciudad Juárez, and at night could pick up the lights of the electric street cars marked 'Mexico' that ran across it. It was in El Paso that he collected his first news of the great storm that was gathering south of the border. A long report had been sent to him at Sproat's request by Knowles from Mexico City. Knowles had it all down on paper, as neat and tidy as Knowles himself, dry as dust but containing facts that were very different from those presented to visiting foreign dignitaries who were not allowed to look closely enough to see the cracks in the Porfirian façade. Díaz's government, in fact, had become one of old men and the country lay in a straitjacket that prevented progress. With the Press under his thumb and the Church and the Legislature aligned with him, there was no liberty and little genuine justice.

El Paso was full of newspaper correspondents, mostly American but a few Europeans, too, and the air was thick with talk of scoops, hoaxes, interventions, and stories of the Balkan wars and the Messina earthquake. They were all busy equipping themselves with cases of wine and spirit, primus stoves, typewriters, tinned food, umbrellas, cameras and papers.

Aware that Mexico was high and could be cold, Harley acquired an overcoat, gloves, a South African veldt hat, a Norfolk jacket, a Webley 45 just in case, and two Yaqui cargadores to lug his kitbag and typewriter. The cable editor of the El Paso newspaper agreed to accept his telegrams and pass them on to New York for transmission to London, and he left money for cables from London to be forwarded to wherever he happened to be. The American was interested in his background. 'At least,' he said, 'you'll know something about the place. Most people in Europe think Mexico's in South America.'

He offered a run-down on the situation. 'Half the goddam country's owned by less than three thousand families,' he said. 'A lot of 'em foreigners, too. If half the good old USA was occupied by Mexicans, *I'd* be as resentful as the Mexes are. Especially if all that was left was desert or jungle as it is in Mexico.' He offered Harley a long green Mexican cigar and lit one for himself. 'If these big families did anything with their property it might help. But they spend all their time in New York, London and Paris. And the little guys who lost their land to Díaz's boys have to work under conditions that aren't much better than slavery. The poor lousy bastards are born, live and die without hope.'

'Is it going to come to civil war?' Harley asked.

'The place's like a hornet's nest. The exiles are sneaking back and the guys who come here to work learn what freedom is and go home with smuggled news-sheets. They say the trade of the peón is labour, but that for the educated mestizo there's nothing except to start a revolution.'

'What do Americans think of it?'

The newspaperman grinned and chewed at his cigar. 'The ones along the border who know what's happening are in favour. The ones up in New York who think that Mexico's somewhere south of Panama don't give a good goddam. The ones who have investments in Mexico would like to see the US take the place over.' He shrugged. 'Mebbe it'll only be a sporting affair anyway. Mebbe even a comedy revolution. Mex revolutions usually are.'

'And the revolutionaries? Where can I find them?'

'Hell, cross the border and you'll trip over 'em.'

'What about this chap, Madero?'

'Funny-looking guy. Jewish-Portuguese origin. Family's wealthy. Seems an unlikely candidate to me but you never know. At least he has sincerity and a willingness to take the lead. In my book he's no politician but they've had enough of Díaz. Go see Carranza's agent. He'll give you the dope.'

'Who's Carranza?'

'There's not just Madero in this, bo. There are guys with him who've been in politics a long time. Some have dough and want for nothing except political freedom. Venustiano Carranza's a landowner and a senator. You'll recognize him immediately. Wears blue-tinted glasses and looks like Moses come down off the mountain with the tablets of the law. Take the street car into Juárez and ask for Isídro Devoto. There's a bar called Los Emocións. You'll find him there.'

Ciudad Juárez was very different from El Paso, with muddy potholes on every corner and only dim sinister lights illuminating the dark streets at night. Occasionally, above the soft Spanish speech, there was an explosive phrase in rough cowboy English, while an automatic piano seemed to play incessantly out of sight in some cantina. Everything smelled damp, and prostitutes – both Mexican and American – waited near taverns that were loud with the noise of gambling. Yet the high sidewalks lay alongside walls painted in soft colours and the outlines of the houses were stark against a sky blazing with stars. It seemed to Harley that he'd known it for years.

He found Devoto without difficulty. He was a judge who had been forced to flee for saying what he thought of Díaz and was now earning a living as a typist. He provided letters of introduction to Carranza.

'Things are stirring,' he said. 'Before long it will be a tempest. Don Venustiano's insistent that nobody should escape. You can find Madero in San Antonio, Texas, with his brothers.'

Returning to El Paso to acquire transport, Harley had to make do with a brass-bonneted Ford. It was painted black and had a typed notice pasted to the dashboard – 'For best results this car should not be driven faster than 20 m.p.h. for the first 500 miles.'

'That don't matter at all,' the man who was offering it for sale said. 'It's already done two thousand.'

There was a carrier at the back for two spare tyres, a luggage rack on the running board, and a radiator topped with a glass-faced instrument that indicated the temperature inside the bonnet. Loading it with his equipment and the two Indian cargadores, Harley parked it outside his hotel while he went in for a meal. As he was asking at the desk for the dining-room, a girl who had been talking to the cashier turned to him.

'That your flivver out there?' she asked.

She was tall with a pale skin. She wore a brown riding habit and divided skirt, and her black hair, done in a heavy bun behind her head, was topped with a wide-brimmed Chihuahueno hat with a feather. Her eyes were a brilliant green and remarkably hostile.

'Yes,' Harley said. 'It's my flivver.'

'Are you this English lord?'

'Which English lord?'

'The Marquis of Harley.'

Harley smiled. 'You've got it wrong. That's my name not my title. I'm Harley Marquis.'

The hostility went out of her expression a little but she didn't unbend much, still ramrod straight, her eyes fixed on his face.

'This is the Señora Ojarra,' the woman behind the desk said.

The black-haired girl regarded Harley steadily. 'You're going over the border, they say,' she announced. 'To watch the fun?'

'*I* wasn't expecting it to be fun.'

'You're sure right. It won't be. You *are* English, aren't you?' It was becoming an inquisition.

'That's right.'

'I'm Irish.'

'Is that supposed to be significant?'

'My grandfather had to leave Ireland because of the English.'

Harley smiled. 'For your information, my father had to leave Mexico because of Díaz. It gives us something in common. He changed his name from Márquez.'

She stared back at him, then she gave him a grin of pure electric brilliance that transformed her face.

'We've got more than that in common,' she said. '*My* name wasn't always Ojarra. It was Mehaffey before I married. Kathleen Angelica Mahaffey. I was born in Georgia.'

'You live here? Or in Juárez?'

'Both. I've got orchards and stock near San Gabriel in Chihuahua, a gunny cloth mill here in El Paso, a coffee plantation in Cuernavaca, vanilla in Veracruz, rents and a house in Mexico City. Some I inherited, some I married. My husband's family came down here to get away from the carpetbaggers after the Civil War. We got our dough from jute, fruit and loot because my husband won the plantation in Cuernavaca gambling. He's dead now. He was killed a month after we married. His horse put its foot in a hole and broke its leg. *He* broke his neck.'

It all came out, defensive and defiant at the same time, in a breathless rush as if she had to let him know everything there was to know about her before he interrupted.

He drew a deep breath. 'Doesn't it worry you being in Mexico just now? I gather they're none too keen on foreigners with large land holdings.'

'Rats, I'm as Mexican now as they are!' she said hotly. 'And we're not big enough to worry about, anyway. You should see some spreads. We'll be okay.'

'It seems to me,' Harley said, 'that I've been talking to the wrong people. Were you about to eat?'

'Sure was.'

'Why not join me?'

She agreed enthusiastically and they found a table. 'You got a wife?' she asked as they sat down.

'Why do you ask?'

'You're old enough,' she pointed out bluntly.

'No,' he said. 'I don't have a wife. Do you have a new husband?'

She grinned at him again, the wild electric grin that lit up her face. 'There are guys who'd like to marry me but I was left a lot of dough and I'm cautious.'

'Anyone in particular?'

'Sure. One. He says he's going to join the revolution but whether that's to impress me or because he wants to make sure the revolutionaries don't set fire to his place I don't know.'

'Will it come to that?'

'It could.' She gestured. 'You'll need help. Mexico's a big country.'

'Can you suggest someone?'

'Tamsy Flood's free, I heard. He knows everybody. Landowners. Government officials. Politicians. He's worked for newspapermen before.' She glanced through the window at the Ford. 'You intending to go in that?'

'That was the general idea.'

'You'll need something bigger. The roads are terrible. You'll also need something with four legs. Do you know about horses?'

'Enough to be aware that both ends are more dangerous than the middle.'

'You'll need good ones.'

'Which, doubtless, you'll be able to sell me.'

She grinned again. 'No. But I'll tell you where to get 'em. Better than buying 'em from some shady horse-dealer you don't know. Where are you going?'

'I'm told Madero's in San Antonio and that whatever happens will start there.'

'It's started. There's been shooting in Puebla, south of Mexico City. There've been a lot killed.'

'Have you got sources of information?'

'I have business interests. They're just as good.'

'Where are the arms coming from? Who's financing them? The States?'

'Not on your life! We expect to get what we need by capturing them.'

'We? Are *you* in on it too?'

'Everybody in Mexico who's got a heart's in it. And when it starts it won't be just the *Mexicans*' revolution. A lot of other people will be interested, too.'

'They are already,' Harley said. 'Me, for one.'

3

Tamsy Flood was a small man with legs that looked as if they were bowed from too much riding, but, though he said he knew about horses, his chief claim to fame was that he knew how to handle motor cars.

'If it'll go at all,' he said. 'I'll make it.'

He had a poacher's face with blue jowls and bright bird-like yellow eyes, and Harley put his age at roughly his own. He was intelligent with the quickness and alertness of a terrier and had served in Cuba during the Spanish-American War. Since then, because he spoke Spanish and knew Chihuahua and the border country, he had acted as stringer to a variety of foreign correspondents.

'Last guy was Sam Yancey,' he pointed out. 'He got shot during the trouble at Río Blanco. But it was okay, I guess. They were aiming at the strikers.'

'He'll stick by you,' Angelica Ojarra said. 'But watch him. He sometimes gets drunk and if he does that's the last you'll see of him for days.'

If Angelica Ojarra knew Tamsy Flood's reputation, Tamsy Flood also knew Angelica Ojarra's.

'Watch her, Boss,' he advised. 'She's bad medicine. She's a great guy – rides a horse like she hates it and she's got no fear – but she's like a catherine wheel that's come loose. She's got no direction and she's always in too much of a goddam hurry.'

True to her promise, Angelica found horses, one a big chestnut with a bad temper and a tendency to kick with its near hind leg. They crossed the International Bridge to Juárez the next day to place the horses in a box car with the two Yaqui guards and the Ford behind on a flat. Despite the brilliance of the sun and the deep blue sky, empty of cloud except for the small puff balls that hung over the distant line of hills, there was a bitter wind blowing out of the north that forced Harley to put on a heavy coat and drove the Mexicans to the sunny side of the streets.

Small boys hurried through the waiting carriages, offering pink lemonade, beer, fruit and pear drops. The platform was crowded, everybody standing well away from the train because, in Mexico, if you stood too close you could be hit by orange peel, a chicken bone – sometimes a chicken carcass – tossed from one of the windows, or even by someone emptying his bronchial tubes: the Mexicans were great spitters and the Americans called the raucous clearing of throats the Mexican National Anthem.

While the Yaquis were struggling with the horses, a taxi came roaring into the forecourt and Angelica Ojarra climbed out. She was going to her property at San Gabriel and was travelling to Chihuahua City where she was to be met. She brought news.

'Madero's due to cross from San Antone into Mexico,' she said. 'His uncle's got three hundred men waiting for him and they're going to capture Piedras Niegras along the border east of here. After that, he expects them to increase in numbers all the time as they move south. They say there are rebel forces near Ceruloso.'

'Will you be safe on your own?' Harley asked.

'Sure I'll be safe. I look after my people so they look after me.' She didn't seem entirely sure, all the same. 'In some places they get treated worse than animals and the only thing they want to do is slit somebody's throat.' She shrugged. 'But I guess they're too apathetic to do much and mostly they stay where they are, ruled by the priests, the overseers, the jefe políticos and the Rurales. You seen the Rurales?'

'Not yet.'

'You sure will. Suede uniform decorated with silver. Licensed killers. Practise the ley fuga – the law of flight. It means they can shoot their prisoners and then say they were trying to escape. A few get away all the same. Villa did.'

'Who's Villa?'

'Pancho Villa. He's a bandit. He's supposed to have declared for Madero.'

The train was slow, moving down a single track to the south through bare brown country covered with low scrubby bush and cactus which changed from time to time from the maguey, from which the Mexicans made their pulque, to yucca and the huge tree-like saguaro round which the dust was whipped into flying clouds by the wind.

Harley stared from the window with hungry eyes. It was a bare brown land tawny as a lion, its mountains the knuckles of its spine, and it seemed without life, without movement, without sound. He had somehow expected Mexico to be more beautiful, more colourful, more romantic with flowers and twanging guitars. The descriptions he'd heard from his father had never mentioned the emptiness, the bitterness of the wind and the dust. But it was *his* country, the land of his fathers, and the knowledge that he was on the soil where his ancestors had trodden gave him a strange sensation of belonging.

Chihuahua City was situated in a valley under the slopes of the Sierra Madre. From the pens alongside the railway track came the smell of cattle dung and a haze of dust as bawling steers were loaded aboard the box cars. The wind was still filling the mouth and eyes with grit. Along the platform people were waiting for trains, their children sleeping at their feet on spread sarapes in whose folds the drifting dust collected. In their faces were generations of patience and suffering.

Angelica was met by a huge Stutz tourer waiting like a battleship among the rickety victorias pulled by rabbit-sized ponies. It had a klaxon, nickle-plated hubcaps, and vast headlamps built for acetylene gas but converted to electricity.

'Come and see me,' Angelica said. 'La casa de usted. My house is yours. In Mexico the house is always the visitor's, because he might turn out to be God.' There was a hint of wistfulness in her voice, almost as though she were sometimes lonely and, finding her hardboiled exterior hard to support, longed for company. Then she opened her hand and held it out. It contained a small silver medallion on a chain. 'It's a St. Christopher medal,' she said. 'The Catholic Church has a lot of useful saints. He'll take care of your travels. Wear it round your neck.'

Harley was touched by the gesture but, as the train jerked, she turned abruptly and, without looking back, headed at a brisk stride for the big automobile. As she disappeared he stared after her.

'The Ojarra hacienda, Tamsy,' he said. 'Is she right in saying it's in no danger?'

'What Angelica Ojarra says often ain't right, Boss,' Tamsy admitted. 'The fact that she looks after her people don't mean everybody feels the same about her. After all, whatever *she* says, her name's O'Hara not Ojarra because her husband's name was O'Hara. What's more she ain't Mexican, she's a gringo, and a lot of people this side of the border don't like gringos. Still an' all, I guess she's safe from Villa's boys. He once hid at San Gabriel from the police and her husband found him. Instead o' turnin' him over to the Rurales, he gave him food and a horse. Villa's never forgotten.'

The countryside seemed empty of people, though occasionally they saw a ragged old man on a donkey, plodding slowly alongside the track, and once a splendid figure on a black horse, dressed in charro costume of fine yellow leather, silver braiding on his vast sombrero.

'Could be one of Villa's boys,' Tamsy said. 'They been chasin' him for years but the people are behind him because to them he's the symbol of the freedom they ain't got, and a lot of what he steals from the big haciendas goes to the poor because he was a peón himself. They say he became a bandit because he killed a hacendado's son who raped his sister. Mebbe it's not the truth but it could be.'

Ceruloso, where Harley decided to leave the train, was well built-up in the middle but its paved streets soon gave way to white dusty outskirts whose narrow alleys were piled high with filth and inhabited by pigs, chickens and children. Round the Plaza de la Constitución in the more civilized centre, huge old jacarandas dropped their leaves into a crumbling fountain standing in a paved area in front of a magnificent baroque church. The hotel, once the home of a wealthy businessman, was a large square building among the flat-roofed shoe-box dwellings that surrounded it. In colonial style, it had a colossal tiled courtyard with palm trees and a garden wall spilling over with bougainvillea. Tamsy knew the owner and his family who lived in the downstairs rooms and brought the news that revolutionaries further along the line had sacked the town of San Jacinto.

During the evening, a band of Federal soldiers in shabby blue and red uniforms played spirited marches in the bandstand opposite their bedroom, then just before dark they heard bugles outside and the clattering of hooves. An automobile escorted by mounted men wearing the grey suede of the Rurales stopped outside the hotel and a man in a frock coat wearing the sash of the jefe político entered, followed by army officers and police. From their room they watched him pass along the corridor to a wide balcony which was obviously the place where public proclamations in Ceruloso were read. A crowd was gathering among the purple-painted public seats of the Plaza de la Constitución.

'There is no danger here from the revolution,' the jefe político announced. 'The lives and interests of everybody are secure. There has been talk – but nothing else – of trouble in Puebla and other places, but it is only rumour and everything is completely in order.'

There were shouts of angry disbelief and the official was obliged to dodge back from stones that were thrown. As the police moved forward, a few excited boys were dragged away and the band climbed back on to the bandstand and started to play again.

The following morning, finding one of the hotel maids weeping in the corner, they learned that two of the arrested boys had been shot and that one of them was her nephew.

As they set off for the jefe político's office, proclamations were being posted which stated that the boys – the proclamations referred to them as 'men' – had been executed for attempting to overthrow the government and that their 'accomplices' had been imprisoned.

'Without trial?' Harley asked.

It's always without trial under Díaz,' Tamsy said flatly.

The news of revolutionary troops in the area had brought other journalists from Chihuahua and, catching on to the fact that Harley had been an eye-witness to what had happened, they followed him closely, the whole lot eventually congregating outside the jefe político's office for a statement.

Nothing was forthcoming and there was a strange silence to the requests for information on what was happening in other parts of the country. Growing suspicious, Harley began to see the proclamations as a shoring-up of confidence more than the truth, and the shooting of the two boys as a nervous reaction to the imminence of danger.

'This is getting us nowhere, Tamsy,' he said. 'We've got to find somebody who really knows what's going on.'

'Angelica Ojarra might. She's in touch with the anti-reelectionists. I know her place. I went there for the *El Paso Times* when her husband was killed.'

From Ceruloso there was a good road running to Chihuahua and they rolled out of the town in a cloud of dust, the rear seat of the Ford filled with cans of water, oil and gasolene. As they roared through a small adobe village half the population turned out to watch, only for them to halt humiliatingly with a tyre punctured by a horseshoe nail.

The sun was brassy in a steely sky as they started again and the barrenness of the land gave way to a spiny vegetation of cactus and mesquite through which they rumbled along a straight road that climbed across the umber desolation as far as the eye could see. They passed a man driving a few lean cattle, beside the road the remains of other cattle, with more bones and dried empty hides in the little arroyos where animals had fallen and died among the rocks and cactus. The alkali dust choked them as they slogged doggedly upwards and the motormeter on the bonnet began to move from 'Good Average' to 'Higher Efficiency' and finally to 'Danger', and steam began to screech in the radiator and jet in clouds from under the bonnet. It was half an hour before they could take off the radiator cap and considerably longer before they dared add water.

'Hell,' Tamsy said. 'Mexico was never made for automobiles.'

They arrived at San Gabriel towards the end of the afternoon in a cloud of dust from which jets of steam were spurting. Though the hacienda stood in a barren area of desert, in its immediate vicinity the presence of water had produced an unexpected greenery and there were trees and even stretches of grass.

Angelica was standing in the shade of a tall eucalyptus by the corral watching her foreman sorting out calves. As the Ford arrived, she turned, her face alight with pleasure.

'I didn't think you'd come,' she said as Harley climbed down.

Tamsy was uttering murderous threats as he stalked round the Ford, kicking at the tyres. The wind had dropped completely now and the late sun was blazing down as he stared at the car with a crimson furious face.

Promising help and the loan of the Stutz, Angelica led the way into the house. It had been built originally as a monastery but had been acquired at the time of Juárez from a family which had made the mistake of supporting the Emperor Maximilian. The walls were enormously thick to keep out the summer heat and the bitter winter cold, and everything about it was as solid as a fortress. It had long corridors, vast rooms, unexpected balconies, its own small church and shop, and huge yards and outbuildings. Alongside it was the village of San Gabriel and in the distance a small group of neat white buildings.

'That's a Mormon colony,' Angelica said. 'They've been there twenty years now. They're worried that outlaws might visit them. There are plenty taking advantage of the situation to pick up anything that's lying around loose.'

The San Gabriel peóns had once been obliged to work for the hacienda but now they all had their own small patches of maize for which they gave several days work a year in lieu of rent.

'The Toral spread next door was different,' Angelica said. 'I warned them to change their habits and they did.'

'Because of the revolution?'

She grinned at him. 'No. Because Féderico Toral's the guy who wants to marry me. He's the son. Féderico Constante Toral. He runs the place. I call him Faithful Fred.'

They were still there the following day when Toral appeared in person. He was a handsome man, younger than Harley, beautifully dressed and riding a fine bay horse. Swinging from the saddle, he kissed Angelica's hand, then looked up as Harley appeared on the steps behind her.

'Who's this?' he asked in smooth suspicious Spanish. 'One of your relatives, Angelica?'

'Yes,' she said, lying cheerfully. 'Harley Marquis. Cousin by marriage. He works for a newspaper. He's English.'

Toral switched to flawless English. 'I went for three years to an English school,' he said. 'Stoneyhurst, the Jesuit College in Surrey. It's essential to learn the language when you do business with the Americans.'

'Harley came to write about Madero's revolution,' Angelica said.

Toral shrugged. 'It's over – finished before it started. Díaz issued a proclamation to be read in all the major cities. I heard it in Zacatecas. I've just come from there. He says there's no danger. You need have no fear, Angelica.'

'I never did have.'

Toral's face was expressionless. 'Díaz is a strong man.'

'He goddam must be,' she snapped. 'To stay in power for thirty years.'

'The American newspapers say his régime's made civil war unattractive.' Toral seemed imperturbable. 'I think Mexico's too busy making money for Mexicans to fight each other these days. I'm wondering, in fact, if it wouldn't be tactful to send a message of congratulations to the President. A lot of important people and societies are doing so.'

'Trust you, Féderico,' Angelica said, 'to make sure your bread's buttered on both sides.'

The following day they heard that Porfirista agents and troops had raided revolutionary headquarters across the country. Hundreds of students and business and professional men had been thrust into prison or toppled into dusty graves in front of blood-splashed walls. Those who had been warned in time had taken to the hills.

It began to look as if Toral was right and the revolution *was* over before it had started. Aware that Sproat would be wanting to know what he was up to, Harley cobbled a story together. He was conscious of indulging in the age-old game of writing about something he hadn't witnessed and he made as much as he could of the shootings in Ceruloso. He sent Tamsy into Chihuahua to despatch the story north.

Tamsy returned from the telegraph office full of information.

'Madero crossed into Mexico okay, just as planned,' he said bluntly. 'But he lost his way and had to spend the night in an Indian hut. He's now back in the States.' He grinned, showing brown broken teeth. 'There was no sign of the three hundred men his uncle was supposed to bring, nor of the American guns and ammunition he'd paid for. When his uncle finally turned up, instead of three hundred men, he only had ten. Fifteen more arrived later, but he decided it wasn't enough so he crossed back into Texas without firing a shot. I brought your cable back. You'll need a rewrite.'

The next day Toral reappeared, full of smiles. 'You may go home, Señor Marquis,' he said. 'There's nothing to write about.'

'I expect you're goddam pleased,' Angelica said harshly.

'Who wants civil war?' Toral gave an elegant shrug. 'I hear Madero's decided to go to New Orleans and from there to exile in Europe.' He smiled at Harley. 'It's usual in Mexico for leaders of coups that fail and there's little else he can do. His finances are exhausted and he's reduced to one meal a day and darning his own socks.'

Toral's sources seemed impeccable, but just as news of disasters travelled quickly, so did the news of triumphs and they were still digesting what he'd said when Tamsy Flood, who had been into Chihuahua in the Stutz for a tyre for the Ford, came thundering back in a cloud of dust.

'It's not finished, Boss!' he roared as he scrambled from behind the driving wheel. 'Holy Biddy, they've kicked Díaz's troops out of San Andrés!'

'Who has?' Angelica ran on to the patio to listen.

'Villa! Pancho Villa! He drummed up five hundred men.'

'Where from?'

'Half of them were his own boys. I got it in a bar in Chihuahua. The place's going crazy. The garrison consisted of a captain and a few conscripts, most of them related to Villa's gente. They were shouting "Viva la revolución" and "Viva Madero" outside the cathedral when I left.'

'I think it's time I went back to Chihuahua,' Harley said.
Angelica was rushing round the house, collecting her possessions, as excited as he was. 'Hold your horses, kiddo,' she said. 'I'm coming too.'

4

Tamsy Flood's gift for exaggeration had run away with him. Chihuahua was not going crazy. In fact, it was subdued and wary.

Called by the Tarahumara Indians, who lived in the nearby hills, 'the place of workshops', it was the nerve centre of the area. Alongside the railroad tracks that ran to the mines, were belching chimneys and the whirr and thump of machinery. There were government troops and Rurales in the barracks there and, though the underpaid, overworked labouring classes were willing enough to support the revolution – *any* revolution – they clearly considered it wise to move carefully.

In the bars in the narrow streets round the towering brown edifice of the cathedral, however, it didn't take Tamsy long to pick up news of further successes. Guerrero had fallen to revolutionary troops commanded by a man called Orozco but nobody expected the rebels to hold on to either Guerrero or San Andrés, because they were desperately short of guns and ammunition, and troop trains were already rushing north from Mexico City. Nevertheless, their example had started further uprisings and other rebel groups were now operating in Sonora, while in southern Chihuahua State more were gathering round Parral. The long-expected revolution was under way after all.

Although the guerrilla bands were still all that Madero could raise in the way of troops, they were upsetting the government's calculations by attacking and continuing to attack. Garrisons and railroad junctions were suddenly falling to them one after another and after every successful attack the rebel numbers grew as the enthusiasm increased and the Federal soldiers changed sides.

The news threw the pressmen into complete confusion. They were a raucous hard-drinking lot who had been trying for weeks to find the fighting, taking trains back and forth to keep track of the march of events. But Mexico was a big country of scattered populations, and good stories were going begging simply because they couldn't be in two places at once. And since the attacking armies – most of them no bigger than regiments – made their thrusts out of thin air and disappeared again just as quickly, it left them all in the invidious position of not knowing a thing until it had become old hat.

It was Tamsy who once again broke the deadlock. He had paid a late visit to the telegraph office to find it empty of newspapermen but the telegraphist bursting with excitement, and he returned in a rush to where Harley was eating a late meal with Angelica Ojarra.

'It's Villa, Boss!' he said. 'Himself! He's heading for Ceruloso!'

Standing in the doorway of the hotel – the same hotel where they had listened to the mayor's proclamation – they watched the shabby cavalcade ride into the town. There were cowboys in charro suits, peóns in white cotton, men in city suits, coveralls, shirts, trousers and jerseys, but no sign of uniform beyond curling sombreros and rolled sarapes. Their horses were dusty and ungroomed but, though many of the riders wore no shoes, they all carried weapons – rifles, revolvers, machetes, knives – and were festooned with bandoliers of cartridges.

It was Harley's first sight of the revolution, of the upsurge of anger and passion, of the gathering of frustrated men determined to be free, and he recognized at once the reality of their demands, sweeping as they were. They were mostly poor men, ill-educated and worn with work, but they clutched their ill-assorted weapons with an incandescent enthusiasm, and in their eyes was a light of expectation and anticipation as if they'd seen a goal they'd dreamed of for years but never expected to experience. It seemed to carry the stumbling horses and shuffling men forward as if they were tireless.

Following them were their women, brown, swarthy figures carrying food and cooking utensils on their backs, their children clinging to their skirts. A few of them rode horses and some, with long feathers in their hats, even carried rifles and wore bandoliers of ammunition. And they were all – every single one of them – excited by their success, people who had nothing to lose but their lives and for whom anything gained could only be an improvement in their lot. With them they brought a strong smell of sweat, dust, gun oil and horses.

Already the rebel soldiers were whooping through the town and there were shots, drunken yells of 'Viva la Revolución,' the crashing of glass, the slamming of doors, shouts of laughter and the screams of women. In the zócalo, the main square, the captured Federal military band, wild-eyed and shaking with fear, were playing a lively version of *La Paloma*, rebel rifles pointed at their heads to make sure they did it properly, one of them who had been a little slow stretched, stone-dead and bloody, on the ground in front of them as a reminder.

Round the corner was a car that had been shot up, dripping blood like a slaughtered bull. It contained three corpses and was surrounded by silent gaping people. Then, as more yelling came from down the street, they saw a group of armed men dragging the jefe político and what appeared to be all his male relations and officials and a group of hatless Federal officers. As they approached, a grinning figure appeared from his office with a large portrait of Díaz, and smashed it down over the jefe político's head so that the wretched man fell to his knees, his spectacles crooked, the picture round his shoulders like a huge square collar. Pieces of glass were sticking in his cheeks and his eyes rolled with pain and terror. Hauled to his feet again, he was dragged away still wearing the frame round his neck like some tragicomic character from a play. He could hardly stand as the armed men shoved him from one to another.

'They're going to kill them!' The voice was Angelica's and, swinging round, Harley saw her face was shocked and white.

He gestured at Tamsy. 'Get her away from here,' he said sharply. 'Upstairs. And keep the door locked until the thing dies down a bit.'

Round the square a rough circle of conical-hatted dark-skinned men were lounging in their saddles, laughing as they pushed back the crowd of peóns, cargadores, mozos, railwaymen in blue denim and Indian pedlars from the surrounding villages. Groups of prisoners were huddled together under the trees, swathed in lashings from head to foot, and soldiers were throwing ropes over the branches. A crash of musketry came from one of the side streets and the soldiers began to haul on the ropes. Bodies rose together like grotesque bunches of grapes, writhing and contorted in a slow garrotting, squirming with their feet off the ground like worms on a hook. As one of the groaning branches tore free, the men suspended from it crashed to the ground, half-strangled and choking, but amid delighted yells they were dragged to another tree and hoisted up again, while a chorus of malediction mingled with the shouts of laughter.

Grimly, trying not to look at the swinging corpses, Harley went round the excited men offering cigarettes in exchange for information. Everyone reached forward for them and they all took two or three, some smoking them at once, some putting them carefully away into pockets hidden beneath the bandoliers of cartridges. Eventually, he discovered the leader of the rebel column sitting at a table eating tortillas stuffed with meat, a bottle of warm beer at his elbow. He was a captain wearing dirty white trousers tucked into brown leather leggings over black buttoned boots. Alongside him sat his second-in-command, in a city suit, puttees and spats. Around them ragged men were cleaning weapons or drinking bitter black coffee boiled over fires built from smashed furniture. Bit chains clinked and saddle leather creaked among the stamping horses tethered to the surrounding trees.

'Are you Pancho Villa?' Harley asked the captain.

The officer looked up with a hostile expression. 'Who're you?' he demanded.

'My name's Marquis. I'm the correspondent of an English newspaper.' For safety Harley produced every scrap of documentary evidence about his identity: his passport, his press pass, letters from Sproat, flamboyant recommendations he'd written about himself in Spanish and stamped with every stamp in the *Courier's* office to make them look official, and finally the letters Devoto had given him in Ciudad Juárez for Carranza.

'Who's this Devoto?' the man at the table said.

'Agent to Carranza.'

'Carranza!' The man at the table spat. 'He calls himself a general but he's never had a bullet near him.'

'I'm not interested in people like him, anyway,' Harley said. 'I want to write about the people who're doing the fighting, what *you're* doing, how you're winning your battles, what you intend to do with Mexico when you throw out Díaz. Everybody's talking about Villa round here and I want them to know about you in London.'

The captain grinned, showing a mouthful of tortilla. 'Not me, mi amigo,' he said. 'I'm Rafael Aguílar. Until a couple of years ago I was a foreman in the railway yards in Torreón. I had to leave because the police were after me and when this lot started it seemed a good way of sorting things out. If we win there'll *be* no police. If you want Villa you'll have to move quick. He tried to attack a train carrying reinforcements from Chihuahua City against Guerrero but he picked the wrong one. It was carrying five hundred men of the 12th. Infantry and they were well led and had bolt-action Mausers. He lost around forty dead.'

'Where is he now?'

'Lying low. In bed with a woman. How do I know? The last I heard he was in San Andrés licking his wounds, and recruiting and drilling men.' Aguílar gestured. 'And he needs men, because if no one else realizes that we shall never win this struggle by attacking places like Ceruloso, he does. This is chicken feed, my friend. We need the railway centres. Chihuahua City. Torreón. Juárez on the border. Especially Juárez, because that's where the American guns come from.'

'Are you going there from here?'

The captain laughed and scratched at his leg. 'No, mi amigo. From here, we shall melt into the mountains and the government will assume once more that the revolution's just a few disorganized fights.' He banged the table with his fist. 'But it isn't, my friend! It's more than that. A lot more.'

Twelve hours later, the captured band, by this time grey-faced with fatigue and barely able to stand, were still pounding away at their instruments. The killing had stopped, however, and the pressmen were wondering where to look next.

Out of date telegrams arrived from Sproat, suggesting that, since the revolution appeared to have failed, Harley should return to London. Harley ignored them all. He had been to the Guerrero area and spoken to Orozco, the man who had captured the city, a tall, gaunt man from the mountains whose mixed mestizo and American parentage showed in his brown, freckled and handsome features. He had news that Villa was heading towards the Camargo-Santa Rosalía area. Though the two cities numbered only a few thousand inhabitants, they ranked fourth in population and commerce in the sparsely-inhabited state of Chihuahua which was the key point of the northern campaign because of its proximity to the United States. Moreover, while Santa Rosalía was little more than an Indian village, Camargo was a vital junction on the National Mexican Railroad, and an important military centre for cattle and mining enterprises in the surrounding valleys.

'We're going down there, Tamsy,' Harley decided. 'Pack the bags and get us train tickets.'

They were glad to get out of Ceruloso away from the grisly horrors still hanging in swaying bunches on the trees. Just off the square, against a bare adobe wall, there were several swollen bodies, one of them that of the jefe político, his face covered with dried blood, still wearing his sash of office and the picture frame round his neck to prop him up in a curiously living posture, his smashed spectacles on his nose.

They found Camargo calm but nervous because the news had already arrived that rebel troops were in the vicinity. Noticing there were no other newspapermen in town, Harley hoped to be able to witness Villa's arrival alone. The rebel leader had been heard of further north and they hired a car without difficulty because a lot of people, nervous of the revolution, were bolting to Chihuahua or Juárez which were handy for the American border.

The road was dreadful, a twisting pale scar winding

through a carpet of brush and cactus, and the dust was enough to choke them, but they roared along as fast as Tamsy could drive, a great yellow cloud hanging in the air behind them.

They camped the night alongside the road. Their rations were running short and they had to fall back on tortillas and a large tin of pilchards but, as they cooked, several Mexicans looking for Villa joined them. There were the usual elaborate exchange of Spanish courtesies and offers of food, and the Mexicans, feeling they had to accept out of politeness, eventually rode away with a great deal of friendliness, leaving Harley and Tamsy ruefully eyeing the remains of their meal. However, their guests had brought news that Villa was near Moquí further along the road, and the following day, thundering through the flinty red hills, they found themselves looking down on a narrow valley containing a huddle of squalid adobe buildings surrounding a church.

Reaching the bottom of the slope, they ran on to the plain and roared into the town. But as they reached the first shabby, mud-splashed crumbling houses along a street paved with flat stones, they found themselves among a mass of armed men who surrounded the car immediately.

'Alto!'

As they drew to a stop, they realized they were staring at a circle of rifle muzzles. The men behind them were in uniforms of khaki cotton, their headgear old-fashioned French-style képis which looked as if they were ex-United States government issue dating back to the Civil War. A young man in a blue tunic and wearing a sword pushed forward and, thrusting the muzzle of a revolver under Harley's nose, cocked the hammer with a deliberate movement before carefully removing the weapons they carried.

'Out,' he said in English.

'You Villa's lot?' Harley asked.

'No.' The officer smiled. 'But I expect *you* are. We've just shot three of them. We'd better shoot you, too.'

5

'I'm not one of Villa's men,' Harley said. 'I'm a newspaperman. I'm English.' He fished in his pocket to produce his documents but the young officer merely smiled and waved them away.

'That's what they all say,' he claimed. 'They're newspapermen. They're businessmen. They're agents. They own land in Mexico. They're American, British, French, Spanish, German. Señor, if I believed everybody who told me that story, Mexico would be swarming with Madero's agents.'

He gestured at the men surrounding them and they moved aside. Beyond them, three figures were lolling against a blood-splashed, bullet-pocked wall surrounded by flies and sniffed at by nervous dogs. All three of them wore soiled bandages.

'Americans,' the lieutenant said. 'Part of Madero's so-called Foreign Legion. *They* claimed to be businessmen, too, but they couldn't explain how they came to be wounded. They were left here after Guerrero to recuperate. We hanged the man who gave them shelter.'

The soldiers were going through Harley's car as the officer talked, sharing out what was left of the tinned food and the beer, kicking his typewriter and smashing the camera.

'For God's sake,' he protested, 'that's my equipment!'

'You'll not need it, my friend,' the officer said politely. 'Not where you're going. I regret this deeply, señor, but you are under arrest and will be shot. We don't worry too much about trials. The charge is causing insurrection. I am

Lieutenant Del Castillo and I shall be in charge of your firing squad. Please follow me.'

They found themselves – almost as if they were being shown round the village – walking between two files of stiff-faced soldiers, and suddenly it dawned on Harley that this was not a grotesque joke, and that Del Castillo was in deadly earnest.

'Tamsy,' he muttered. 'Do they really mean it?'

'Sure do, Boss,' Tamsy grated. 'If I get the chance I'm goin' to cut an' run.'

As they were pushed up against the wall alongside the lolling corpses of the Americans, Harley's thoughts were darting about wildly. Sproat would be pleased. Ever faithful to the newspaper. Even unto death. He'd like that. There'd be large headlines in the *Courier*. CORRESPONDENT SHOT BY FIRING SQUAD. MEXICAN TROOPS MURDER ENGLISHMAN.

He could see Tamsy's cunning little yellow eyes flickering about them, but he knew that attempting to escape would help nobody. The Mexicans would invoke the ley fuga and bring them down as they ran. But they couldn't stand still and be shot *without* running.

'I demand time to say my prayers,' he said loudly. 'I demand to see a priest. No good Catholic can refuse a man the last rites.'

Del Castillo sheathed his sword and turned to one of the crowd which had begun to gather. 'Fetch the priest,' he snapped.

The priest was an old man in a dusty cassock, his feet bare beneath it.

'Father,' Harley whispered. 'Tell this idiot that I'm not a rebel. I'm English and my friend here's American.'

The priest looked nervously at Del Castillo. 'There's nothing I can do, my son,' he said. He nodded at the three corpses. '*They* said they weren't rebels. But they were. I know they were. One of them was a Catholic and I heard his confession.'

'Then, listen, Father,' Harley said urgently. 'Make it last a long time. Pray that something will turn up, and make sure He hears you.'

Watched by the crowd, the priest raised his hand in blessing, his head bowed in the yellowing sun. As he muttered, Harley tried to think quickly. Alongside the dead Americans was an adobe wall roughly the height of a man's shoulder. Beyond that was thick foliage, then a few scattered flat-roofed houses and a group of trees. He was just eyeing the wall, wondering if he could be over it and into the undergrowth before the firing squad could recover from their surprise when he heard shouts in the distance and a ripple of musketry. The crowd began to disperse hurriedly and a soldier on a horse came thundering into the square, scattering the dawdlers.

'Villa! Villa!' he was yelling.

As Del Castillo swung round, the heads of the firing squad followed and for a second they were not watching. Giving Tamsy a shove, Harley started running. A few scattered shots whined over their heads as they leapt at the low wall and rolled over the top, then they were flat on their faces in the undergrowth on the other side. Face-down in the foliage, getting their breath back, they realized no one was shooting at them and that the firing in the distance had grown heavier and the shouting had become louder. No one had followed them so they scrambled to their feet and started to push through the undergrowth, their clothing torn by thorns, then, crouching for a while, they realized that the firing was coming now in sporadic bursts and they began to run bent double between the scattered houses.

Children watched them solemn-faced as they scrambled over walls and bolted down stony alleyways hedged with cactus, and an old woman hurtled out of a doorway to scream maledictions at them. Halting again to draw breath, they noticed that the firing had stopped now and that they could hear shouts of triumph through the trees. Nudging Tamsy, Harley set off again, scrambling over piles of discarded tins and bottles humming with flies, and as they finally broke free they found themselves in a small square filled with heavily foliaged trees and once more surrounded by armed men. Horses were plunging and rearing in a cloud of whirling dust, dogs were barking frantically, a black sow and its litter were bolting for cover between the legs of the horses and there were feathers and dust everywhere as chickens burst into the air with clattering wings to avoid grabbing brown hands. Somebody fired a shot, and once again Harley found himself covered by rifles, but this time the men behind them wore shabby rebozos, gaudy kerchiefs and tiger-striped sarapes vivid against the faded pinks, greens and mauves of the houses. There was the same reek of horseflesh, sweat and gun oil about them that he'd smelled in Ceruloso, and a strong sense of menace that didn't come just from the guns. Lean men in wide sombreros on gaunt sore-backed horses, brush-scarred and with splintered hooves, some even with open wounds, milled about them. Some of the men had bare bronzed feet wearing a single spur, but they carried carbines and were weighted down with bandoliers of ammunition. A small man wearing breeches, a campaign hat and a moustache like a Chinese mandarin, pushed his horse forward and pointed his revolver.

'Alto!'

They had stopped dead, panting, huddled together away from the circle of trampling nervous animals.

'Funcionarios de Díaz.' The little man spat. 'We'll soon put you where you ought to be. In Heaven.'

The shooting seemed finally to have stopped completely and there was an ominous silence over the little town. As they were pushed back into the square, they saw Del Castillo, without his hat, his eyes wild, standing against a tree, a noose round his neck. There was blood on his face but he was trying to hold his head up proudly, and when one of the men surrounding him tried to push him, he spat in his face.

The men in sombreros were shouting a ribald ditty about what villains they were ' – Todos los alzados, y los forjidos, y los deliciosos – ' then someone yelled and the man in the campaign hat turned to Harley. 'You're lucky,' he said with a grin. 'Pancho Villa himself has come to see you off.'

Beyond the crowd, Harley saw a huge high-spirited black horse, and a man swinging from a silver-mounted saddle. He was of medium height but built with the chest of a gorilla, with short bowed legs and the pigeon toes of a life-long horseman. His hair was reddish brown and, like most Mexicans, he wore a large moustache and was dressed in a leather charro suit, a peso-studded sombrero, enormous jingling spurs, a sarape, and the extra Indio finery of a scarf and vermilion sash looted from a Rurale.

Halting in front of Del Castillo, he stared at him with steady topaz eyes. There was a long silence then he turned to the man in the campaign hat, speaking pelado, the crude Spanish of the poor.

'What about his men, Tómas?'

'They've been given the opportunity of joining us or being shot, mi jefe. They've agreed to join us.'

'Not much of a choice, was it?' Villa turned to Del Castillo. 'And what about you, mi amigo? Are you ready?'

Del Castillo said nothing and Villa grinned. 'Better this way than one of the others,' he said. 'There are some who'd have you smeared with molasses and staked out over an ants' nest, or strung out over a maguey plant so that it shoves its spike through your belly as it grows. What do you say?'

'I demand a firing squad.'

Villa's heavy face darkened. 'Your damned gachupín honour, I suppose? Nobody ever considered it worth worrying about the honour of people like me. String him up!'

'This is murder!' Del Castillo gasped.

Villa gestured at the three corpses still lolling against the wall beyond the crowd. They were surrounded now by a group of tough-looking men in stetsons who were speaking in English.

'Get rid of him,' he snapped.

They had hoisted Del Castillo on to a chair now and tightened the rope round his neck, so that there was no slack. Villa stared at it, then with a sweep of a heavy arm, he dragged away the chair. The branch above Del Castillo creaked but the rope round his neck was not tied in a hangman's knot and there was no drop so that, as the noose tightened, his death came from slow strangulation, his feet kicking, his hands fluttering convulsively. Villa stood watching, his eyes filled with grim satisfaction, then he turned to Harley, studying him with an inscrutable stare that seemed to go right through him.

'And now you, mi amigo,' he said. 'There are more hats around here than we need.'

The whole lunatic drama started again, with Harley

arguing fiercely as the noose dropped round his neck. 'I'm English,' he insisted.

'You speak good Spanish for an Englishman,' Villa snapped.

'My father was a Mexican! He had to flee from Mexico! Look at my papers! You'll see his name on them. Lázaro Inés Márquez.'

Villa frowned. 'Papers mean nothing to me.'

The man in the campaign hat had fished in Harley's pocket. 'That's what it says, mi jefe,' he admitted. 'Lázaro Harley Marquis. It gives his father's name. Lázaro Inés Márquez.'

'He was well known in Chihuahua,' Harley gasped. 'He came from Parral.'

'I don't believe you,' Villa growled. 'Up with him'.

As the rope tightened round Harley's neck, he began to yell, the veins on his neck standing out in his fury. He jerked his head at the body of Del Castillo alongside, now still but swinging slightly. '*He* tried to shoot me because I was an American fighting for Madero! I can't be both!'

Villa looked baffled, his head down like an overgrown schoolboy presented with a difficult problem.

'I'm a newspaperman,' Harley insisted. 'People want to know what's happening here.'

'A revolution's happening here. We're going to make Francisco Madero president.'

'I want to write about it! I want to tell the people in Europe about it so that their governments will recognize him.'

They were still arguing when they heard the honking of a klaxon and the crowd parted hurriedly. Beyond it Harley saw Angelica Ojarra's Stutz. As it approached one of the Villistas jumped on the running board, his immense spurs ringing, and leaned over her, his hands pawing her at her bosom. As she clapped on the brakes and the car stopped abruptly in front of them, the man rolled into the dust. As he scrambled to his feet, his eyes angry, Villa whipped out his gun.

'No! Don't shoot him!'

As Angelica screamed, Villa looked puzzled. Then he

reversed the gun and held it out to her, butt foremost. '*You* want to shoot him?'

'Nobody's going to shoot him! He didn't hurt me.'

Villa frowned then he shrugged and swung the weapon to send the cringing man flying. As he picked himself up, Villa pointed the gun at him. 'You do not insult Pancho Villa's friends, mi amigo,' he said. 'Get out of my sight before I send you to your Maker.'

As Angelica climbed from the car, her eyes fell on the body of Del Castillo still swinging gently at the end of the rope and her face twisted in disgust. Villa saw her expression.

'Cut him down,' he snapped. 'He's not very decorative, anyway. Get rid of him. Together with those.' He gestured at the dead Americans, then he removed his sombrero and held it to his chest to face Angelica. 'Señora Ojarra.'

She indicated Harley and Tamsy Flood and let go a torrent of impassioned Spanish so that Villa seemed to back away from her fury.

'Release those men,' she snapped. 'They're not Díaz people. They want to write about you.'

'I don't like people who write,' Villa growled as the ropes were released. 'I'm not interested in writers. It's soldiers I want.'

'*They've* been soldiers. Both of them. They can help you!'

She turned to Harley. 'Why in God's name didn't you tell me you were looking for Don Francisco?' she said. 'I could have sent someone with you. He trusts me.'

'Well, just make it clear to him that we've got a car in the square over there. We want a guard on it.'

She spoke to Villa who swung to the man in the campaign hat.

'He says there'll be a guard on it and there'll be nothing missing.'

Just along the street from the square was a flat-roofed little cantina. Its name – Las Puertas Celestiales, the Heavenly Gates – was painted in square-ended Victorian lettering on a lopsided board over the entrance. It was a flat-faced structure without doors and from inside came the smell of food and the hum of flies. Along the front was a verandah surrounded by a wall where an ancient bougainvillea swelled against the sky.

Villa pulled forward a table with cast-iron legs and a marble top and gestured to chairs. Wine and tequilla appeared – though Harley noticed that Villa didn't touch either – followed by a meal on earthenware plates of chicken, corn, tortillas and frijoles, the inevitable beans, and a dish of chilli sauce.

As they ate, Villa's troops stood watching them under a luminous opalescent sky, on one side a grinning man whose face was practically lost under his vast sombrero twanging on a guitar. Among them was the group of young Americans.

'My machine gunners.' Villa indicated them proudly. 'They know how to fire them and clean them. Soon we shall have guns for them.'

A burly sphinx, he sat watching for a while, then he leaned towards Harley. 'Is it true what she says,' he asked. 'That you are simpático and know about soldiering?'

'I've been a soldier.'

Villa frowned. 'I have only been a bandit. I know how to fight, but in small numbers. I need to know how to drill men. And aren't there doctors with armies to look after the wounded? And if we're to capture Camargo, I'll need men who know how to handle railways. Once we have a railroad, we can move troops by train. But I'm only a peón. I can't even read or write.'

He shifted uncomfortably in his chair, embarrassed by his own thoughts, then he went on fiercely. 'But I'm no longer the compañero of the camp fires,' he said. 'I've been given a commission as a captain in Madero's armies. Abraham González gave it to me. He told me the revolution needed me. He pointed out that I could do what he couldn't do, what Madero couldn't do, what a lot of the talkers couldn't do. I could ride and shoot. He talked to me a long time. He told me things about my country I never knew. He told me how Madero was trying to free the people, how they needed soldiers. I'd always thought that all the rich could do was gather corn and hold it in their fists so that only the shedding of their blood could make them open their hands to the poor. But González was different. Mi amigo, he painted great visions on my heart.'

He spoke with a sincerity that was strangely touching. A man of no education, he was nevertheless obviously greatly moved by the thought of freedom and the fact that he, a bandit, had been asked to help.

'I have to work with Orozco who's been made a colonel,' he went on. 'So I must know what to do. Can you tell me? I'll give you stories for your paper and you can be right at the front where you can see everything.' He grinned. 'You might get shot. That would be a *very* good story.'

'Not as good as being hanged.'

'That was a mistake, mi amigo.' Villa's laugh died and the earnest visage of a man struggling to express himself reappeared. 'We *need* people to tell the world of our struggles, to show them we are in earnest, that we've been living in slavery. We need education not banquets in Mexico City for Díaz and his hangers-on.' He banged the table and looked intently at Harley. 'And we need proof that we have the power to get what we're asking. The capture of Camargo will give it to us. You must come and take pictures with your cameras.'

'I can't take pictures. Del Castillo's men smashed my equipment.'

Villa shrugged and turned to the man in the campaign hat. 'Find him a new typewriter, Tomás. There'll be one somewhere. And a camera so he can take our portraits.'

Ten minutes later the man in the campaign hat was back with two other men, one carrying a typewriter, the other a huge plate camera.

'I can't use that,' Harley said.

'I can.' The speaker was one of the Americans, a fair-haired youngster with a snub nose, blue eyes and a wide innocent smile. He wore a Norfolk jacket with a celluloid collar and string tie, on his yellow curls a huge wideawake hat.

'I can handle a camera,' he said. 'I can even handle a movie camera.' He took the apparatus from the man who was carrying it and began to examine it, his eyes all the time on Angelica so that he was addressing her, not Harley. 'I worked in the movie studios in Los Angeles before I came down here. There's a guy there called Carl Laemmle making moving pictures. Long ones. Two-reelers. Love stories with Theda Bara and Mary Pickford. That sort of thing. Johnny Cox, that's me. John Claverly Cox. I worked for him.'

'Then what in God's name are you doing here?' Angelica asked. 'Why aren't you *still* making moving pictures?'

Cox's wide disarming smile had the innocence of a naughty small boy's. 'I got drunk,' he said. 'Spoiled the whole goddam shoot. Had to remake a whole reel. But I know how to take pictures. Laemmle said I was good at it. That's because I'm an artist, too, I guess. Trained for it. Used to draw cartoons for the *Jonesville Herald* before I went to California. I'm good at that too.'

6

Strung out towards Camargo across a wind-whipped winter desert, Villa's army was in reality no more than a few hundred raffish, ragged men, on horseback or riding in stolen waggons, the rear brought up by an ancient stage coach which looked as if it had come from the Wells Fargo stable and was drawn by mules that tried to kick it to pieces every time they were harnessed to it.

It was a tattered army of pink shirts, yellow shirts, green shirts, white shirts; gaudy Indio scarves; bright sarapes; stetsons, sombreros, city hats – even an occasional bowler; coveralls, charro jackets, tight vaquero trousers, an ancient frock coat split up the back to give freedom of movement – the only common denominator that they all had guns and wore four or five cartridge belts.

Surrounded by an aura of sweat, grease and horses, they were dusty and primitive-looking, many still bandaged from their last skirmish. Drunk and excited, whooping and waving carbines of every age and type, they were a ragtime horde, scruffy, uneducated, romantic, noble and foolish, but murderous in intent, even if stirred by vague idealistic images of freedom they could barely understand. Ahead, the vanguard rode in a ragged coil of smoky dust, led by a Mexican flag carried by a man in a floppy sombrero stolen from some murdered hacendado, decorated with an incredible weight of tarnished gold braid and adorned now with wilting flowers and a picture of the Madonna.

Angelica had wanted to be with them but Villa had refused to allow it. 'This is no job for a woman,' he had said.

'There are women with your troops,' she had snapped.

Villa had answered her sheepishly, embarrassed by her demands, and it had ocurred to Harley that though he didn't want her he had no wish to offend her. 'They are peóns' women,' he had pointed out. 'With cooking kettles and babies. You are different, Dona Angelica. Una grande señora.'

'I don't want to be different,' she said. 'I don't want to be grand. I'm Mexican. I want to fight Mexico's battles.'

She was finding it hard to check her temper as she passionately tried to lose her upper-class identity and merge with what she considered her people, and Harley had caught the anguished look Villa gave him.

'Señor,' he had said and shrugged his shoulders helplessly. Then his face had lit up and he had turned to her again. 'There are other things to do,' he insisted. 'I need medical supplies. I need tents to use as hospitals. And *I* know nothing of these things. You can buy them in El Paso for me. Good things. American things. That is *your* job, señora.'

It had brought the light back into her eyes and as she headed for the Stutz to make a list of what was wanted, Villa had given Harley a look that was almost a grimace.

'Dona Angelica is a determined woman, compadre,' he said. 'I'm glad I'm not married to her.'

They halted for the night at a village called Dolores, a scattering of low adobe huts among lean little fields of rock, dust and cactus round a mission church where black-clad figures of women carried ollas of water from the stream. There were the usual pigs in the street, a solitary goat chewing at a newspaper, and a faint smell of urine over everything. Chickens scratched in the doorway of the church and a woman nursing a baby sat on the steps picking lice out of the hair of a starry-eyed five-year-old that looked as if it hadn't been washed since birth. Others crouched over the perpetual task of grinding corn in stone troughs, while the men squatted by the walls – except for a murmured 'buenas noches' as if made of stone – and the whole place was silent, in a silence that went with the dust and the veil of evening stillness that lay over the place.

The inn was little more than a cantina smelling of cooking food and sweating humanity. It was hung with festoons of jerked meat, peppers and drying clothes, and was haunted by bats and birds, and the chickens, pigs and children wandered in and out. As dusk fell, candles flickered on haloed images in dusty pictures, and the inevitable painted plaster Madonna standing on a chipped commode with a drawer missing.

As the light faded, women lit fires and started to slap at tortillas, while their menfolk came to life and gathered in a ring for a cockfight. A boy wearing sandals and one yellow sock started throwing out challenges. As it grew darker, the laughter stopped and the firefly glow of cigarettes began to catch the angles of dark faces, the gleam of buckles and rifle barrels, and the shiny wood of rifle stocks. Round one fire where a slaughtered sheep was being cooked the men watched hungrily, scratching at their flea bites, the tall sombreros making them seem even shorter than they were. From somewhere among them came the wheeze of an accordion.

Villa, who despised self-indulgence and had a fierce instinct for health and self-preservation, drank only milk and ate little beyond half a sweet potato. Over the meal, his fingers in his hair as if trying to get at the thoughts inside his head, he began to pick Harley's brain.

'Who are the British fighting at the moment, amigo?' he asked.

'Nobody.'

'Nobody at all? How do they pass the time without a war to fight?' He paused. 'How do they fight their wars when they have them?'

'Badly on the whole,' Harley admitted.

'But they always win them, I think.'

Harley smiled. 'That's because the other side's usually worse than we are. We take a long time to learn. There are grocers in all armies.'

Villa's brow twisted. 'Grocers?'

'Soldiers who don't learn from their experiences as you have.'

Villa shrugged. 'Nowadays I don't allow my people beyond the camp unless they're fully armed. Then if they're surprised, they can act alone, and the noise they make will alert the rest of us. They also have orders not to head straight for camp so as to give us time to be ready.' He frowned. 'I understand that one should have reserves. What are reserves for?'

It was clear he had learned a great deal already. He had no educated advisors so that he had had to work things out for himself, but he had already fought several small actions, trying out the scraps of military knowledge he had picked up in his years as a bandit. He knew how to set ambushes and use rendezvous points so that if his men were split up they could regather at some prearranged spot where fresh arms, ammunition, horses and clothing were available.

'One man can wear out three horses escaping,' he explained.

He had also taught his men how to keep an open formation when moving forward, and his knowledge of terrain, acquired in his years beyond the law, was vast and his espionage system unmatchable.

'The people are on my side,' he explained. 'Because they are *my* people and I see they're well rewarded. I've often paid their debts or left a few pesos for a pair of new shoes or to help with a wedding or to celebrate the birth of a son. Now, when the Rurales ask for me, they can never remember which way I went.'

'Even Señora Ojarra?'

Villa frowned. 'One day the government – some government – will shoot her.'

As Harley laughed, Villa went on soberly. 'But make no mistake, mi amigo, Dona Angelica is one of us. The man she married gave me a horse when I was running from the Rurales. It meant the difference between life and death and I don't forget. I owe her a great debt and it taught me all rich people are not the same. Abraham Gonzáles, for whom I would give my life, is also different. He respects me as a man, not just because I could shoot him dead if I wanted to, and he trusted me and made me a captain in Madero's army. Madero's another. He's the Redeemer come to save Mexico.'

With a thin mist over the plains, the column moved off again. Villa was among the first to his feet and, stiff with the night-time cold, was pushing horses between shafts and kicking at the stomachs of recalcitrant mules while other men were still blinking themselves awake. As he swung on to his horse, the old woman who owned the inn, moved forward to kiss his foot.

'God, His sainted Mother, the Blessed Niño, and Our Lady of Guadalupe protect you, Don Francisco!'

As they swung eastward under a milky overcast that thinned the sunlight, small groups of men kept joining them, lonely charros who thoughtfully brought their employers' cattle along for food; miners with a pack train of dynamite; small knots of campesinos from every village they passed. They had all heard that the revolution had come and that Villa was leading it and they cantered up on sway-backed, ungroomed horses, mules, even donkeys, clutching ancient rifles, shotguns, muskets, sometimes just machetes. Some were joining the revolution because they wanted a meal, some because they wanted a pair of pants, some because they just wanted a gun and an excuse to blow a hated master to pieces.

It was different from other revolutions, it seemed to Harley. Its leaders had no sturdy peasantry to support them, no guilds or trade unions, no organized workmen, no disciplined body of citizens, only a mass of illiterate, superstitious villagers and scattered campesinos who had long since worn themselves out trying to force a living from their arid parcels of land. They weren't even of common blood, tongue or tradition, but represented half a hundred different racial lines distinct in type and speech, from the savage Yaqui bowmen to the aristocratic Mayans of the south, men who knew little of their own history, let alone that of the other groups. Without leaders, without money, weapons, foreign support, or even trained soldiers, it was a starveling revolution that seemed by its poverty doomed to failure.

And, after European armies, it was strange to live among the ingenuous peasant soldiers. They were boastful and noisy about their courage, their skill as soldiers, their attraction as lovers, but despite their talent for bombast and display they were far from stupid. They were doing what they were doing with cold unsentimental logic, making allowances for the colourful descriptions of their friends and even their own embroideries. They expected exaggeration in themselves and everybody else but this never deterred them from making decisions when they had to be made. Only poverty had made them apathetic and now they had an aim and an objective they were eager and energetic. And, despite their ferocity, they were surprisingly sentimental and loyal. Several times Harley was accused of being a spy but there was always someone to explain that he had come thousands of miles to tell of their fight for liberty. And, though their houses were built of the soil they tilled, though their food was the corn they grew, the clothes they wore were spun from their own wool and their crude sandals cut from the hides of their cattle, though they possessed nothing, they never attempted to steal from him.

Sometimes the column sang, sometimes it moved in silence. Sometimes a coyote slipped across their path and the whole of the vanguard, yelping with delight, sarapes flying, hats bouncing, took off in pursuit, raking their horses with their spurs until they finally yanked them to a staggering halt with bleeding mouths in a wild confusion of dust, horses and men. As the wind rose, the blown sand stung their faces and they hoisted up their sarapes so that there was little to see beneath the huge sombreros beyond a pair of glittering eyes. As the gusts increased, the wind blew shrilly and bitterly, then a fierce storm sprang up and the head of the column was battling against a hail of fine sand that reduced visibility to nothing, while those behind faced an icy rain that streamed down on the wind. Hands froze clawlike on reins and, as the wind increased to a gale, wailing in from the west, it foiled all attempts to cook, filling the cooking pots with sand or bowling them along in the squalls that struck at the backs of the horses, whipping their tails and forcing the riders to clutch their sarapes tight against them, the brims of their sombreros lifting and rolling in the gusts. And as they tried to sleep at night the cold of the high lands got into their bones and stayed there even through the next day when the sun came up.

On the fifth day, with the storm subsiding and the rasping sound of the wind and the flying sand dwindling to a mere irritation, they came to the railway track, two shining steel lines dwindling into the distance, and turned north along it. Not far ahead of them now was Camargo, close to Chihuahua City, railhead of the National Railroad, a military post and shipping point for the cattle and mining enterprises of the Conchos and Florida valleys. Villa had divided his men into groups equivalent to companies and placed them under old compañeros of his bandit days like Ochoa, Salas Vaca and Tomás Urbina, or new men who had joined him because of the revolution like Aguílar and Fierro, the railwaymen, and Maclovio Herrera, the businessman.

At every halt, he gathered them round him and talked in a low voice, drawing lines in the dusty earth with a stick.

'Can you do it?' Harley asked.

'I have to do it,' Villa admitted. 'Or I remain a mere bandit commanding a group of bandits.'

As the distant town became visible, they drew rein at the village of San Pedro. The villagers brought information that the Federal troops were expecting them and were far from nervous.

'Well,' Villa said, 'neither are we.'

Johnny Cox looked up at him. By this time he had acquired a car and several cameras, one of them a movie camera with a crank-handle on the side. He had also organized a small dark room from a tent and blankets, where he could develop and print his stills, and had somehow acquired permission to represent a group of Arizona newspapers so that he rarely left Harley's side in case he missed something. He knew how to write after a fashion, and Harley suspected he was more than willing to steal any item of news he couldn't dig up for himself. But he fitted in easily, dropping the machine gun group in a way that suggested he found it easy to switch loyalties, yet, with his wide smile and innocent manner, difficult to dislike. He had little patience, however, and, liking comfort, was looking forward to the pleasures of a town.

'How about some pictures, Don Pancho?' he asked. 'Before you start. Get your men to pose. Like they were in a battle. Go forward. Fire their guns. I'll run off some film.'

Villa grinned. 'I'll do better than that,' he said. 'I'll bring the real battle forward so you can film that.'

He called his leaders together and explained what was in his mind. Then, splitting his force, he sent half of it to the right under cover of the rolling terrain while the rest dismounted and deployed opposite the Federal trenches that lay across their route. As he rode to the top of a little rise to watch, Harley, Tamsy Flood and Cox followed with his staff.

'I've taught my gente what you had to say,' he pointed out to Harley. 'And explained what they're to do. We'll see now if any of it went in.'

Sitting with a dusty booted leg over the horn of his saddle, he gestured with his sombrero and the wave of men began to move forward, bent low as he'd taught them, their weapons at their sides, the brims of their tall hats flopping in the brisk wind. They had little experience of war and were totally without engineers or artillery, but Villa knew his own people and the villagers had brought fresh news that told of disaffection among the Federals.

With Harley watching through binoculars and Johnny Cox standing up, indifferent to the chances of being hit, cranking away at his camera, the revolutionaries pressed forward, firing as they went, their steps growing faster until they were running. When they were almost within pistol range, Harley saw Federal officers rise in the trenches and the flash of the sun on their raised swords. As musketry rattled out, obscuring the position with grey smoke, the Villistas began to waver, their officers scurrying among them, using their fists to drive them forward. At the second volley they broke, turned tail and began to run.

Looking quickly at Villa, Harley saw he was sitting unmoved, his leg still over the horn of his saddle. The sound of bugles came over the thin air and the blue-coated soldiers climbed from their trenches and ran forward, but, as they ran, the main body of Villistas rose from their cover on their left with a volley of enfilading fire. Cut off from their defences, the Federals milled about in confusion, their flanks crumbling, their officers wildly beating at them with the flat of their swords. As the trap was sprung, they went down like maize before a scythe.

Screaming 'Tierra y libertad,' Land and liberty, the rebels

swept into the town, breaking into the bars and thrusting the rifles of the dying into the eager hands of the new recruits who swarmed about them. The whole centre round the zócalo was filled with horses and waggons, and as drunken dusty men brandished bottles, fired their rifles into the air, smashed windows and grabbed for the women – all women, any women – the prisoners were set to work under the hovering vultures to collect the dead. Near the barracks stood queues of prisoners and one of them calmly told Harley they were waiting to be shot. They seemed unconcerned with their fate, however, and were even quarrelling over their last cigarettes.

Somewhere nearby bugles were sounding the *Diana* – the Mexican melody of victory, the tune they played for executions, the tune they had played on the day they had executed the Emperor Maximilian at the Hill of Bells in Querétaro. Then, as Harley turned away, an officer touched the arm of the man he had spoken to and the group followed him out of sight. The *Diana* finished and seconds later he heard the crash of the volley.

Though the victory was chaotic, bloody and cruel, it was not just a triumph for Villa. It was a tremendous moment for the revolution because it was the first successful assault on a strategic centre and, though due as much as anything to the poor quality of the Federal soldiers, it seemed to be the first welding together of a hundred little uprisings all over northern Mexico.

Camargo had a telegraph office and, as the town was taken over by the mob, Harley sent off a long despatch describing his meeting with Villa and his near death by hanging. With some pleasure he headed it 'With the Revolutionary forces'.

'Will you tell your English newspaper about my victory, Inglés?' Villa asked.

'I've already told them,' Harley said.

'You wrote all this out? All those words? Already?'

'*And* sent it to England. They'll be reading it in the newspapers as soon as it arrives.'

'Can you get me one of these newspapers? So I can see my name in print. Francisco Villa. Properly spelled and written. And you will point it out?' Villa rubbed his forehead frustratedly. 'One day I shall learn to read and write and then I shall know how to tell Madero what I am doing. How is my name written?'

As Harley wrote the name on the table cloth, Villa studied it with the absorbed frown of a child faced with its first spelling lesson.

'That is not my real name,' he pointed out. 'I was born Doroteo Arango. I changed it because it sounds like the clanking of chains. Could you teach me to read? So I could use big words?'

The town was still packed with men and horses when Angelica Ojarra arrived. She had been buying in El Paso – tents, drugs, bandages, blankets, mattresses, bedpans, surgical instruments – using her own money in her usual impulsively generous way. They came rolling into Camargo in a convoy of a dozen high tonneaued lorries, eyed with awe by the dusty bloodstained soldiers. Then Angelica herself arrived in the Stutz, to slide to a screeching stop outside the headquarters Villa had set up in the jefe político's office. Her face was alight with triumph.

'See what I got,' she yelled at Harley. 'Tents, drugs, bandages, blankets, surgical instruments.'

'To be used by whom?' Harley asked.

'Surgeons, for God's sake! Who else?'

'And have you brought those, too?'

Her face went blank and he realized that the idea of recruiting doctors and nurses simply hadn't occurred to her.

She brushed the point aside to be investigated later. 'Never mind that,' she said. 'We've got Camargo and Rosalía.'

'And a lot of people have died,' Harley pointed out flatly. 'It's something that happens in war. They don't just go out of the room. Their lives end. One-two. Just like that. Not all of them bad people. Some were murdered after it was all over. Shot in cold blood.'

Her enthusiasm vanished at once and she looked at him, startled by his attitude, as if it were something that hadn't occurred to her before.

'They were Porfiristas,' she said. 'What else could happen to them? In wartime.' The enthusiasm returned. 'Nothing's going to stop us now. The lid's going to come off.' Then her expression changed yet again as she watched his face – first to bewilderment, then to anger. 'My God, you goddam po-faced Limey,' she said desperately, 'you've spoiled everything for me!'

7

Despite the successes, the revolution was still burning only with a fitful flame. The telegraphist at Camargo, as eager as anyone to see it succeed, had information of powerful reinforcements moving against the rising in the north. Spirits were further deflated by news of a serious reverse at Cerro Prieto in the west and the information that Orozco had had to abandon Guerrero, and had suffered a thumping defeat at Ciudad Juárez and another at Bauche a few days later, his humiliation witnessed by crowds of El Pasoans who had turned up to watch the fighting.

Villa was just beginning to wonder whether to bolt for the hills when the gloom was lifted by Tamsy. He had been to the railroad looking for gasolene and, with the telegraph wires repaired, had learned that Madero was back in Mexico.

He had been met by women carrying armfuls of flowers, and, considering his arrival equal to a dozen victories, Villa decided to remain where he was. Banishing his men from the town centre, he began to distribute food to the poor and appoint committees of anti-reelectionists to official positions, even executing a few of his men for looting or molesting the citizenry.

'I am no longer a bandit,' he explained grimly. 'I'm an officer in Madero's army.'

The town's bandstand was cleaned up and a band composed of policemen who had changed sides, a few of Villa's men and anybody else who could play an instrument, crowded into it and began to thump out a spirited programme of revolutionary tunes, even the old ribald *Mama Carlota*, sung in the days of Maximilian.

Order had just been restored when they heard of a new and more disastrous setback. Madero had thrown a weak force against the town of Casas Grandes but the battle had seemed won and white flags had appeared in the Federal lines when reinforcements had arrived and the firing had started once more. The victory had turned into a rout and there had been heavy casualties, one of them Madero, who had been hit in the wrist.

The pendulum had swung once more because Madero had been regarded as a miracle worker. With him in flight, the blow to morale was tremendous and the revolution seemed to be flat on its back again when, at the telegraph office with a long despatch on the failures, Harley picked up fresh and unexpected news.

Spurred on by the victory at Camargo, Sonora, South Chihuahua State and Laguna had sprung to life and fighting had started in Morelos, south of Mexico City, where previously there had been no sign of trouble.

When Harley returned to the town centre, he found Villa had changed his mind yet again and his bugler was blowing an assortment of calls on a cracked bugle. He had been ordered to sound assembly but, because he didn't know which it was, he was wading through them all. Near the depot, the sound of engine whistles was interrupted by the thump of dynamiting as the track was destroyed. The telephones and telegraph lines were being cut and engines with chains and hooks were tearing up the lines on both sides of the city so that troop trains could not move up from Mexico City and Torreón. Chihuahua City was effectively cut off from the south.

Villa was in a bad temper because the anti-reelectionists in the town were objecting that the damage being done would ruin their businesses, and was stamping up and down, yellow fire in his eyes, his sombrero pushed back, swinging in a fury at any object within reach of his huge hands and sending it flying.

'They talk so much, these committee men!' he shouted. 'That's all they do – talk! Even when they know what needs doing, they have to make a speech about it! I didn't make speeches when I attacked Camargo! Now, because we're going, they're starting to whine.'

His face changed as he heard Harley's news and his temper vanished at once. 'What!' he said. 'Those lazy bastards south of Mexico City have come to life, have they? Put their noses out of their trees and flowers? Pues bien, we stay! Madero will be sending me orders.' He swung round and began to shout commands to halt the destruction. 'We'll let the correctos have their way after all.'

The orders he was expecting arrived later in the day, carried by a man on a staggering horse. Villa was eating an orange, the juice running down his chin as he bit into it unpeeled like an apple, chewing the rind and pith with the fruit and spitting out the pips. He frowned at the bundle of papers.

'I can't read them,' he growled, thrusting them at Harley. 'Here, Inglés, read them for me. I can trust you. You have no axe to grind.'

Harley took the papers. 'One's an official greeting from Madero,' he said. 'Welcoming you into the revolutionary army, congratulating you on your successes at San Andrés and Camargo and asking you to restrain your troops from excesses.'

Villa's expression changed. 'Excesses? What excesses?'

'I expect he means killing civilians and prisoners of war.'

Villa looked surprised. 'They'd have killed *me* if they'd captured me,' he said. '*And* any of my men. What's the difference?'

'The difference is the rules of war.'

'There are *rules* for war?' Villa looked bewildered.

'In civilized warfare there are. One of them is that you don't shoot your prisoners.'

'Not even when they're Porfirista officers and officials who've been preying on such as me for the whole of their lives? You fight strange wars in Europe, Inglés. What else does he say?'

'He wants you to preserve the good name of the Revolution so it can be presented to the world as clean and decent and honourable'.

Villa scowled. 'All I did was hang one or two. Everybody

who was there approved. And why are we at war if we're *not* to kill Federal officers?' He was sitting at a table now, brooding angrily. 'What else?' he asked.

'There's also a military order from Orozco. It says you're to leave the smallest possible garrison here compatible with its safety, and report with your command at Fresno for an attack on Chihuahua City. Madero's at Bustillos and he's summoning all loyal revolutionaries to meet him there. Are you going?'

Villa looked up, his heavy head hanging, his whole body filled with an air of primitive force. 'Of course we'll go,' he said. 'He's the leader, isn't he?'

With flurries of snow coming down from the hills, Villa's little army began to head northward. Villa rode in the lead, with Harley alongside him among his staff, Tamsy Flood just behind, clad in a flat cap and made-up bow tie, surly and rebellious at not having a steering wheel to grip.

Suddenly the revolution was not only standing on shaky legs again, it was even beginning to take steps forward. From the cold dusty north to the humid south, the knowledge was exciting the whole country, and broad-minded hacendados who could see no future under Díaz were joining unlikely forces with labourers-become-generals. In the sugar state of Morelos close to the capital, a man called Emiliano Zapata, a farmer from Anencuilco, had rallied a ragged group of peasants round him and, reddening the earth with the blood of the hated gachupíns in a campaign unmatched for bitterness and cruelty, was recruiting men with the slogan that it was better for them to die on their feet than live on their knees.

'That's a good slogan,' Villa said enviously. 'I wish I'd thought of it.'

On the third day, while the main body of the army was drinking its breakfast coffee, news came that the vanguard, scouting far ahead, were sacking the town of Morillo and the nearby hacienda. Flinging his tin mug down, Villa yelled for his horse and started to kick dust over the embers of the fire. Then the whole lot of them were off, whooping and yelling, strung out across the desert in a long straggling column moving at full speed.

They found the vanguard milling around in the middle of the square and the sky darkened by smoke where houses were burning. Hauling on the reins, Villa started to shout orders and, dragging at his pistol, he swung round and dropped a man dragging a half-naked girl from a cantina.

'Por Dios!' he yelled. 'You're soldiers of the army of Madero, not bandidos!'

The ill-disciplined men were going through the place with drunken delight, riding their horses through the wide corridors of the hacienda, hacking at priceless chandeliers and shooting the eyes out of the portraits on the walls, ripping furniture and hangings with machetes and threatening the occupants with death if they didn't produce their valuables. Villa went raging among them with his fists and his feet and his pistol until he had restored order. He made no attempt to comfort the wealthy family of the hacendado but at least he got his men under control again, cowed, scared-looking, and with three of their number stretched dead in the dust.

But there was no holding the insurrectos now. For the seventh time in a century ragged armies were trailing across the landscape as Mexico came alive with rebellion. A crimson wind was beginning to sweep across the country and Díaz supporters were being spirited away in the middle of the night and their bodies found hanging from telegraph poles the next morning. Small towns and haciendas like those at Morillo were looted with glee and foreign residents were being held at gun point until a ransom was paid. Mormon colonies were attacked for their possessions by bandits posing as revolutionary soldiers, while trains were stopped by whooping, unruly drunken men who robbed the passengers of all they owned, often leaving them – men and women alike – in nothing but their underclothes – sometimes even less – and, with the engine wrecked, forced to walk along the line to safety.

Killing had become common and behind it came the anarchy of disorder. Insurrectos were running amok and tattered figures were streaming across the northern plains clutching looted vases, pictures, clocks or clothing. There were women as well as men, and girls from the captured towns were ordered to strip to the skin because some rebel wanted their clothes for his girl friend. They were drunk not only on alcohol but also on success and power and a sense of freedom they had never known before.

As the rebels began to realize that at last the yoke was being lifted, they grew even bolder. Posters demanding Díaz's resignation appeared on the streets and newspapers criticizing the government were no longer immediately suppressed.

Díaz was now between two great unexploded bombs with the fuses well alight. And incredibly the rebels were finding the opposition was less than they had anticipated. With Villa nervously waiting the arrival of Federal reinforcements, Harley made enquiries of the railway despatching office. Learning no troop trains were expected, he wired Knowles in Mexico City to find out if some carefully-planned encirclement was on its way. Knowles' reply startled him. No reinforcements had been sent because the capital had been emptied of troops long before.

It finally dawned on him that what was happening in Mexico was what he had seen happen in Spain in 1908 when the Catalan nationalists, expecting swift retribution for their rising, had realized that the government had used up its resources during the Spanish-American War in Cuba and against dissident tribes in Morocco.

'There *aren't* any reinforcements,' he told Angelica. 'They don't exist. Everybody's been accepting Díaz's dictatorship simply because it was there. He *has* no reinforcements. The generals have been padding the rolls for years.'

It was true. When they despatched telegrams to check on the theory, they discovered that the army, on which an enormous part of the country's finances had been expended, was only a hollow sham. Officers had embezzled the pay and ration funds of their soldiers, and the muster rolls were filled with the names of men who no longer existed; the rank and file, ill-fed, ill-clothed and only occasionally paid – their chief ambition to return to the families from which they'd been dragged by Díaz's press gangs – had no stomach for opposing men with whom they not only had sympathy but to whom they were also often related. Díaz *had* no army.

Madero had set up his headquarters in a hacienda on a wide sandy plain south of Juárez. Near it rebel bands had begun to gather until a sprawling dusty camp of more than three thousand men covered the surrounding land. For the most part they were short of food, clothing, weapons and ammunition, and most of them were simple peasants from the plains and mountains who amused themselves with guitars, exhibitions of horsemanship and boasting of their courage, so that the camp looked more like a fiesta than the gathering of an army. Among them were miners, city dwellers and a few intellectuals caught up by the ideal of freedom, and they sat in groups, cleaning weapons, currying horses or drinking coffee boiled over fires that filled the air with mesquite smoke.

There were many non-Mexicans: Guiseppe Garibaldi, the polished grandson of the great Italian liberator, and General Viljoen, a Boer leader who had fought against the British and was now a resident in the United States. They were leading Madero's Foreign Legion, tough young men who saw the revolution as an adventure they could not miss, among them a French artilleryman, neat to the point of dandyism, but desperately short of guns; a Jew who had fought in other revolutions and couldn't get them out of his blood; a Canadian machine gunner; a New Yorker who had learned to wreck trains and now couldn't stop; and a doctor who had accepted a commission as chief surgeon.

In addition, there were newspapermen from all over the world. Mostly they came from the north, representing the sharp magazines that caught the urgent spirit of the young United States, crisp, sparing with words, cramming everything into blunt paragraphs that pulled no punches and strove for sensation, itching always to find some scandal they could scream out. But among them also were men representing smaller papers, groups and press agencies, a few rabid socialists trying to make anti-capitalist copy out of the occasion, French writers determined to find gory stories, and men from London feeling the situation was made for disaster and anxious to pass it on to the public with their breakfasts.

They packed the hotels, jammed the bars, hired all the available transport, quarrelling at the cable office and every telegram station, and waiting – always waiting – for a statement or for something to happen. Among them was Johnny Cox, suddenly draped from head to foot in cameras. He had acquired a team of Mexicans to carry his equipment and had clearly discovered his true element. He was busy with lenses, notebooks and drawing pads, producing photographs and – where he couldn't take photographs – making sketches of what was going on. He moved about the sprawling camp like some paladin of the press, listening with his wide innocent smile for other people's discoveries and bribing telegraphists to let him see other people's despatches. He had already been offered a punch on the nose by the *New York Times* man and one of the Frenchmen had threatened to shoot him. It left him with his smile totally undisturbed.

Harley regarded them all with a jaundiced eye. No one was better at the job than he was and he knew he could always write a commentary nicely tinged with sarcasm, but this time, somehow, sarcasm seemed out of place. He was witnessing a war of little people fired with a spark of greatness.

With the border open to all but Mexicans, it was easy to cross into Texas to send long despatches home, and with that magic by-line at the top, 'With the revolutionary forces', he gave them all he had. What he wrote was strong, meaty stuff containing all he had seen at Camargo and around the camps. It included a long pen portrait of Villa and other revolutionaries, and the gleeful comment, especially for Sproat, that what he was witnessing wasn't Sproat's 'bit of an uprising' but a full-scale rebellion.

There were letters for him – including several from Isobel Hartnell, asking petulantly why he had left England without seeing her. She seemed to think he had disappeared to outer darkness and to imagine that he was somewhere in South America. There were also cables and packages, among them copies of the *Courier*. To his surprise, on the page headed 'Imperial and Foreign Intelligence', his despatches merited no more than mere paragraphs among the outbreaks of violence in Europe, North Africa and the Middle East. Clearly Sproat's conference had decided that Mexico was too distant and the minor uprisings nearer home demanded more space than a convulsion three thousand miles away across an ocean. There wasn't a single mention of Villa and he sheepishly burned the papers in case Villa demanded to see them.

He caught his first sight of Madero when he called a

conference to meet the press who were vociferously beginning to demand facts. He was small, slight and clearly delicate. A beard hid a weak chin and he had a broad forehead, receding hair and a high-pitched voice that occasionally rose almost to a falsetto. He was a vegetarian and had just finished a meal of biscuits and beans as the newspapermen gathered round him.

All the men whose names Harley had heard over and over again were with him – his father and brothers; the political men, Maytorena, Vázquez Gómez, Abraham González and Carranza, who turned out exactly as Harley had imagined him, a heavily-built, pompous man wearing blue-tinted spectacles and a bowler hat who constantly combed his beard with his fingers; the 'generals', Orozco, Blanco – and Villa, awkward and clumsy in his charro suit and decorated sombrero, aeons apart from the thinkers with his dusty clothes and gauche manners. He had obviously taken a strong dislike to Orozco, whose handsome face was always blank, as if a dozen and one plots were going on behind it all the time,and to Carranza, who, cold, unfeeling and self-satisfied, jarred even with Harley.

There were also a few so-called enlightened witnesses from Mexico City who, Harley suspected, had come less to help than to protect their own interests. Among them was Féderico Toral, smart in a city suit with a straw hat to give him just that touch of informality he felt the occasion demanded. He greeted Harley with reserve and claimed he had arrived to offer his support. 'It's clear,' he said, 'that the Díaz regime's on its last legs.'

'That's always a good time to desert it,' Harley smiled.

Madero gave what details he knew and described the recent battle for Agua Prieta, which was divided only by the width of a street from Douglas, Arizona. When rebel troops had steamed through the Federal defences on a captured train, flying bullets had killed several of the hundreds of Americans who had swarmed to watch the battle, so that finally a troop of American cavalry had crossed the street which formed the border and, offering asylum in the States, had persuaded the Federals to surrender. Civilians had poured across in their cars to give first aid to the wounded of both sides. Despite the victory, Madero seemed irritated.

'That's because it's been lost again,' whispered Tamsy, who knew everything. 'The guy who captured it – name of Lopez, a former rustler – was whooping it up with his buddies on the American side of the street when Federal reinforcements arrived. When he got over his hangover, he found his troops had thrown in their hand and he'd lost both his army and his prize.'

'The country is aflame,' Madero said in his high-pitched voice. 'And every day more men flock to our cause. Every day brings worse news for Díaz and the wind that is sweeping Mexico becomes a storm.'

As the meeting finished, Harley found Villa standing alone, frowning at his feet. Holding off the Federal cavalry thundering out of Chihuahua City to harass the movement of the revolutionary troops, he had been the last to arrive. Large, clumsy and smelling of horse-sweat and leather, throughout the meetings in front of men like Garibaldi, Viljoen and the Madero family, he had been over-awed by their education and surprised that they didn't know, any more than Orozco, what to do next.

'He lectured me about Camargo,' he growled. 'He said I hadn't to hang Porfirista officials or shoot their officers because men could learn to behave themselves under good conditions.' He scratched his head. 'It seems to me, mi amigo, that it is the *men* who make the conditions, not the conditions that make the men, and if you don't kill the hawks, they will kill more chickens. He's too trusting. One day they'll betray him.'

He frowned. 'He worries me,' he went on. 'He doesn't want to use force, he says. Por Dios, how does he expect to shift Díaz *except* by force? He seemed so innocent, he made me weep. But he told me that tears of the heart are like the benediction of heaven and can wash away sins.' He drew a deep breath and gestured angrily. 'And that lot! There are too many talkers among them just looking for places in his government. They say we must have organization, but organization to me always seems to end up in graft. What we need is a scheme to distribute power so that the poor and the uneducated aren't just unthinking battalions, exploited by a few pushers, self-seekers and crooks.'

Harley looked at him quickly. More used to the open air

than the council table, there were nevertheless times when Villa showed himself capable of deep thought.

'They asked me what I felt,' he continued slowly. 'But that old fart, Carranza, because I'm just an ignorant peón, kept saying they had a lot to discuss and time was short.' He flicked a murderous glance at the bulky white-bearded figure. 'It put me off and when they asked what I had to say, all I could think of was to say I'd finished.' He drew another painful breath that made his great chest heave. 'We listened to a lot of talk about putting on demonstrations and holding strikes. What do *they* mean to Díaz? He only understands battles and killing. I said we should attack Juárez. Seal him off from the border; he'd understand that.'

'Did they accept it?'

Like a huge raw animal, Villa turned sullen eyes to the group round Madero, jealous of their proximity to the leader and his own inability to speak their language.

'They said Juárez was too well-garrisoned and that they'd already been warned by the Americans about stray bullets crossing the border. They're afraid, amigo, afraid of an American invasion. I told them ordinary Americans were on our side – haven't we got a lot of them actually fighting for us? – and I said that what we needed was un solo golpe terífico – one terrific blow – that will shake Díaz off his throne.'

Villa's ideas, though only the promptings of an undeveloped mind, nevertheless seemed to be those of the Americans in the camp. They had been coming across the border for days, among them Angelica back from another spending spree, full of passion, but totally lacking direction – as Tamsy had said, a spluttering catherine wheel of irresponsibility.

She was wearing a wideawake hat with a cockade of feathers and a dark green habit that looked like an attempt at a uniform. She was eager with enthusiasm and devoid of fear but irritated by the presence of Féderico Toral who, Harley noticed, always seemed to be within reach. She had brought with her a group of women – a few Americans, a few city dwellers from Chihuahua, a few of the Mormon women from San Gabriel, a few Indian women, a few wives whose men had gone to join the armies – and had smuggled them past the Federals in Chihuahua to Juárez. She had also formed a troop of what she called 'boy scouts,' a para-military organization designed, she said, to fight for Mexico's independence. A crack shot herself, she had taught them to use revolvers and rifles in the empty desert, and brought them to Madero's camp.

'They're children,' Harley said. 'Mere boys!'

'In Mexico,' she snapped back, 'boys grow very quickly into men. Besides – ' she seemed to become aware that she had probably been too enthusiastic and was trying to excuse herself ' – they're only intended as messengers. The weapons are purely to defend themselves, though they're trained to fight and if necessary they will.'

'And the women?'

She was a little disconcerted. 'You said armies need nurses.'

'You don't look much like a nurse. I suspect you're enjoying all these heroics.' Harley smiled. 'You know what they think of you? That you're a high-born dabbler who'd be better off raising a family.'

'Is that what *you* think?'

'I said that's what *they* think.'

'And I asked what *you* think.'

'I think you'd be better marrying again.'

She flushed and for a moment her manner softened, then she stiffened abruptly and turned away. 'Well, I wouldn't marry *you*,' she snapped, 'if you were the last man on earth!'

8

Villa was right, and to everyone but Madero it was becoming clear that deeds not words were what were needed. All the words Madero had uttered had clearly made no impression on the old dictator in Mexico City. The reforms he had promised had come to nothing. He had replaced a minister or two and made a few concessions but he still showed no sign of resigning.

And now, like Díaz's own army, the revolutionary army, sadly lacking from the start in weapons and finance, was beginning to run out of steam. The insurrectos had mostly brought along their own weapons – Winchesters, Mausers, Remingtons, Krags, Sharps, Mannlichers, Colts, Lebels, Springfields, Mondragóns, even shotguns and old Martini-Henrys – and it was impossible to keep every man supplied with cartridges.

'If only one rifle and one calibre bullet had been invented,' Villa growled, 'we could have taken Mexico in ninety days.'

Even an American Civil War brass muzzle-loader which stood at the entrance to the town hall in El Paso but found still serviceable by a group of American enthusiasts, had been attached to the back of a car and towed across a ford of the Río Grande.

It was possible for foreign newspapermen to go in and out of Juárez without trouble and Harley saw reinforcements being pushed aboard trains for Chihuahua where the next blow was expected to fall, the officers standing at the carriage doors with loaded revolvers to prevent desertion. From

Juárez it was also easy to move into El Paso, which was like an armed camp with barbed wire everywhere and twenty thousand American soldiers taking up positions to safeguard United States soil.

The revolution had drawn so many sightseers south that the place resembled a circus. Trains brought them in every day, with still more newspapermen; commercial travellers and arms salesmen coming in with their wares on what was known as the drummers' express, eager to sell; tourists; college girls with new box cameras looking for excitement; movie cameramen from California; boys wondering if they dare join in; self-styled soldiers of fortune – most of them frauds who were after the girls and the money and had no intention of going near the fighting; middle-aged women eager to see a Mexican bandido; and elderly spinsters who at any other time would have been inspecting the ruins in Rome or journeying out to Herculaneum or Pompeii.

It was a crazy atmosphere. The revolution was a bonanza and the inhabitants were making money hand over fist. Mexicans posed for pictures and American soldiers signed their names to postcards that were held out to them. As Harley telegraphed his despatches to Europe, Johnny Cox was negotiating the sale of his film of the fighting at Camargo and, in the atmosphere of a rodeo, owners of property on high ground were offering viewpoints and bullet-proof rooms to anyone who wanted to see the battle brewing across the border. Because, despite Madero, it *was* brewing. Every newspaperman in the area who was interested in headlines was encouraging it. Eager for film, Johnny Cox had even inserted claims in the *El Paso Times*, purporting to come from the Federals in Juárez, that the rebels were afraid.

A few people had already witnessed fighting, and in quiet corners of the hotels women chattered over their coffee about the dead men they'd seen hanging from trees and the way a man spun round when hit by a bullet. Angelica was still there, still spending wildly – from her own resources because the rebels had nothing to give her – heeding Harley's words enough to recruit doctors and nurses, and contemptuous of the gossiping women who were organizing tea parties to watch the coming battle.

Passionate in her devotion to what she called 'The Cause',

she was perpetually waiting for a call to action, but since so far there had been no fighting and the army was more concerned with eating than dying, nobody wanted her. She turned her frustration on Harley.

'What are you telling them in London?' she demanded.

'That we're winning,' he said.

Her eyes lit up and the taut, bleak face became warm and beautiful at once. 'You think we are?'

'We will if Villa can persuade Madero that the border's important and that if he goes for Juárez instead of Chihuahua it'll cut Díaz off from the States.'

'Are they going to start a siege?'

'Villa wants an out-and-out attack. Madero favours discussion.'

'And you? What do you favour?'

Harley smiled. 'I favour waiting on the sidelines to see what happens.'

She sniffed. 'You're half-Mexican,' she said contemptuously. 'And you're regarding what's going on as if you've got ice water in your veins.'

Harley smiled. 'That's my English mother,' he pointed out. 'The English are noted for their phlegm.'

Returning across the river, he found the revolutionary army had moved closer to Ciudad Juárez, their camps stretching along the Río Grande on either side of the International Bridge. Madero was still unwilling to agree to bloodshed and was pinning his hopes on a surrender, but his troops had learned that General Navarro, the government commander in Juárez, had shot not only rebel prisoners but also anyone who was suspected of sympathizing with them.

As the rebel forces increased, the view in El Paso was firmly that there would be an attack, and people began to gather on the tops of tall buildings, railway box cars, along the banks of the Río Grande, and on the nearby Franklin and Krazy Kat mountains. When no battle began, they trailed away again, disappointed and angry.

Madero remained hesitant, unwilling to risk everything in a single attack. While success would give them the north, defeat would destroy the revolution in one blow, and he persisted vainly with the idea of approaching Navarro personally to demand him to relinquish the city.

A ten-day truce by which the rebels were allowed to import food and clothing from the States through Ciudad Juárez was suggested and for the first time the rebel army was properly fed and clothed. No one was worrying about arms, which could be smuggled over the Río Grande – American sympathisers even threw silver dollars across the narrow parts of the river – and when the truce expired, Madero extended it by a further five days so that Angelica began to boil with impatience.

'Just let a few Americans get across there,' she said. 'We'd clean the goddam place up in twenty-four hours!'

'Perhaps they prefer to do it on their own,' Harley pointed out gently. 'So that when it's over they can say it was a *Mexican* revolution.'

She stared at him. 'You sound like a Mexican.'

'You sound like an Irishman.'

Returning to the Mexican side of the river, Harley found Villa arguing again in favour of an attack and tempers beginning to grow frayed.

'They're well armed,' Garibaldi was yelling. 'With French machine guns and mortars!'

'There are only five hundred of them!' Villa yelled back. 'Plus about three hundred civilians!'

'Their defences have been carefully worked out.'

'A mouse can get through a small hole! There must *be* a small hole!'

'We have no artillery.'

'Then let us make some.'

Later in the day Harley came on Villa raving against Orozco, for whom his dislike had developed almost to detestation.

'He's nothing but a mule-skinner, a storekeeper!' he shouted, stuffing pieces of orange into his mouth so that pith and juice flew as he spoke. 'He can't even control his own men! We should be on the move but they refuse to budge!' He gestured angrily. 'Madero talks now of abandoning the siege and moving south! He sees visions of us marching the length of the country, picking up supporters as we go until we appear at the gates of the capital to frighten Díaz off his throne. It won't work! We'll pick up no more supporters until we show we can *knock* him off!'

Villa's absorption of an idea was always tremendous in its force and Harley suddenly realized his men were packing saddlebags and filling carts, their women stamping out the cooking fires.

Following him to a jerrybuilt armoury, he found him overseeing his men stuffing tin cans with powder, stones, ball bearings and nails. Capped with a short fuse, they were being stored in a dugout carved out of the bank of dirt between the river and an irrigation canal that ran parallel. Incredibly, the space between the two waterways had been left unguarded and the high ridge of hard mud dug from the canal during a recent spring clean provided a convenient cover.

'That,' Villa said, 'is our mousehole.'

Madero was just explaining his intentions to a noisy group of newspapermen when a crackle of firing started. It came from no more than a dozen rifles but immediately a nervous answering volley came from the city, to be answered again with redoubled energy. For every rifle that fired, ten more took up the challenge, then twenty, then fifty, until in no time there was firing along the whole line.

Madero stood and listened with a shocked look on his face and shouted to one of his aides. 'Stop it,' he yelled in his high-pitched voice. 'Stop it at once! There must be no attack!'

A mounted officer with a white flag galloped off, but even as he broke out into the open his horse was shot from under him.

Madero began to grow frantic.

'Where's Villa?' he was shouting. 'Where's Orozco? Somebody stop this shooting! I shall court martial any officer who lets his men get out of control!'

But he had already lost his audience. With a better sense of news than he had, the newspapermen had bolted for their automobiles and headed towards the source of the firing, and he frantically began to despatch aides and dictate messages to be sent under a flag of truce to Juárez requesting a renewal of the armistice.

Tamsy arrived in a cloud of dust with the car he had

acquired in El Paso and, as Harley scrambled aboard, they headed towards the canal. Volley after volley was being fired by both sides now, the whole front alive with flame and smoke. With the rolling drum-fire in their ears, Tamsy stopped the car and they ran forward, crouching below the bursts of machine gun fire that ripped through the trees. Sombreroed soldiers were moving cautiously into position.

Villa was squatting in the little ravine near his armoury. He had a group of fifty men, all heavily loaded with ammunition bandoliers and canvas pouches stuffed with the home-made bombs. In each hand he held a piece of cowhide into which had been sewn a stick of dynamite surrounded by nails, screws and stones.

'They look like tacos,' he grinned. 'But they'll be a bit more indigestible than that.'

His soldiers were lined up, grim-faced swarthy men in sombreros, weighted down with the armament they carried.

'Is the battle on?' Harley demanded, ducking down as a burst of fire clipped the top off the ravine.

'What battle?' Villa grinned. '*Is* there a battle? I heard that there wasn't to be one. This is just a bit of loose firing.'

Night was approaching but the firing didn't die down and agitated movement in the lines opposite showed that the Porfiristas were expecting an attack.

'If anybody asks,' Villa said, 'tell them I'm trying to stop the shooting. But don't tell them where.'

Leaving Tamsy with Villa, Harley dashed back to Madero's headquarters to find Madero and his advisers holding their troops back with difficulty. By dawn it was obvious nothing could stop them. They had decided for themselves that there was to be a battle, and Garibaldi was pleading for a chance to give them their heads.

Madero threw up his hands. 'We have no option,' he said. 'But first I *must* inform the enemy that the truce is at an end.'

Garibaldi's eyebrows rose. 'I thought it came to an end last night,' he said.

Hurrying back to Villa's position, Harley found marksmen emptying the Federal trenches. His fifty bombers, their rifles and pistols loaded, were gathering in position. Johnny Cox had arrived ahead of him, struggling with heavy equipment, his two assistants, their eyes scared, crouching in a ditch with their heads down. He indicated the roofs and upper windows of business blocks on the south side of El Paso across the river crammed with spectators, the rising sun glinting on field glasses and telescopes.

'This is the grand finale of the circus they've been enjoying for months,' he said.

Even the Mexicans seemed determined not to miss the excitement and a group of them in sarapes, their eyes shadowed by the brims of their huge hats, had also begun to gather. Villa was vainly trying to persuade them to head for somewhere safe.

'But, mi capitán,' one of them said earnestly, 'this is where we stood when Orozco tried to take Juárez.'

Villa threw up his arms and turned to his marksmen, explaining what he wanted. He had a gift for explaining things simply to simple men so they could understand. 'Listen, amigos,' he said. 'We're going out there to blow them out of their holes. We can't go fast, so wait until we're halfway over, and when you hear the bugle let's have heavy fire along their parapets to keep their heads down.' He looked at Harley. 'You wish to be with us, Inglés? You came to see the revolution. Now's your chance.'

He began to distribute cigars to his bombing squad. 'Light up. When you see me signal, start throwing. You'll have five seconds. Let's go.'

Running awkwardly, deploying in clumsy fashion to cover the whole line of trench opposite, the men began to scramble into the open. A drumroll of rifle fire paralyzed all movement opposite as the heavily-laden men stumbled through the smoke. They were half-way across when the Federals came to life. As a machine gun chattered, several fell but the rest pushed forward, glowing cigars stuck in their teeth. Then, as fuses were lit, the tin can bombs began to fly through the air, black specks in the sunshine, and the Federal line erupted in a slam of explosions that threw up flame-tinted yellow dust. Flat on their faces, they had barely time for a second throw before the main body erupted from cover and swept forward.

'Oh, boy!' Cox yelled, hoisting himself into the open with his camera. 'This will wow the folks back home!'

One of the French officers from Madero's contingent of mercenaries was trying to get in the line of his viewfinder and every time Cox swung it to follow some group of running figures, he moved to one side or the other, smiling and posturing, to be in the picture. As Cox continued to ignore him, he finally swung his squad of men round and halted them directly in front.

'Goddammit!' Cox yelled. 'It's not you I want pictures of, you stupid bastard! Get out of the way!'

Because there was no uniform, the rebel officers wore the national colours of red, white and green on their sombreros. There was also no regimental order and the attackers moved in no recognizable formation, just a confused stream of men in large hats with rifles, their shadows flung by the low sun on to the clouds of dust and smoke that moved across the lines.

'Rats! The sun's in my eyes!'

The voice made Harley turn. Angelica was alongside him wearing her green 'uniform'. As she lifted her head to see better, the Federal machine gun began to swing and Harley grabbed her and thrust her face-down on the muddy earth. As she twisted under him, there was a smear of dirt across her cheek and fury in her eyes.

'Goddammit,' she snapped. 'Take your hands off me!'

'It seems you don't have to be a Mexican,' he snapped back, 'to feel the compulsion to drench the ground with your blood.'

'Mexicans are willing to drench the ground with their blood, you goddam cold-hearted Limey,' she yelled, 'because it's *their* land! If anybody knows that, *you* ought to!'

As she sat up, he thrust her down again just as the scythe-like sweep of the bullets started to send up spurts of dust along the top of the bank. Johnny Cox, exposed to the flying metal but magnificently indifferent to the danger, gave a hoot of laughter.

'Let me up,' Angelica grated in a harsh whisper that was as near to a scream as it could get. '*He's* up there!'

'*He's* mad!'

Cox gave another yell of laughter but he didn't stop cranking the handle of his camera and, as Angelica struggled to free herself, Harley grabbed her arms.

'Are you *trying* to get yourself killed?' he grated. 'Because in a battle you don't have to try very hard.'

Her eyes focussed at last on the spurts of dust that were being kicked up just above her head and it dawned on her what they were. Her eyes widened and the angry reply she was about to make died on her lips. Then Cox finally decided it was becoming too dangerous and, folding the legs of the camera, he jumped down the bank and crouched on the ground beside them, flinching with them as dust was thrown over them from the striking bullets.

'Let her look, Harl',' he said. 'It's something she'll never see the like of again.'

'This isn't an entertainment put on for her special benefit,' Harley said. 'She's no damn different from those bloody women on the other side of the river who're holding tea parties to watch the battle from their roofs!'

The running men in front had fallen into the Federal trench by this time and it became a shambles of tangled figures hacking with clubbed rifles, machetes, knives, axes, pruning hooks, anything they had been able to snatch up. Federal soldiers began to scramble out of the trench. More followed until they were boiling like ants from a disturbed nest, racing for the city walls and throwing away their rifles as they ran.

Angelica made no attempt to raise her head until Harley did and, when she did so, it was without any sign of triumph in her eyes as she stared at the silent conical-hatted figures sprawled in front. By now, the whole revolutionary force was in action, advancing from two points at once. There were only two guns in the rebel armoury, one of them the stolen civil war cannon from El Paso. The first shot from the Mexican gun missed the town altogether. The second hit the water tank. The third wrecked the gun.

In the heat of the afternoon, as the firing died away, Harley pushed Angelica into an adobe house where Mexican women who had been watching the fighting had been forced to take shelter. She made no objections but her expression was sulky.

'And stay there, for God's sake,' he said.

She pretended to touch her forelock. 'Yes sir, Mr. Marquis. Sure I will, Mr. Marquis. Anything you say, Mr. Marquis.'

In the heat of the afternoon, Villa's men began to move down the banks of the river on the north side of the town.

While the Federals sprayed the men advancing from the south and south-west with shrapnel, they dared not fire to the north for fear of their missiles landing in El Paso. Nobody, neither Porfirista nor Maderista, wanted the Americans to join in and Villa had made the Americans his ally.

As he pressed forward down the steep bank of the Río Bravo, Blanco's men were working their way northwards and westwards towards the international bridge which was guarded by machine guns and heavy sandbag barricades. Fresh rebel bands, drummed up by local chiefs in Salamayuca, Zaragoza, Mesa, Mendes and Flores, were beginning to arrive. They had been en route for some time and were streaming forward, constantly moving into battle and out again as they tired. Garibaldi kept trying to force them to go forward together, but they knew what they were doing and, while the Federals, lacking sleep and water, grew more exhausted, the rebel army always had a nucleus of men fresh and ready for action.

Villa had hidden his main force in a curve of the river. In front of them a machine gun was chattering, then a bomb trailed an arc of smoke through the air and, as the thunder of the explosion silenced the gun, every man was on his feet and scrambling forward in a chaos of crashes and shouts of rage. Blackened, bloody men stumbled ahead, then the reserves charged forward in a furious mass assault, and within minutes the Villistas were swarming over the barricades among the human fragments and the mutilated dead and wounded. A few scorched and wounded prisoners crouched against the sandbags and, incredibly, a man on a bicycle holding an open umbrella against the sun and obviously unaware of the danger, rode straight across the front through the flying bullets and wasn't touched.

By sunset it was clear the Federals were in difficulties because people from the city were beginning to pour across the Río Grande into the States with their families and whatever they could carry. By this time also, water and electricity supplies had been cut, and as the black puffs of shrapnel shells were silhouetted against the yellow afterglow, smoke-blackened, dirty and crawling with lice, Harley watched the Foreign Legion heading for the bullring, the first of the rebel army to enter the city. Orozco's men were pushing into the north-western outskirts and had gained the railroad and the Customs Building, while Blanco's men were pushing through the maze of narrow streets in the south-west.

As darkness came, the firing died away, with Villa finally halted in a district of narrow streets. At dawn the shooting started again. The first men to push forward were swept away by machine gun fire to sprawl like broken sawdust dolls in crumpled heaps on the pavements, their faces hidden by the wide brims of their sombreros. From a rooftop, rifles snapped back at the machine gunners but they were answered by an artillery shell that flung roof, rifles and men aside in a shower of dust and curling yellow smoke. With the houses built wall-to-wall, there was no shelter for any attacker and they were pinned down in the shelter of the narrow cross streets.

Just in front of them was a massive barricade of heavy timbers and sandbags bristling with machine guns, and both sides of the street presented a solid wall of shops, cafés and cantinas. Streaming sweat, blood-stained, smoke-blackened and red-eyed, his jaw hanging open, his great chest heaving under a torn rag of shirt, Villa peered round the corner at it until a bullet, gouging out plaster, made him withdraw his head sharply.

'We can't attack that from the front,' he growled.

'Why not go through the houses?' Harley suggested. 'I heard that's what they did after the battle at Omdurman to avoid the snipers on the rooftops. They blew in the walls and moved from one house to the next, all the time under the cover of the roofs.'

Villa's eyebrows lifted. 'Where is this Omdurman?' he asked. 'Somewhere in England?'

Harley tried to explain but Villa's grasp of geography was limited. 'The walls in Mexican houses are only built of mud,' he said.

'So were the walls in Omdurman.'

'Won't the roofs collapse on us?'

'Not if you blow *little* holes.'

Villa was impressed. Calling up his explosives experts, he explained what he wanted and the dynamite was brought forward. Alongside them was a bar with the sign, El Templo del Amor – The Abode of Love – painted above the door with the advertisements for pulque, the 'No Posters' sign half-plastered over with sheets advertising lotteries and old bullfights, and he indicated it with a grin.

'Let's start there, amigos,' he said. 'The roof looks sound.'

As they began to climb in through the open window, Tamsy gave Harley a look of alarm. 'Holy Biddy, Boss,' he said. 'What I do to earn a livin'.'

As they crammed into the narrow little bar, a hole was drilled in the wall that separated it from the house next door, and a stick of dynamite inserted. The crash filled their eyes with dust and grit, flung down bottles and glasses, and sent a cloud of smoke puffing through the windows with the stink of explosive.

Wall by wall, they began to cut their way through the houses alongside the barricade until they reached a cross street beyond. As the barricade fell, using narrow alleyways, windows and bomb-holed walls, they pushed forward again, wrecking whole streets as they went. By nightfall on the second day every part of Ciudad Juárez except the bullring, the church and the army barracks was in rebel hands. As the last defences were reduced by mortar fire, the Federals decided they had had enough, and Garibaldi, who happened to be the only rebel officer on hand, accepted Navarro's sword in surrender.

As people began to step out into the open, dazed by the gunfire and deafened by the blasting, Angelica appeared. Her green habit was bedraggled, her hair had come unpinned, her face was dirty, and her shoes were muddy.

'You can go home now,' Harley said shortly. 'And hold a tea party to tell all your friends how you watched the battle.'

'Okay, goddammit,' she snapped back. 'So I made a fool of myself! I was wrong and in future I'll be a good girl and keep my nose out of men's affairs. You don't have to rub my goddam face in it.'

Part Two

1

The sky was full of the wheeling shapes of vultures as Tamsy Flood edged the car through the red mud of the shattered streets. The wounded lay with the stiff carcasses of horses in every doorway and behind every wall.

The looting had already started and every shop they passed had had its windows smashed and its merchandise strewn across the streets among the shards of shattered glass. Grimy blood-splashed men in sombreros, still swathed in bandoliers of cartridges, rummaged among the debris, indifferent to the dead. At one shop a group of them had found a drawerful of coloured silk shirts and they were grinning with delight as they dragged them on, one on top of another. Next door, others were scrambling among a pile of shoes trying to find two that would fit. One man carried a sewing machine and another pushed a brand-new perambulator, which, he said, he had acquired the day before and had pushed about with him all through the fighting. Another wore several sombreros one on top of the others, two shirts and a pair of bright yellow button boots.

A stiff breeze was fanning the flames started by Villa's bombing, and the Federal Medical Corps had been unable to function under the ferocity of the attacks, so that the American Red Cross and others were bringing blankets and bandages from across the river. But they were struggling with a task beyond their numbers, and a stream of walking wounded and terrified and homeless non-combatants was pouring across the International Bridge to the internment camps on the American side.

Dynamiting was still going on to collapse wrecked buildings, and a long coil of dark smoke hung over the stricken city, but the final mopping up had finished and the wounded were being carried from the doorways where they had been propped up out of the firing to the emergency hospitals set up in hotels. A soldier staggered in with his jaw shot away, his pink tongue flapping stupidly from his mouth, and a small knot of men carried a heavily-laden blanket from which blood dripped steadily to the ground. They came like drunkards, leaning on each other, one of them a mere boy staggering under the weight of his dead father, behind him an exhausted horse, its head down, two bodies flopping across the saddle, behind them on the horse's rump a man with a gaping wound in his thigh shouting with pain at every step the horse took. Mexican and American doctors were slaving over the injured of both sides while the Federal prisoners were lifting the dead into carts and driving them to the fields on the outskirts where they were thrown into shallow graves. From one of them, hurriedly dug and as hurriedly filled in, an arm protruded.

The conditions were unbearable and in the terrible hospitals, the wounded still wearing the filthy bandages that had been applied during the fighting, lay exhausted among the dirty blankets, too worn to rise from the puddles of water and blood to combat the fires that sometimes raged around them. In the street outside the prostitutes had emerged from their shelters and were offering their wares among the excited rebel soldiers.

Harley found Angelica in one of the hotels. Outside, the proprietor's staff were already painting its new name, *Hotel Francisco I. Madero*, over the old one, *Hotel Porfirio Díaz*. Her face was still smudged, and there was blood on the hem of her skirt. All round her small dark men lay in rows, some of them moaning, some of them stiff and still, among them occasionally a woman or a child caught by the bombardment or the crossfire. Swarms of flies hovered over them, the air loud with their humming, and the smell of sweat, blood and excrement was nauseating so that she looked as if she were on the point of vomiting.

'Some of them have been here since it started,' she said in a stark voice. 'There's typhus among them, too. The Federals brought it with them from the south and there are cases lying among the wounded. Some of them are already dead of neglect or starvation.'

Her eyes were wide and scared so that, for a moment, caught up in something that was suddenly too big for her, she had lost her self-assurance and looked like a young foal in the presence of fresh blood. She never seemed able to burn with an even light of steady endeavour but erupted in a series of explosions and suddenly she had been damaged by one she had helped to make. As she stared at Harley, her nostrils flared, her face peaked with unhappiness, he longed to put his arms round her, brush the damp hair from her face and calm her with soothing words.

'It's a different revolution from the one you expected, isn't it?' he said gently. 'This is the bit without the banners and the glory and the fine speeches.'

She was scared enough to misunderstand his attempt to be kind and flashed a bitter glance at him. 'It was necessary.' Her voice was shaky and she was trembling, as though fighting with her courage. 'For Mexico.'

'And now?' he asked. 'Where will you go now? Mexico City? To see the celebrations?'

'Yes.' She stiffened as if getting a grip on herself, and flashed him an anxious appealing look. 'What about you?'

It wasn't his job to go to Mexico City, he knew. Knowles, the *Courier*'s man there, could cover the departure of Díaz and the arrival of Madero when it occurred. His own job was to stay with the armies, to see them win the final victories. But he was going to the capital, nevertheless, and suddenly he knew it was because he wanted to be near Angelica Ojarra.

'Are you a Catholic?' she asked in a small voice.

'Not a very good one.'

'Come with me to church. Somebody ought to offer up some prayers.'

He agreed and she put a shawl over her head and they joined others in the cool interior. It was a long time since Harley had been to church and he studied the dusty figures of the Madonna and the Christ, conscious of a guilty feeling of having neglected something that should have been part of his life. Angelica knelt alongside him, as beautiful as a Madonna herself, her face calm and composed, her turbulent spirit quiet for once. Whatever she claimed to be, at heart she was a good Irish Catholic, awed by the saints and frightened by threats of damnation.

As they left, they became aware that church bells were pealing all over the city, so that the whole centre seemed to be vibrating with the clamour. Hurrying to the door, they saw Madero had appeared in the street, surrounded by his staff and political backers. They were clean and neat, unlike the blackened, bearded, wild-eyed scarecrows in their torn and burned shirts who had done the fighting. But nobody seemed to notice and as the cheering started rifles and pistols were fired into the air in an ecstasy of triumph and admiration. Even the captured Federal soldiers stopped their grisly task and began to strip off their uniforms and shout 'Viva la Constitución.' For the most part the men behind Madero seemed unmoved by the tragedy but Madero himself, a tiny figure alongside the bulk of Carranza, looked sick and shaken at what he had caused.

Behind the official party came the swarms of the curious, the souvenir hunters and the looters. They had hurried across the border bridges and the shallows of the river and were helping themselves to anything portable that hadn't already been taken. They were scurrying away with Federal weapons, flags, belts and caps. One of them had a jacket bearing a sergeant's insignia, covered with mud and stained with blood, which he had picked up in the street.

One of the American doctors shouted at him. 'Put that down,' he roared. 'Some of these men have typhus and typhus is carried by fleas! You could take it back across the border!'

The man dropped the jacket as if it were red-hot but it was immediately snatched up by another man and spirited away.

The first announcement about Madero's plans was made later in the day. Johnny Cox brought the information. He had spent all his time since the fall of the city bribing Orozco's soldiers to put on their armouries and filming them charging, grimacing, waving their rifles, falling 'dead' in mock attacks which he could sell as the real thing to the American newsreel companies.

'They're providing Navarro with a car and he's to be allowed to cross the frontier into the States,' he said. 'Garibaldi and his Foreign Legion are to be Madero's bodyguard. Carranza's to be Minister of War.'

A headquarters had been set up in the old Customs Building, and Madero, in Norfolk jacket and breeches, was making speeches outside from the back of a car surrounded by insurrecto soldiers. A few politicians also made speeches, and there was a lot of music and cheering, then, moving inside, at a massive table surrounded by chairs Madero sat with his advisers, his father, his brother, Abraham González, Carranza, and a few others, among them, Harley noticed to his surprise, Féderico Toral. Watching them from the door was a crowd of newspapermen and El Pasoans who had crossed the river to see the fun.

'This, gentlemen,' Carranza announced, 'is the first meeting of our cabinet – at the moment one day old.'

As he spoke, the people crowding the doorway were thrust apart as Villa and Orozco burst into the room. For the first time Villa had put off his yellow leather charro costume and was dressed in a clean shirt and store suit, a watch chain across his stomach, his pigeon-toed horseman's feet, more used to sandals, crammed into tight shoes, a new American campaign hat on the back of his head in place of his sombrero.

Madero smiled. 'Don Francisco,' he said. 'You look like a politician in those clothes.'

Villa glowered. He was obviously in a towering temper. 'Salas Vaca and Tomás Urbina found them for me,' he growled. 'If I have to talk with politicians, I have to look like one.'

'You need something?'

Villa and Orozco looked at each other then Orozco backed away and it was Villa who had to step forward.

'We've heard you've agreed to let Navarro go.' His face grew dark. 'He should be executed! You insult our dead by letting him go.'

Garibaldi tried to intervene but Villa's hand dropped to

the gun at his hip. 'Tell this foreigner to mind his tongue,' he snapped at Madero. 'You insult those of us who fought by making him leader of your guard of honour. What's wrong with our own men?'

The impact of his rage silenced the room. Nobody moved or spoke and for a moment the atmosphere was electric with menace. Then one of the newspapermen started to scribble down what he saw and his action was immediately followed by all the others.

Madero hadn't moved and Villa went on, still in a fury of anger. 'You've appointed him – ' his thumb jerked at Carranza ' – as Minister of War! What's wrong with a man who's done the fighting? He's never fired a shot in his life!'

Madero rose. 'I have here,' he said gently, 'your commission as a colonel in my army and Orozco's commission as a brigadier-general.' He leaned over the table, signed the papers and passed them across. The action silenced Villa and he stared at the paper as if he suspected a trick. Then Madero went on in a quiet voice, explaining that a Minister of War wasn't a soldier but a bureaucrat who had to be used to handling public affairs, while there was still fighting to be done by the men who *were* soldiers. Villa's great head sank forward, his heavy brow wrinkled with bewilderment, baffled by the correcto manners of the men round the table.

'We have to remember,' Madero went on in a low voice, 'that General Navarro fought at the side of Benito Juárez, our great leader, against Maximilian of Austria, and it's no fault of his that, in the performance of his duty as a loyal soldier to the state, he now finds himself against *us*.'

'He's been given a car and allowed to leave!' Villa growled. 'He's to get his freedom.'

'The car's been borrowed,' Madero pointed out. 'And he's crossed into America. He gave his promise never to take up arms against us again.'

'People like him butchered women and children at Tomochic, Papantlá and Orizaba.'

'Do you wish that we should prove to be of the same calibre, Don Francisco?'

The argument went on for some time, Villa towering over Madero, watched by the silent men round the table who seemed mesmerized by the duel of wills.

'You risk your whole future, mi presidente,' Villa grated. 'Gallantry to a man who would have executed you if the boot had been on the other foot is foolish.'

Madero refused to let go, clinging stubbornly to his principles but arguing quietly and with force, his expression always one of saintliness and hope. Slowly the angry redness in Villa's eyes dispersed then, suddenly, his mouth twitched and he was grinning, infectiously, admitting he was wrong. Orozco, equally uneasy, cleared his throat and did the same. As Villa gave the little leader one of his huge abrazos, enfolding him in his arms, a small neat figure against his own bulk, chairs were carried from the room and everybody went outside to have their photograph taken as a group, the revolutionary leaders and their generals, Madero in the middle, with Vázquez Gómez and Abraham González on either side with Maytorena, Carranza – looking like a university professor – and Orozco, his campaign hat cocked arrogantly over his eye, confident, shrewd and cunning. Behind them were the Maderos, father and brother, Blanco, rubbing eyes that were still red with smoke and tiredness, Garibaldi and Toral. Villa, awkward in his city suit, was pushed unwillingly on the end, and stood with his hands in his pockets, looking as if he wanted no part of it.

Johnny Cox set the occasion on record. There were no other cameramen present because the rest had suddenly discovered they had been deserted by the men carrying their equipment, and Harley found himself wondering if Cox had bribed them to disappear.

Villa's quarrel with Madero had been an awkward moment and Madero had overcome it by sheer personal charm, but the newsmen, more worldly-wise, saw the problems at once.

'Well, that's that,' the *New York Times* man observed as the cameras stopped clicking. 'But it sure shows how brittle this goddam revolution is. The little man's going to find running this country a damn sight harder than capturing it. He shouldn't have freed Navarro, he *should* have had Mexicans as his bodyguard, and he *should* have appointed some representative of the boys to the cabinet. And he sure as hell shouldn't have given the Ministry of War to a guy who only last year voted for Díaz.'

The whole Díaz structure was crumbling. Villa had been right. Ciudad Juárez was the beginning of the end.

In a dozen states, guerrilla chiefs were on the warpath and Zapata was reported at the very gates of Mexico City. Torreón, the most important railroad and military centre in the north, fell to Villa and immediately there was a massacre of Chinese settlers who had set up their shops and little businesses there. At once it was blamed by the correctos, who despised the riotous guerrillas, on Villa's troops; and one newspaperman sent off a story saying they had got drunk on brandy and had run amok, shooting and stabbing and tying their Chinese victims to horses by their pigtails.

Villa stormed in on Harley. 'Tell them the truth, Inglés!' he yelled. 'Por Dios, tell them the truth! It was started by the laundrywomen because the Chinese had taken away their business!'

After Torreón, Chihuahua went, then, with the whole of the north and part of the south falling, the end came. At midnight, eleven days after the fall of Juárez, Madero and his cabinet gathered at a collapsible table placed for them in the street in front of the half-wrecked Customs building. There was still no electricity and cars were called round to provide illumination with their headlights. Tamsy edged the hired car forward, and they were in the forefront as Díaz's emissary announced that his master would give up the presidency. There was a whoop from the watching crowd but the men round the table said nothing, and Madero stood up to announce that, having agreed that the presidency should be held by the Mexican ambassador in Washington until an election could be held, he was giving up the title of provisional president until he could be properly elected.

'The guy's out of touch,' Tamsy growled. 'Holy Biddy, that ain't the way they do things in Mexico. They like a president to *grab* power. By the scruff of the neck.'

Angelica was still at the hotel but order was being restored now and, lacking nursing skill, her presence in Juárez was no longer urgent because there were plenty of local women eager to play their part.

'You still going to Mexico City?' she asked shortly.

'Yes,' Harley agreed. 'I'm going to Mexico City.'

She paused. 'And afterwards? When it's all over. When Madero's elected president and the revolution's finished. What then?'

'I go home.'

The green eyes flashed. 'This is your home,' she said unexpectedly.

'England's my home.'

She shook her head, her eyes dangerously bright and angry. '*This* is more your home than you know,' she said. 'If you go home now, you'll only come back. If not this year, then next. If not next, then some time. But you'll come back.'

He knew what she meant. Hungry, half-starved, backward, desperate for stability and education, Mexico could offer him little in comparison with powerful, sophisticated, expert Britain, but he had been aware from the moment he had set foot over the border that it possessed something that was important to him.

The capital, looking like a little Paris with its tree-lined Paseo de la Reforma, its French architecture, its champagne and the splendour of its new opera house, was jittery as Harley arrived. The streets were crowded and, stripped of troops to counter Zapata's attacks in the south, the city was nervous.

In the newspaper, *El Independiente*, there was a cruel cartoon showing a terrified Díaz, portrayed as a rabbit, hiding behind a boulder while Madero searched for him with a shotgun. It was boldly drawn, striking and modern, and Harley commented on it.

'Me,' Johnny Cox said. 'I often drew 'em for the Los Angeles papers to make a little dough.'

Knowles, the *Courier*'s man in the capital, showed little pleasure at Harley's arrival. He was a stringy, moustached man with a face devoid of expression, as though he had spent all his life cultivating a no-comment attitude to what he saw. He was formally dressed in a high collar, suit and watch chain, his only concession to informality in the increasing heat a boater with a red and white ribbon.

'Mexico City's *my* territory,' he pointed out stiffly.

Harley soothed him gently. 'I'm not interested in Mexico City,' he said. 'But I've been following Madero around. I need to know how he's received here – in case anything happens.'

'What can happen?'

Harley shrugged. 'Nothing, I suppose,' he said. 'He made it.' But somewhere at the back of his mind was the uneasy feeling that among those advisers of Madero's he'd seen at Juárez were a few who would have preferred being the leader to being the led.

Knowles agreed to include him in anything he did and even found an apartment for him and Tamsy with a woman to clean for them. But he had a telegram from Sproat for him, too. It confirmed what Harley had expected. '*War over,*' it said. '*Return London soonest. No interest anything that drags on too long.*' It was tantamount to an order but he was determined to see the last act of the drama.

Leaving Tamsy to handle the luggage, he went with Knowles to Díaz's home in the Calle Cadena. The newspapermen were already keeping the death watch there and almost the first person he saw was Johnny Cox, who gave him a wide grin from behind the tripod camera he had set up in the back of a landau across the road.

There was a huge mob outside the house yelling that it was time Díaz went. There were shouts for Madero and the Revolution and demands for the president's head, but no real violence. At the station the Científicos and the men who had given their support to Díaz were collecting with their families, servants, luggage and personal possessions, and brawls kept breaking out with Maderistas and yelling youngsters from the university who had become revolutionaries overnight.

The following day the demonstrations were larger. Starting in narrow backstreets teeming with people, crammed with carts and waggons and smelling of decay, urine and horse dung, the mobs grew until they numbered thousands, then they burst out into the wide avenues, following military bands or improvized orchestras of violins snatched from cafés and playing national airs. With still no sign of the dictator's departure, the shouts were fiercer now and students and workmen patrolled the squares, beating empty petrol cans and yelling for resignation.

'Down with Díaz! Viva Madero! Viva la revolución!'

In the wealthy areas of the city, the correctos had barricaded the doors and were keeping well away from the windows, and Tamsy, prowling round the bars, brought the news that a march had been planned on the National Palace.

'There's going to be trouble!' he said as Harley reached for his coat. 'They've got soldiers on the roof. Several companies, Boss. With machine guns. There are more on the south side of the square.'

The demonstrations were flowing towards the Zócalo, the great open space fronting the vast flat-faced edifice of the National Palace. The crowd had attempted to reach the Díaz home again but, driven back by the Rurales, was collecting in front of the Cathedral. Yelling men were standing on boxes – students, socialists, Maderistas, Zapatistas – all enjoying the wild exhilaration of the freedom of speech. As he struggled to force his way through, Harley found himself alongside Angelica.

'What are you doing here?'

She gave him a hot glance. 'I want to be here when Díaz goes. I want to cheer him on his way.' She was dressed as usual in a green that matched her eyes and looked magnificent in her anger.

'Is Faithful Fred here?'

'Faithful Fred's doing a lapdog act for Madero,' she muttered. 'He wants a job in the Cabinet.'

Harley smiled, openly admiring her. 'He doesn't realize what he's missing,' he said.

She looked sharply at him to see if he was teasing and, realizing he wasn't, she blushed. Then someone knocked her hat on one side and she pushed it straight with a fierce gesture.

'Féderico Toral means nothing to me,' she snapped. 'You know that. And that isn't why I came to Mexico City. I'm here because this is what I've prayed for, for years, what I spent money on, worked for, hoped for. It's the end of a corrupt régime.'

'Spoken like a good American,' Harley smiled.

'I'm not American,' she grated furiously. 'I'm a Mexican. A dago. A greaser. I made myself one. Nobody forced me.'

She spoke too earnestly and he had a suspicion that she

wasn't sure what she was. Despite her wishes, she couldn't throw off her heritage any more than he could.

He indicated the crowd and the police in front of the Palace. 'Make sure you haven't picked the wrong spot,' he warned. 'This is no place for a woman.'

'Nobody's going to make me miss it!' she said. 'Not even you! I'm going to watch Díaz leave even if I have to stay here all night.'

He pulled her aside. 'I think you've got plenty of time,' he pointed out. 'It isn't going to happen just yet and we can watch what happens from the café under the arcades over there.'

The café was crowded but they found a table and she sat opposite him, her face defiant, even sullen. 'I don't need looking after,' she snorted.

'I think you do,' he said. 'Are you hungry?'

She said nothing for a moment then she nodded. 'I've been here a long time.'

Catching the eye of a waiter, Harley ordered food and they sat watching the crowd outside, aware of the warm human roar of people determined not to miss the fun. There was still no anger, only curiosity, though from time to time there were periods of turbulence as some more virulent speaker stirred up his section of the mob.

The sun disappeared by the side of the cathedral and in the west the clouds were building up and the sky was darkening. Angelica had relaxed a little but she was still prickly and hostile.

'What happens now?' Harley asked. 'Now that the revolution's at an end?'

'A new one's beginning. One of education and freedom.'

'Don't get too involved in it. You're flesh and blood, not a bill passing through Congress.'

She reddened. 'What's it to you?' she demanded. 'You're already spoken for. Isobel Hartnell, isn't it?'

He wondered how she knew. Had she pumped Knowles? Or had Johnny Cox found out and passed it on for reasons of his own.

She gave him an angry glance but she made no attempt to go. Then they noticed that the crowd outside had become so packed it had become almost immovable. Almost at the same time, they became aware of a hush, as though at some menace, and Harley rose to his feet. Angelica pushed with him to the door and they forced themselves into the edge of the crowd which was suddenly no longer cheerful, but demanding Díaz's head again.

The sun had gone completely now, and the sky was prematurely dark. As they watched they saw a squad of mounted police emerge from the main entrance of the Palace. The roaring increased and the horsemen were forced back by the density of the crowd. As they retreated, they were followed by yells of derision with which were mixed fiercer, angrier cries at this last demonstration of the fading dictator's power.

Three more times the police tried to force a way through but each time they were driven back. Then, on the fourth attempt, one of the officers nervously fired his pistol over the heads of the crowd. It was a mistake because several others immediately followed suit and at once any good humour that was left disappeared. Bunching, the crowd charged.

Over the teeming heads, Harley saw horses' heads high in the air, their ears laid back in fright, their eyes bulging, their riders struggling with people trying to drag them from the saddle. A man went down, yelling, then a horse crashed to the ground, and, looking up, Harley saw men running along the roofs of the Palace and movement round the machine guns.

Grabbing Angelica, he began to elbow his way towards a doorway, using fists and feet to make a path between the screaming people.

'Let me go!' she yelled at him. 'I want to see! I came to see!'

Fighting to throw off his grip, she swung at him with her handbag until, in the end, he snatched it from her. He had just thrust her into a doorway and crouched against her, covering her with his body, when the roar of the crowd was cut across by a stuttering crash as a volley was fired. The shouting died in a sudden shocked silence, then it started up again in a mixture of angry yells, agonized screams and wails of terror. Faces which had been watching from upstairs windows were hurriedly withdrawn and shutters were slammed to.

There were thousands of people in the square, massed so tightly there was no hope of flight and no need for the riflemen to aim. Milling and trampling on each other in panic, people fell in rows and groups. Almost at once the Maxim guns started and the screams rose higher. Clutching Angelica in a corner of the doorway, his cheek pressed against hers, Harley heard the clink and clatter of bullets striking the brickwork and whining off into the air. Her face was white and shocked, her eyes wide and terrified and blinking at every burst.

The firing lasted a full five minutes, coming in gusts and ragged volleys. Though it killed and maimed, it didn't disperse the crowd. Infuriated, intent now on murder, they hurled themselves at the Palace, determined to get to the men who were shooting at them. But then the clouds, which had been building up all evening, opened. Black as velvet, they tossed down the first drops of rain, hot and huge, so that they splashed on the pavement in great splodges of water. They were followed by a roll of thunder that drowned even the firing and, in a flash of purple fire, the heavens opened and a solid wall of water crashed down. It was so heavy it snatched at the breath and the crowd stopped dead, drenched to the skin in a second.

There was a wild stampede for shelter and in a moment the square was deserted, except for huddled groups in doorways, the sprawled figures of the dead, and the slow-moving shapes of the injured. The water sluicing across the square washed away the bloody pools as figures fled past the doorway where Harley crouched, trying to shelter Angelica from the downpour. Among them a man swung round and fell slowly to the ground, his fingers clawing at the wall. As he subsided to the pavement, blood from his breast daubed a red smear across the stonework.

Vehicles decorated with red and white crosses began to swing into the square, searching for the wounded dragging themselves like slugs across the stones. A few newspapermen were moving about, startled by what had happened, and Harley saw Knowles standing in a doorway, looking shocked, and Johnny Cox on the steps of the Cathedral, a wet sketch pad in his hand, drawing as if his life depended on it.

'For Christ's sake!' he yelled. 'Why couldn't the lousy bastards do it before dark so I coulda taken a picture?'

The square was still full of drifting smoke and people kept darting out from doorways to drag away dead and dying. Stretched on the ground in front of them, the man who had been hit was breathing in a heavy snore. Bending over him Harley saw an artery had been severed and his fingers were reddened with his blood. As the man's head fell back, he looked up to see Angelica kneeling alongside him, tears in her eyes, her wet clothes clinging to her body, shining strands of hair sticking to her white cheeks.

Sitting back on her heels, she put her hands to her face. 'Damn Díaz,' she whispered above the moaning. 'Damn him! Why couldn't he go in peace?'

2

The massacre in the Zócalo wrote the end to Díaz's reign.

He was informed by his followers that they could no longer be responsible for his life and as the journalists bolted for telephones and motor cars to break the news to the world, a huge parade started to snake round the city centre – police, peóns, students and soldiers from both sides.

The press were at the station to see him go. Accompanied by his grim-faced wife and followed by his children and grandchildren, he had quitted his house in the Calle Cadena, leaving behind everything he possessed. Pressmen and railway officials watched in silence as he headed towards his carriage. Ahead of his train another, hissing steam and crammed with soldiers, waited to lead the way in case of an attempt against his life. There were a few handshakes, then General Huerta, in command of the guard, a stumpy squarely-built man with a blank Indian face, round wire-rimmed spectacles and a reputation as a brandy drinker, indicated the soldiers. 'These represent the only portion of the country that hasn't gone against you,' he pointed out.

Like the rest of the press corps, Harley had been on his feet without rest for almost a week now, snatching what sleep he could in trains and between the events pouring over Mexico one after the other. With Díaz gone, Madero was moving down from the north with his staff, his advisers and the main body of his troops, and there was time to catch up.

Angelica had been to see him, subdued, no longer angry, somehow loath to see the end of it all.

'I owe you an apology,' she said unwillingly. 'You saved my life, I guess. I shall watch Madero come then I shall go back to San Gabriel.'

'To do what?'

She shook her head in perplexity. 'I don't know. I could open a school but my husband's family opened one years ago and there aren't enough children for two. I could open a hospital, or at least somewhere they could go when they were sick, but I know nothing about nursing. What about you?'

'I'm not sure. It hasn't finished here yet.'

'It will have when Madero arrives.'

'Will it, Angelica?' Harley was thinking of the hard-faced men surrounding Madero, all of them more experienced in politics than he was.

'For God's sake,' she said angrily, 'what else can happen? He's won! He's coming! He'll be president! There's no one who doesn't want him to be. He could rule for a lifetime if he wished. He's the only honest man there is.'

Harley shrugged. 'Either way it'll be none of my business. I'll be going back to England. Why not come, too? Take time off for a holiday. Come and stay at my home for a while.'

She gave him a sad look, as if she'd hoped for more, and shook her head slowly. The spirit seemed to have left her. 'I don't think so,' she said flatly. 'I've heard about your family. Gachupín here. Upper crust in England. Class either way. What would they think of me? Bog-Irish Mexican-American. A dago. A greaser whose only qualification is having some dough.'

He didn't reply because it was true that his mother's family didn't even consider the fact that he worked for a newspaper – or even at all – quite proper. *The Times* might have been all right but the *Courier* was beyond the pale.

She shrugged. 'It was my own choice,' she said. 'When I married and came to live here, it seemed wrong, things being what they were, to be anything else. There were too many goddam gringos profiteering from the poor bastards. I couldn't be another. I said I was Mexican and gave them good wages and good conditions. I can't go back on it now.'

Madero's journey was becoming a processional as every little wayside station and halt was jammed with dark-faced, cotton-clad crowds waving sombreros and rebozos and drowning the hiss of the train with the rocking waves of their cheers.

'Viva Madero! Viva la revolución! Tierra y libertad!'

Because Madero insisted on halting wherever a group had gathered to welcome him, it was a slow progress. As the train stopped, women ran forward to deck the engine and the carriages with garlands of flowers, and girls offered bouquets and snatched the ribbons from their hair to tie them to the rear platform of the observation car. There was no sign of triumph in his speeches, however, only an earnest plea for patience and goodwill in the difficult task of remaking Mexico. Nobody listened. All they asked was to be allowed to see him, to touch him with their fingers.

There was a semi-royal reception in Chihuahua, presented with cynical realism by men who not long before had backed Díaz, but the roars of approval as Madero made a speech from the balcony of the Governor's palace came not from them but from the peóns and the campesinos who had flocked in from the surrounding plains and hills. At Torreón, only recently ravaged by the mobs, he was welcomed as a saviour, and as the slow procession dropped into the valley of Mexico, the crowds became so dense it was almost halted. Strangers crowded the villages through which it passed, bringing flowers and gifts of ancient Aztec craftsmanship. There were cries, tears, blessings of a people transported with relief and delight because they felt that once more they owned the ground they stood on. Touched by Madero's mystic aura of goodness, they packed the bridges, the stations, the level crossings, and climbed the water tanks just to be able to look at him. Women held up sick babies, firmly believing he could cure them. Madero was not just a conqueror. He was a saviour. He was Christ come again.

There were dozens of newspapermen in the capital waiting for his arrival. The Mexican papers didn't seem sure what line to take – one of welcome, doubt, concern for the country's future, even contempt for his inexperience. In *El Independiente* there was a cartoon of him with Carranza and Vázquez Gómez with instruments but all playing different tunes. In the background was Orozco looking like an organ grinder's monkey and Féderico Toral and a few others as puppets manipulated by the ghost of Porfirio Díaz. It was clever and cruel and Harley recognized it at once as one of Johnny Cox's.

As the city prepared for Madero's arrival, the streetcars were having to push with clanging bells through the crowds that poured out of the narrow back streets to where they could see the newspaper kiosks, the sweet and balloon-sellers and the flower vendors' baskets. Beneath the rococo buildings of the French Second Empire, thousands of Indians, who had trudged in by foot or ridden in on carts and donkeys, prepared to spend the nights in the plazas and streets and parks, sitting round their little charcoal fires, clapping their hands as they fashioned their tortillas and lying in dusty bundles under the shelter of the walls.

Nobody seemed to want to go to sleep and the streets were full of strollers. Knowing that within days Harley would be on his way home, he and Angelica had eaten together, both unwilling to say goodbye. They drank their coffee under the trees in the Paseo de la Reforma and as they started to walk across the wide lawns of the Alameda Park, Harley suddenly felt her hand in his.

All round them, people were stretched out on blankets and sarapes, or squatting in groups talking in low voices. There were the clink of bottles and the movement of restless bodies. All the way from the station to the National Palace, triumphal arches had been erected, some of wood, some of branches. Topping them were the Mexican eagle and serpent and the streets were filled with flags and banners and strips of bunting.

Just before dawn they became aware of dogs barking. Despite the chilly night, the air seemed stuffy and strangely full of menace. A horse neighed and in a nearby street they heard a donkey bray. Then suddenly the birds sleeping in the trees began to twitter and then to crash away in a blind blundering flight.

Harley had stopped dead and Angelica had moved closer to him, so that he could feel her body brushing his.

'What is it, Harley?' she whispered.

The next second there was a violent rumbling sound like thunder that seemed to come from beneath their feet. Flung together as the earth lurched, they clutched each other as a great fissure ran across the ground less than twenty yards away. Dozing people sat up and scrambled to their feet. In a moment everybody was yelling with fright.

'By God!' Harley yelled. 'It's an earthquake!'

The shaking seemed to go on for an eternity and, clutching coats and dressing gowns to them, people were appearing from the houses around, hurled out of bed by the movement. With a crash a wall collapsed in a roaring cascade of bricks that enveloped a group of people running for the safety of the park, and trees shook as if there were a high wind. The Alameda was filled with screaming people as roofs collapsed one after another, then a power cable fell, crackling and sparking, the noise drowning the clamour of the streetcar bells as the whole area was blacked out.

Holding Angelica to him, Harley waited for the movement to stop, watching the earth rising and falling around them. New fissures appeared, running swiftly away on every side so that the whole city seemed to be bowing, swaying backwards and forwards, and water shot into the air in great fountains from burst mains. Finally it stopped. The silence was immense after the din, then the wailing and the screams started again.

As she became aware of Harley's arms about her, his face only inches from hers, Angelica's trembling stopped and she became stiff. Flushing, she pushed him away roughly.

'This is becoming a goddam habit,' she said. She stared about her at the yelling people, the collapsed buildings and the torn and tortured earth. 'My God,' she went on quietly. 'Madero's enemies will say it's God's vengeance on us for turning Díaz out!'

The excitement had died by the time full daylight came but there was wreckage all over the city. The Church of Santo Domingo had fallen, killing people praying for the health of the new president, and the San Cosme barracks had collapsed, crushing over thirty soldiers. The streetcars had been halted by twisted tracks and fallen wires, the central railway station had crashed to the ground, and there was a new and massive crack in one of the walls of the Palace so that the arch through which Díaz had passed daily during the long years of his reign had a distinctly cock-eyed look. Only the imminent arrival of Madero quelled the panic.

At his express wish, troops were not called out, but within hours the streets had been cleared by his supporters and the dead and injured removed. Fresh tricolour flags sprouted everywhere and people began to return to line the sidewalks with their ribbons and bouquets.

The fear was swept aside by the welcome. Moving a yard or two at a time through the vast roar that filled the air, it took four hours for Madero's cavalcade to cover the two miles to the Palace from the railway station where he had stepped imperturbably over the fissures caused by the earthquake. As the excitable Mexican blood surged, the crowd tossed up hats, waved rebozos, and yelled themselves hoarse. From windows and balconies flowers and bouquets were thrown, and hysterical people constantly broke into the procession.

The parade was led by Madero in a two-horse carriage driven by top-hatted, high-booted postilions who only a week before had been driving Díaz. Orozco, in the fourth car and clad suddenly in the gold lace of a general's uniform, rose from time to time and swung to right and left with stiff salutes. Villa was with Blanco, looking acutely ill-at-ease and uncomfortable, and as the crowds, recognizing him from Johnny Cox's pictures that had appeared about the capital, began to shout his name, he rose sheepishly, called for a cheer for Madero and sat down again hurriedly.

That evening the press were allowed with their photographers and cameras into the National Palace where Madero, tired-looking but flushed with happiness, was trying to smile as flash gun after flash gun went off. The air was filled with white magnesium smoke as he stood with his entourage for the occasion to be set on record. Alongside him were his immediate colleagues, immaculate in evening dress, boiled shirts and gloves, and behind them the soldiers, epauletted, pomaded and hung with medals, all crowded into the audience chamber.

Villa was unimpressed. Civilian-suited, clumsy, struggling to be on his best behaviour, he eyed them with suspicion. 'They look exactly like the gang we just kicked out,' he growled.

As they watched, a small slender man with a thin sensuous face half-hidden by a large moustache arrived. His eyes were hard and dark as obsidian and, making no attempt to ape the politicians, he was dressed theatrically in charro costume. He wore a well-fitting black jacket and tight trousers trimmed down the seams with silver, and in his hand was an enormous decorated sombrero. Villa stared at him with narrowed eyes.

'Who's he?' he demanded.

It was Zapata, the man who had won the south for Madero, cold, distant and wary of the men he saw about him, even of Villa and the northern leaders. Introductions were made, Zapata calm, dignified, his eyes burning with black fervour, Villa awkward, looking more like a small farmer on a day out than a soldier.

Suspicious, preferring his own territory, Zapata had made the journey to the capital to meet the man who was supposed to be about to change things in Mexico, and he was still wearing a gun. Madero stood alongside him, eyeing the weapon with disapproval, as if he knew it didn't fit the image he was hoping to present to his divided country. Eventually he drew attention to it.

'We must put our arms aside now,' he urged. 'We need them no longer.'

Zapata's black eyes were expressionless. He fingered the watch chain Madero wore. 'If I were to use my gun to take your watch by force, mi jefe,' he said, 'would you have the right to ask for it back?'

Madero nodded, his air one of goodness and hopefulness, as if he felt he was getting through to this man who had such a terrible reputation.

'Of course, of course,' he said.

There was no change in Zapata's expression but there was a note of triumph in his voice. 'Then you'll understand why I carry my weapons,' he said. 'That's what I'm doing about my soldiers' land. They were robbed of it by the hacendados who employed armed men for the job. They want their land back – and they want it back *now*.'

Women dressed in evening finery had also been invited to the reception but were confined to a separate room where they were gathered round Madero's wife. In the doorway, Harley bumped into Angelica. She was dressed in green, her neck and throat bare, egrets' feathers in her hair, and he was staggered by the sophisticated beauty she presented.

'Angelica,' he said softly. 'You look magnificent!'

She looked faintly embarrassed. 'Faithful Fred asked me to come,' she said. 'I think he's after a job in the government and wanted support.'

'And what splendid support he's getting!'

She eyed him warily. 'I don't get you, Harley Marquis,' she said. 'One minute you're slapping me down like a first grade infant. The next you're behaving as if I were your wealthy Great Aunt Martha from Peoria.'

He smiled. 'It seems to be a fault in both of us,' he said. 'Faithful Fred's a lucky man.'

'Damn Faithful Fred,' she snapped. 'I only got myself dressed up like a Thanksgiving turkey because I wanted to be close to Madero. I wanted to know what he's like.'

'And what is he like?'

She frowned. 'Like the Lamb of God,' she said. 'But with the wolves about to come down on the fold.'

What she said was true. Waiting to shake Madero's hand were hard-faced political sophisticates, place-seekers, concessionaires, foreign investors, holdovers from the Díaz régime, men who in their hearts belonged to the old Científico gang but whom he would have to employ because after so many years of Díaz there was no one else with experience. Among them, standing near Toral, was Victoriano Huerta, the general who had accompanied Díaz on the first stage of his journey into exile, dressed in a uniform of blue and gold, his breath smelling of brandy, his bald pate shining, his hard, cruel Indian face an expressionless mask. Though Madero was in the National Palace at last, he already looked an innocent among the cynical, tight-mouthed, low-voiced whisperers who surrounded him. The frock coats had already replaced the khaki uniforms and despite their smiles, their handshakes and their congratulations, Harley had a feeling they were gathering like vultures.

As champagne was produced by white-shirted waiters, he found himself next to Villa among the soldiers and the awkward peóns masquerading as generals.

'What now, Don Pancho?' he asked.

Villa's head was hanging in the way it always did when he was suspicious and disapproving.

'Not this, compadre,' he growled. 'Por Dios, not this!' He tried to explain. His life had been spent in the hills and plains of Chihuahua and he had just ridden for the first time in a train the length of Mexico, seeing things he had never seen before. 'These people talk too much,' he said. 'They'll run rings round him. But the people – the people, señor – they seem to have gained nothing and will probably still gain nothing. I need to do something for them. I shall go back to Chihuahua City and open a string of butcher shops.' He grinned suddenly, the old mischievous grin. 'There are still plenty of fine herds up there owned by the Terrazas family who've kept the people hungry for years. If *they* supply the meat – aware of it or not – *I* can sell it cheaply. When you give to people you're closer to Heaven. Old men will eat meat who haven't tasted it since their wedding day.'

'And Mexico City?'

'They can keep it. Already I have three invitations. To a ball, to a reception and to a luncheon. But I don't know how to use a knife and fork the way they do, I can't go to a reception because I don't drink, and as for balls – I can't dance their modern dances. I shall feel a fool.'

He stared at Harley, frowning heavily. 'I've explained to Madero,' he went on. 'When I charged him with ingratitude at Juárez, it was the doing of Orozco who wants rewards. But I've told him I am ashamed. I committed a black infamy and my heart was between two stones. But he understood my wishes. I asked nothing from the revolution and I've got nothing. Now I'm ready to quit.'

'And the army?'

Villa stared at his shoes and frowned. 'Mi amigo,' he said. 'I am finished with the army. I am going back where I belong.'

3

There were things to tidy up in El Paso and things to close down, and Harley travelled north by train with Tamsy Flood, Johnny Cox and Angelica Ojarra. Angelica sat staring out of the window most of the time, with little to say. She had longed to see Mexico throw off its chains, had virtually changed her nationality to that end, and now seemed at a loss what to do, unsettled and left with a sense of incompleteness after the excitement.

They parted on the station at Chihuahua. The platform was full of people, half of them refugees who had supported Díaz, fleeing to the safety of the United States. But there were others waiting for the train south with the light of glory in their faces as if they believed the arrival of Madero at the seat of power would solve all their problems.

The Stutz had come to meet Angelica and she shook hands formally with Tamsy. Johnny Cox tried to kiss her but her head was turned and it was no more than a brushing of his lips against her cheek. She was pale as she faced Harley. There were no tears, no emotion but, unexpectedly, as he kissed her, she kissed him back fiercely, then, before he could call her back, she was climbing into the car which shot away with a scrape of tyres and a cloud of dust.

'What do you have to do to get that kind of goodbye?' Cox asked. Then he shrugged. 'I guess that's that then. This is where we go our separate ways. I'm going to Douglas and up to Los Angeles. There are guys there setting up news reel companies. Front pages in moving pictures. After what I've been sending 'em, they'll have me like that.' He clicked his fingers and grinned. 'They're going into film making in a big way these days.'

It didn't take Harley long to settle his debts, then he took the train to New York to board the ship home.

As soon as he arrived, Isobel Hartnell was on the doorstep, full of questions about Mexico, but lacking in understanding and even faintly condescending. She was smooth, mannered and correct, and he thought nostalgically of Angelica, involved, abrasive, difficult and passionate in her anger, but never never boring.

In London Sproat seemed well satisfied with what had been done. 'I particularly liked the story of the hanging,' he grinned. 'It isn't every newspaperman who faces execution twice in an hour. You'd better get some rest because you'll be needed again soon. Even if Mexico's come to a stop, the rest of the world hasn't.'

Obsessed by the feeling that events in Mexico were *not* over, before leaving Harley had arranged with Knowles to keep him in touch with what was happening. Knowles had not been very willing but he kept his word and his first report arrived while Harley was in Brindisi waiting to cross the Mediterranean to North Africa, where Italy was busily occupying territory belonging to the old and decaying Ottoman Empire. With his knowledge of Mexican politics, Knowles had left nothing out. Though the Díaz government had been toppled, the Porfiristas had closed ranks and Madero, already showing up as an inept politician, had started to lose support the day he had arrived in his capital. Villa had returned to Chihuahua as he had promised and opened a meat business; but Orozco, dissatisfied by the rewards he'd been given, was muttering with discontent, while Zapata remained unwilling to disband his followers without the land reforms he had been promised.

Knowles' second report came while Harley was in Libya, following hard on the heels of the triumphant Italians who were chasing the Turks towards Derna. With the disbanding of the rebel forces, Mexico was once more slipping into the grip of the regular army which had just shown its inability to defend it. The provisional president, a Porfirista at heart, had sent troops under General Huerta to force Zapata to disarm, and when the revolutionary generals had protested, Madero – always the political dreamer – had told them they must not flout authority, so the clique which had supported Díaz still controlled the army and the executive departments of government.

By the end of the year the war in North Africa seemed to be over and Harley was recalled to London. To his surprise a letter from Angelica was waiting for him.

'Villa got married,' it said. 'He persuaded the bishop of the diocese to perform the ceremony and there was dancing in the streets and as much drink as they could put away. They even produced a song about it, printed and everything.' It sounded exciting and in the chilly London weather made him homesick for the hot-blooded emotions of Mexico, even for the dusty smell of the northern villages.

But then it changed abruptly, and the second half was full of blots, underlinings and indignant exclamation marks. Johnny Cox was back in El Paso, she said, doing odd jobs for the newspaper there. 'He doesn't seem able to tear himself loose,' she went on in her hurried spidery writing. 'I think he even feels there's money to be made because Zapata's finally *come out openly* against Madero, who seems *unable* to see what he's doing wrong and there's been fighting in Morelos!!'

'Poor Madero,' she continued. 'He doesn't seem to know how to do things right. He was seen to *embrace* General Blanquet for his work in suppressing Zapata's rising!!! Not that he did suppress it! But, damn it – ' in her anger her pen had splashed ink across the sheet ' – the rising was by men who less than two months ago were fighting to put Madero in *power*!!! Why doesn't he realize he must show *strength*???? Mexico was never a country for half measures. That's why Díaz stayed so long. Though he promises things, the provisional president ignores him. Yet he never says *anything* because he insists that, until the election, what the provisional president says goes!!! Fighting's been going on in the south ever since *the beginning of the month*!!!'

The letter seemed almost a plea for Harley to return to sort out for her the problems troubling her, as if she were uncertain what to believe and needed reassurance. It spoke of disappointment, disillusion and bewilderment, yet there was no hint of affection for him or any kind of warmth, nothing but information and a passionate belief in her adopted land.

At the end of the year, Harley was sent to the Balkans. He went via Austria and as he waited in Vienna, Isobel Hartnell turned up on a tour of the Continent, hiring guides, dragomen, servants, her arms full of maps and guide books, her mouth full of platitudes.

'Prague's the city to see,' she said. 'And Buda-Pest's the place to have a good time. But Vienna's the place to live.'

It was true. Vienna was a strange place, full of music and colour but somehow, under the façade, wearing the doomed look of a convicted man. It was balancing on the edge of an abyss, hiding its fears with a round of gaiety that seemed frantic in its pace.

They danced and drank champagne to Strauss on the Prater and sipped tokay in shadowy little restaurants to the music of Tzigane fiddles scraped by dark-eyed men. Isobel was beautiful with the cool blonde beauty of a wealthy Englishwoman, sure of herself and her background, never uncertain but also never moved to passion. But it wasn't difficult for Harley to be enticed back to the apartment she had rented and even easier to stay the night.

'We should make it permanent, Harley,' she said. 'We've grown used to each other.'

But after Angelica Ojarra she seemed like milky coffee after the bite of brandy and he took care to ignore the veiled hints she was throwing out.

Another report from Knowles arrived. Even the election that had legalized Madero's presidency had upset his followers because, instead of appointing one of his close supporters as his vice-president, he had insisted on an obscure journalist who had taken no part in the struggle to put him in power. The swearing-in itself had gone wrong. In an atmosphere of resentment, the occasion had dissolved into confusion and bitterness and it was once more being suggested that the United States should intervene. Since then Madero had managed to disappoint more and more sections of the society he needed to back him, and was being opposed by rebellious generals, the Church and Mexican and foreign big business, finally even by some of his own revolutionary groups.

Christmas brought a letter from Angelica, again bewailing the incredible innocence of Madero. He was paying a bitter price for his lack of experience and Zapata was openly defying him with a manifesto of his own in which he demanded the seizure of all property owned by foreigners and hacendados not friendly to the revolution, the execution of all Díaz supporters and the expulsion of all Spaniards. It was a sweeping demand that was impossible to grant.

'*Thousands* are flocking to Zapata's banner!!!' she announced. 'I was in Cuernavaca when his gente arrived. They rode through the place with *armfuls* of bougainvillea and flowers in their hats and belts!! They released the prisoners from the jail – *murderers* as well as políticos!! – and the fighting's increased. Madero makes things *worse* by appointing Huerta to put down the rising and then, just as suddenly withdrawing his troops. Huerta's livid! They say he's gone for the bottle!!! He's also made cabinet ministers of his uncles, cousins and brothers who had no connection with the revolution!!! Mexico *seethes* with anger!!!'

For the next few weeks, Harley moved about the Balkans. Then, a telegram from Sproat caught up with him – 'Return London immediately,' – and, packing his belongings, he caught the train from Vienna back to the Channel coast.

As soon as he arrived in the *Courier* building he was handed a telegram from Isobel, care of the press room. 'We kept it for you,' the girl who gave it to him said. 'We heard you were on your way home.'

Since the telegram was dated two days previously, he could only assume that half the office and half the people who knew his family also knew he was on his way. It requested him to call on her at her London address and, guessing she was plotting to trap him in marriage, he determined to get out of the country again as fast as possible.

He was studying his options when an irritated message arrived from Sproat's office asking where he was. There was no delay as he appeared in the suite where Sproat held sway. The squad of secretaries who guarded his personal domain showed him in immediately. Sproat was just finishing his daily conference and the office was full of tobacco smoke.

He indicated one of the chairs which had been lined up for the conference and began to search among the papers and galley proofs on his desk.

'I thought it was all over in Mexico,' he said.

'*I* didn't say so,' Harley pointed out. '*You* did. Madero was in the Palace when I left, and he was elected president according to Knowles by ninety per cent of the people. There were a few who voted for Díaz, Zapata, Orozco, even a bullfighter or two, but it seems there was no real opposition.'

Sproat looked up. 'Have you been receiving reports from Knowles since you returned?'

'Yes.'

'He's not paid to supply *you* with information.'

'No. But I suspected I'd be going back before long. It seemed a good idea to keep up with events.'

Sproat gave him a long cool look as it he were uncertain whether to admire his cheek or tick him off for it. Eventually, he fished what he was seeking out of the pile of papers on his desk, and sat back in his chair.

'Well, you were right,' he said. 'Take a look through that lot. Our famous Mr. Madero seems to be in trouble already. There's been a rising against him by a general called Bernardo Reyes.'

'Reyes isn't worth much.'

'What about Vázquez Gómez? He was one of the men who backed the revolution but he was sacked from the cabinet for claiming Madero's not fulfilling his promises. *He's* started another. The Americans have thirty thousand troops lining the Río Grande and Madero was so scared of bullets going across the border he ordered the garrison of Ciudad Juárez not to get involved and the rebels took it without a shot being fired.' Sproat paused and drew breath. 'Now his favourite general – the chap who pushed him into power, Orozco – has defected with six thousand men and says he's going to hang Madero from the tallest tree in Mexico City. Your countrymen, Marquis, are a pretty treacherous lot.'

'Bloodthirsty too,' Harley said mildly.

'He's gained control of most of Chihuahua, and Madero has no troops to spare because of Zapata's rebellion in the south.'

'What about Villa?'

'Nothing.'
'He won't sit down under this.'
Sproat smiled. 'That's what I thought.'
'And Knowles can't handle that from Mexico City.'
'That's also what I thought.'
'You want me to go back there?'
'How soon can you start?'

4

It was strange to be back again. Angelica had been right. He felt almost as if he'd come home, and certainly more at ease than he had in the steep little townships of the Balkans.

A telegram to El Paso had Tamsy Flood waiting at the station when he arrived, complete with a Stutz roadster. 'Better than that Ford we started with last time, Boss,' he said. 'I gotta coupla Indians in Juárez to act as cargadores.'

'Where's Villa?'

'Vanished. Just abandoned his butchery business and disappeared.'

'Who's backing Orozco?'

'The Terrazas family. They own all the land north of Chihuahua. And, so they say, a few Americans and British who see themselves losing their property if Madero carries out his promises to give Mexico back to the Mexicans. Orozco asked Villa to join him. Villa sent a letter back to say that if Orozco moved against Madero he'd have to deal with him too.'

'What's it like over the border?'

'Dynamite, Boss. Juárez, Casas Grandes and Chihuahua are full of Orozco's gente. They say Villa sent his family to San Andrés with a strong guard and barricaded himself in the Chihuahua stockyards till he could get away.'

El Paso was already filling up with newspapermen, though this time there was a more professional air about them, and instead of Norfolk jackets and flat caps, most of them had fitted themselves out with campaign gear of breeches, leggings and Stetsons so that they looked like overgrown Boy Scouts. One of the more exotic wore a monocle and carried a gold mounted stick, while yet another was busy fitting up a boxcar for the railway, with the words 'OFICINA PARTICULAR DEL CORRESPONSAL ESPECIAL' daubed across the side. Most of them had brought their own cars and those who hadn't were scouring the town for them.

The cable editor of the El Paso paper welcomed Harley back with a grin and offered one of his green Mexican cigars. 'This time,' he said, 'it'll be a three-ringed circus and a three-alarm fire all in one because now there's bad blood between 'em and they don't just want to slit the throats of the Porfiristas, they want to slit each others'.'

He agreed to act on Harley's behalf as before. 'Same guy?' he asked. 'Spode? Scrotum?'

'Sproat.'

'I got him.'

The following day, Johnny Cox appeared at Harley's hotel. His breath smelled of whisky and he looked a little shabby and sheepish.

Harley studied him. 'What happened, Johnny? Didn't they want you back in Los Angeles?'

'I didn't go. I got drunk. I got a job with the *El Paso Times*. But peace ain't the same as war. There wasn't the money. Nobody's interested in seein' Mexicans when they're not shooting each other.' The old wide grin came, untroubled and innocent. 'I bet you could use a cameraman, Harl'.'

'I've been falling over cameramen, Johnny.'

'None of 'em as good as me.'

'None of them has your cheek.'

'I'd let you have pictures cheap. You'd have the monopoly.'

Harley paused. The boy had appeal and courage. 'All right,' he agreed. 'You can tag along and see what happens.'

'Sure.' Cox was all smiles again, the sheepishness gone in a flood of self-confidence. 'I'll need a few dollars first though, Harl'. To get my cameras out of hock.'

'I'll help. Where's Villa? Have you heard?'

'No, I haven't. I reckon Angelica Ojarra will have, though.'

'How is she?'

'Hadn't you heard?'

'Heard what?'

'She got married.'
There was a long silence before Harley spoke. 'Toral?'
'Who else?'
'Is he with Madero or against him?'
'I guess he's sittin' on the fence as usual.'
'And Angelica?'
'*She's* not the type to change.'

Chihuahua City was nervous. There were a lot of Orozco's men about, the red shirts they wore bright in the brassy sunshine. Tamsy warned that they were quick on the trigger and that Orozco didn't like newsmen and had even offered to stand one sideways against a wall and shoot furrows across his back. The citizens seemed ready to head for the hills, worried that Villa, who had always regarded the city as his home, would sack it for allowing Orozco to make his headquarters there.

There were a lot of Americans about, down from the border, and the line was open to El Paso so they could telegraph despatches north, while Cox was able to acquire fresh film and – despite his promise to Harley of a monopoly – to mail a folder of pictures to a Tucson newspaper which had agreed to take what he could send.

Once or twice they caught a glimpse of Orozco himself at the main station near the river, tall, scowling, his freckled face grim. Carriages and cars were parked near the track as their owners waited for news on the telegraph, and armed men in wide sombreros stood alongside a train that was being put together. As the telegraph began to click they swarmed round the office in a noisy crowd demanding to know what was happening.

They found Angelica at San Gabriel. In her over-enthusiastic way, where once she had raised funds for the revolutionary war chest and drilled ragged peón boys into riflemen, she had now identified with the poor. Baffled because Madero had not measured up to her stringent demands, she had opened a food kitchen in Chihuahua for the families of men killed in the fighting.

She saw the Stutz before they saw her and, as they approached the house, a large chestnut swooped over the brow of a rise and came thundering up behind them.

Harley pounded Tamsy's shoulder. 'Stop this damn' thing, Tamsy!' he yelled. 'It's her!'

The car slid to a stop in a cloud of swirling dust and Angelica drew rein alongside, her horse snorting with excitement.

'You!' The delight was clear in her voice.

Harley grinned back at her as he scrambled from the car and took her hands in his.

She kissed him unaffectedly and turned to Tamsy. 'Hello, Tamsy,' she said. 'He got you again, did he?'

'Sure did, Ma'am.'

'I knew you'd come back,' she insisted.

'Why?' Harley asked. '*I* didn't. What's happening, Angelica?'

She looked sad and disappointed. 'It's started all over again. It's all so horrible. Madero insists everything's to be done legally but the Zapatistas believe his régime's nothing but a house of cards that can be blown away at any time.'

'Is it?'

'Of course it is.' She looked angry. 'He doesn't insist on things and the newspapers spread terrible rumours. Yet he doesn't close them down. He makes dreadful mistakes. Zapata actually disbanded his army and even went so far as to stage a victory parade for him with what they call his "horde." I was at the coffee plantation and saw it. Hell, it wasn't a horde. They looked half-starved, knew nothing about drill and had no uniforms at all. Just straw sombreros and white cotton pants tucked into coloured socks. Every kind of rifle you could think of and one small cannon. There were even women among them, one with a pink ribbon round her waist, and she gave the game away because I kept seeing it time after time. There weren't half as many as they pretended and they were just going round and round the block. But Madero came back and said everything was solved.'

'What went wrong?'

'Zapata expected to be governor of Morelos – chief of police at the very least – but Madero appointed a goddam hacendado who'd done nothing for the revolution, and when the Zapatistas rose again the soldiers he sent against them moved so slowly everybody had disappeared and all they could do was burn the villages. When they came back, there were just that many more Zapatistas. They don't hold parades for him now.'

'And Villa? Where's he?'

She gestured towards the hills. 'Near Parral, I think. We can get a message to him.'

'How many men has he?'

'Not many. But they're coming in. Fierro's there. Urbina's on his way.'

'I'm on my way, too.'

'And I'm coming with you.'

Harley frowned. 'Let's stop this damn fooling about, Angelica.'

'There are soldaderas in all Mexican armies.'

'You're not a soldadera. You're a married woman with a husband.'

'My husband's in Mexico City.'

'Doing what?'

She shrugged. 'He says he's working for Madero. He seems to do the talking. Huerta does the fighting. Madero does the worrying. He has a woman there. Faithful Fred turned out to be not as faithful as he pretended. It didn't work. Not even from the first.'

She stared at him defiantly, scourging herself, daring him to comment.

He studied her. 'Angelica,' he said. '*Why* did you marry him?'

Her eyes flashed angrily and her head came up as she reached for her horse. 'I don't have to explain that to *you*!'

In a blazing heat they drove across country to Parral. The narrow winding streets were full of troops but there was a distinctly nervous air about them because Villa was expected within a matter of days. Always fond of dramatic messages, he had invited them if they were loyal to Madero to march out and meet him, if they were not loyal to march out and fight because he intended taking the town anyway.

One of Villa's old officers, Maclovio Herrera, the businessman turned soldier, had command of part of the garrison. He had opted to remain in the army after the revolution and wore Federal uniform, but he clearly didn't like Orozco and was unhappy with the fact that he and his command had been swept into the rising against Madero by his commanding officer and was now committed to defending Parral against his old chief, Villa.

'It's one of the tragedies of our days, compadre,' he told Harley. 'One finds oneself facing old friends over a gun.'

Harley had acquired a room in a hotel for himself and one for Angelica by offering the desk clerk a large denomination note. The building was crowded with people from outside the town who were afraid to stay at home because of the likelihood of fighting and they were sleeping in the dining room, lounge and billiard room. Harley suffered no remorse for his bribery because he knew perfectly well that if someone came along with a larger note he could be turned out at a moment's notice.

The town was silent as darkness came but everyone knew Villa wasn't far away. Harley had just fallen into a deep sleep when he was awakened by some sixth sense that told him he wasn't alone in the room. As he reached for a match to light the lamp, a hand clamped over his mouth.

'Quiet, compadre. It's me – Pancho Villa!'

As the hand was removed and Harley lit the lamp, he saw him alongside the bed, his clothes dusty, long leggings reaching up to his thighs. 'Are you alone?' Villa asked in a soft voice.

'Dona Angelica's here.'

Villa's eyes moved swiftly over the bed. 'Where?'

'Down the corridor.'

'And you are here?' Villa's look was one of surprise. 'You must be mad, compadre.'

'How did you get in?'

'No trouble. The sentries are Mexican so they were all asleep, and the desk clerk looked the other way for a hundred-peso note. I'm looking for Maclovio Herrera. They tell me he has part of the garrison.'

'That's right. I've seen him. He doesn't like the situation.'

'Who does? Vázquez Gómez was a fool to throw in his lot with that damned mule-skinner, Orozco. Will Herrera change sides?'

'He's not very happy.'

'Where is he?'

Harley told him and Villa grinned. 'Abraham González told me what was happening,' he said. 'Then he went on to Mexico City to help the President while I raised the men. They're waiting outside the town. I'm going now to see Herrera.'

'I'll come with you.'

Villa pushed him back as he started to climb from the bed. 'Stay where you are, compadre. I can persuade him to change sides better if I'm on my own. *You'd* do better to go down the corridor and see what you can do there, I think.'

Harley spent the rest of the night watching the streets through the shutters at the window. There was a lot of movement but remarkably little sound. Slipping out of the hotel at daybreak, he found Villa had succeeded in winning Herrera over and, with his aid, had captured the mutinous Federal officers and netted the most important military centre south of Chihuahua, complete with its garrison and machine guns, without a shot being fired.

He had established himself in Herrera's headquarters, alongside him Herrera and the burly Fierro. In the street outside were the ragged men who had been with him since he had left Chihuahua. They had been on the move continuously under the lurid sun and through the freezing nights and their lips were chapped by the wind.

This time he greeted Harley with an abrazo, clutching him to his chest with both arms and slapping his back as he hugged him.

'Why did you come back?' he asked. 'Did your king send you to find out what was going on? Did he ask about me?' He gestured at the men outside, among them large groups still wearing Federal uniform. 'Until today I was a general without an army. Now I'm back in business. We had five hundred when we started but we grew hungry and half of them disappeared. But most have come back now and the rest will turn up when they know there's a chance of winning.' He gestured at a newspaper on the table. 'Orozco's declared himself Governor of Chihuahua and Supreme Chief of the Revolutionary Forces with Vázquez Gómez as provisional president of Mexico. They won't last but you'd better write and tell your newspaper.'

Harley doubted if Sproat would be that much interested.

Despite his success, Villa was wary and distrustful and Harley picked his words carefully. 'I'm coming with you, Don Pancho,' he said. 'What's next?'

'Nothing's next. We're not strong enough to move yet. But Urbina's on his way and Madero's sending reinforcements. But he can't have many to spare because we've just heard that Zapata's come out for Orozco and started threatening Mexico City. Orozco's sent an army to throw us out of here. It's expected within twenty-four hours. In the meantime, my boys need paying so I'm levying a loan from the Parral bankers. They claim it's illegal but they know better than to refuse. I shall hang them if they do.'

For an uneducated peón, Villa had absorbed the lessons of his last compaign well and had acquired a remarkable grasp of organization and tactics. The naive simplicity of the savage hid an extraordinary native shrewdness and, setting up his outposts and drawing solely on intuition, he had formed his cavalry into small companies of heavily-armed shock troops which could be moved easily about a battlefield. He had placed Herrera's Federals behind barricades, with supporting machine guns in the hands of a group of the young American mercenaries who had been with him the previous year and had hurried to rejoin when they heard that he had taken the field again.

The Orozquistas came at night and Harley woke to the roar of rifle fire and the thud of guns. Dressing hurriedly, he found the reception area of the hotel occupied by frightened people. Angelica was among them, nervous and excited, but for once she didn't argue when he told her to stay where it was safe. Outside, the darkness was filled with the steady thump and crash of explosives.

Moving forward with Tamsy, Harley ran into groups of men firing into the darkness. The fighting was confused and nobody was certain where the enemy were, and the night was lit with the nervous stabbing spurts of flame from rifles and the flickering blue light from the muzzle of a Maxim gun.

Villa was covered with sweat and dirt but he was confident. The Orozquistas' attack had been repulsed.

'They've fallen back,' he said. 'But they're not finished.'

Almost at once the first shells from the Orozquista guns started to crash on to the town and they heard the roar of falling masonry and flying tiles.

'Softening us up, compadre,' Villa said. 'They'll come again at first light and expect us to be ready to throw our hands in.'

They waited in the tense darkness until they heard the sound of the first cock crow, then figures in tall hats began to shuffle into position, their shapes silhouetted black against the faint glow in the east where the sun was still below the horizon. A man coughed, a lucifer flared and there was the glow of cigarettes against the blackness. Then a rifle fired in the distance; they were alert at once and Villa moved along the line, cuffing them from the last vestiges of their sleep.

'There, mi jefe!'

Someone yelled and it became just possible to see moving shapes in the purple shadows. Immediately the whole line of rifles crashed out and there were yells of pain and fury in the darkness in front, then the moving shapes grew larger and they saw bobbing sombreros against the growing yellow light in the sky.

The attack had been slowed almost to a halt and for the most part now consisted of verbal abuse because the rebels had been pinned down, but none of the defenders was willing to risk his neck against what was still an unseen and unnumbered enemy.

While they hesitated, they heard the snort of a horse, and the clatter of stones under hooves, and they saw Villa moving forward, his stetson as usual on the back of his head, a pistol in his hand as he urged his mount on. Behind him there was a group of men from his bodyguard.

'On your feet, you lizards,' he was yelling. 'While they're hesitating! Come with me and I'll show you what we'll do to these pigs of Orozquistas!'

His energy, his enthusiasm, his qualities of leadership lifted the yelling men to their feet. Scrambling up, they grabbed stirrups and horses' tails and were swept forward to where the distant figures, now more clear as the sun rose higher, had come to a complete stop. A machine gun brought down several groups, but they swept over the Orozquista position as if it didn't exist and Villa was among the rebels, fighting like a madman. In no time, the foothills were filled with fleeing men, the mounted Villistas chasing them with rifles, pistols, and captured swords they didn't know how to use, swinging and slashing and clubbing until the scattered force thinned out and finally disappeared.

As Villa trotted back, they counted noses and found their losses were few. A lot of Orozquista bodies were dragged out with a few moaning wounded. Though there was a chance some of them might have survived, they were given no chance. Those who looked as if they might summon up enough strength to crawl away were shot where they lay. No bullets were wasted on the dying and the barefooted Villistas were already removing their boots and clothing to leave them moaning and naked in the pools of their own blood in the cold morning air.

As the light increased, Villa sent mounted men forward. Harley went with them but, apart from the body of an occasional wounded man who had crept into an arroyo to die, there was no other sign of the Orozquistas. The sombreroed horsemen wound in and out of the shallow ravines outside the town, hoping for the sport of flushing out a fugitive but there was nothing, though they learned from a wounded man before they shot him that Orozquista reinforcements, supported by cavalry and artillery, were on their way from Chihuahua. Outgunned and outnumbered, Villa couldn't hope to hold the town, but it seemed impossible to let it go without a fight, so, drawing lines in the dust, he indicated his tactics. 'Orozco controls the railroad in Jiménez,' he said. 'But we know the desert so we'll go through the hills to head south towards Torreón.'

A group of the young Americans agreed to hold Parral with their machine guns to enable him to withdraw. 'We'll be okay,' their leader told him. 'We're American. Orozco knows better than to harm us if we're captured.'

Villa was uneasy but he agreed and, to make the Orozquistas believe they were stronger than they were, corpses were propped up round fires, complete with scarves, sombreros and bandoliers; then, under cover of darkness, the little army, hardly bigger than a regiment, withdrew. By morning they were trailing into the hills, horses, mules, and commandeered carriages, everybody with their heads down against the flying grit, the brims of their sombreros bouncing in the gusts as they trudged westwards.

The tail of the column consisted of carts containing the wounded, where Angelica laboured over the moaning men with the soldaderas. Only those who could ride or walk had been brought away, the worst cases left behind with local doctors. Reaching a Tarahumara village, they unloaded the men who had died en route, and gave the Indians looted brandy to bury them. They left them all drunk and later learned that the Indians had merely poured pitch on the bodies and set them on fire.

They were well into the hills when a cloud of dust appeared on the horizon behind them. It turned out to be a solitary messenger on a lathered and stumbling horse. The Orozquistas had recaptured Parral and shot all the Villista prisoners, including the Americans. The wounded had been lashed to chairs to face the firing squads and the doctors who had cared for them had been hanged.

Villa's heavy face grew dark with fury. 'From now on,' he ordered, 'no Orozquista, officer or man, is to be given the chance of joining us. For them all there's only one question: "Where do you want the bullet"?' He turned to Harley. 'You can tell that to your newspaper, Inglés. From me. And if your king asks, you can tell him, too.'

For a hundred miles to Villa Coronado through the dusty desert they made their way from the state of Chihuahua into the state of Durango. They crossed the boundary by a small village called Catuhuála which consisted of a huddle of flat-roofed adobe huts against which the sand, drifting in the wind, had piled, and a shabby convent where a few poverty-stricken nuns ministered to the inhabitants and guarded their relics with a feverish asceticism among the cactus and the bare-branched thorn trees.

In the countryside around there wasn't a blade of grass, and the wind was stirring up dust as fine as face-powder. The discouraging landscape was all the same colour from horizon to horizon, and the sun beat down vertically to create mirages and plaster the dust on sweating faces and cracked lips. Some inborn quality that Villa possessed, some hidden drive, kept them going. He watched from the saddle of a stumbling horse, like a yellow-eyed eagle, lost in a brooding silence, but never still as the straggling men staggered on, a long strung-out column on weaving exhausted horses, the riders haggard and bearded, their eyes circled by shadows.

Riding in a cart with his photographic equipment, Cox turned a face greasy with perspiration to Harley. 'For Jesus' sake, Harl', how much longer?'

Silent, enduring, her own face drawn by fatigue, Angelica turned on him. 'Rats,' she snapped, '*you've* nothing to complain about!'

Coming to a drying stream, they jostled for the bitter stagnant liquid lying in the pools among the rocks. It was already fouled by animals but they were all too thirsty to mind, and they fell on their faces in the muddy shallows while the sun, white, clinical and sterile, burned their backs.

Gradually the country improved, then, just outside the village of San Luís Gonsaga they saw another small column approaching, surrounded as usual by a dust cloud of its own making. Dry mouths raised a shout of pleasure as the leading horseman was recognized as Tomás Urbina, Villa's old comrade and fellow-bandit. He was stiff with rheumatism and haggard with the excesses of alcohol and women, but his small face was alive with humour. He had several girls with him and he brought the news that Madero had raised Villa to the rank of honorary general in the Mexican army.

'What's an *honorary* general?'

Urbina grinned. 'An honorary general, mi jefe, doesn't get paid.'

With the appearance of some sort of civilization as they entered San Luís, crude though it was, Johnny Cox immediately became busy with his cameras, setting up the usual mock attacks for filming, crouching, sighting, squatting, taking angle shots and close-ups until the rebel soldiers grew bored with him and wandered away. Villa posed for portraits, however, and Urbina had half a dozen pictures taken for his family: Sitting on a horse; sitting in a chair; eating; drinking; with his arms round a couple of the girls he had brought with him; grimacing in an expression that was meant to indicate determination and heroism; and finally armed to the teeth, his small face peeping over a whole array of ammunition belts and topped by a vast sombrero.

Slipping past the Orozquista army, they made their way by Escalón and Jaralito to Mapimí. With the two columns integrated so that Villa had a sizeable force once more, they began to be joined by young men who, unlike Villa's officers, had started their careers in the Federal army of Díaz, young men with waxed moustaches, puttees and pith helmets, and tailored uniforms that aped the French and Germans, Científicos every one of them, down to their fingernails. Won over by Madero's attempt to clean up his country, they were indignant at Orozco's treachery and eager to support the shaky régime. Though they made no effort to hide their education and sophistication, they also made no attempt to impose their views on the crude, virile peón who was leading them.

'Everything he does is larger than life,' a Colegio Militar graduate called Navarrete explained to Harley. 'Though his excesses are no worse than anybody else's. Díaz's generals shot their prisoners. So did Huerta. So did Zapata. So why does everybody point the finger at Villa? Simply because he's crude, ill-mannered and uneducated, and everybody expects it of him.'

At Mapimí several other European correspondents and a colourful bunch of Americans joined them. Villa was always popular with the Americans because he could always be expected to provide better stories than anyone else and his territory was handy for the border so their copy could travel more quickly. What they couldn't find out they made up. More than one was willing to fictionalize lurid stories for the sensation-seeking newspapers, knowing well that Villa would never read them, while others, working for capitalist or foreign interests, were outrageously slanting their copy to provide a terrifying picture of murderous Mexican armies.

As these new journalists arrived, Johnny Cox suddenly vanished. He had never been driven by faith in victory and, feeling Madero was bound eventually to be overthrown, had been anxious for some time to have pictures of the opposition. Quietly he helped himself to a roadster belonging to one of the German correspondents and disappeared towards Mexico City.

Suspecting he had learned something, Harley decided that, with Villa happy to sit tight for the moment in Mapimí, it might be worth trying to get to Morelos to see what was happening there. Two of the American newspapermen learned what he was up to and insisted on joining him.

'We go, too,' one of them said. 'That way we reduce costs, and increase efficiency. We tell no one but each other, okay?'

There wasn't much choice so they tossed their belongings into the back of the Stutz and Harley had Tamsy drive them to Rellano to catch the next train to Mexico City. Rellano seemed quiet as they drove in but the station was full of Orozquistas, almost as if they had set an ambush, and Tamsy had no sooner vanished with the Stutz when they began to pour out of every door and window, grinning at the three startled newspapermen standing on the platform clutching their equipment.

'Maderistas by the look of them,' one of them said. 'Better hang them quickly and get it over and done with.'

'General Campo likes to question all prisoners,' another pointed out. 'Better to let him see them and hang them afterwards.'

They were dragged in front of a small man in a general's uniform who was sitting in the square surrounded by a group of heavily-armed men. There were a few frightening moments as the soldiers yelled for them to be strung up from the jacarandas round the bandstand, but Campo was eager to have the world know his views and decided to allow them to pass through, holding them just long enough to lecture them on his ambitions and intentions.

'You can tell those people in Mexico City that we're coming,' he informed them. 'We know how many there are and we've heard that Salas, Madero's War Minister himself, is bringing an army against us.'

With the orgy of wrecking the revolution had brought, there was a shortage of box cars and locomotives, but late in the evening they found a petrol-driven handcar consisting of four wheels, a motor and a platform big enough to hold half a dozen men. It seemed highly dangerous as they began to rush along the rails in the darkness, the wind lashing their faces, the wheels clicking wildly as they crossed switches, but, with the swaying and the steady throbbing of the motor, Harley was almost asleep when there was a crash and the machine leapt from the track. He landed heavily in the dust with a skinned elbow and a pair of torn trousers. One of the Americans had a broken finger and the other a sprained ankle.

They had struck a cow sleeping across the track and though no one was seriously hurt they were all covered with its blood. The handcar seemed undamaged, however, so they levered it back on to the track and set off again. Reaching Conejos, they decided that they had had enough of the handcar and persuaded railway officials to put together a small train consisting of a shunting engine with a contraption like an enormous jug on the funnel, an ancient carriage with hard seats and a caboose. There was no means of providing food aboard so they bought cooked chickens, jerky and beer, then, with a few additional passengers filling the spare seats, began to move steadily towards the capital.

Mexico City seemed sullen, vastly different from the hysterical, enthusiastic place that had greeted Madero's entrance the previous year, and the newspapers were critical of the régime, demanding that the threatening Zapatistas be put down. *El Independiente* carried a cartoon of Madero dressed as an absentminded professor trying to control a class of unruly pupils, drawn by Johnny Cox who had clearly arrived ahead of them. Nobody appeared to care a damn about what was happening in the north. The north was too far away while Morelos was right on the doorstep.

It wasn't easy getting a train south because Zapata was running Morelos as if he owned it. It was a different area from the northern plains, a hot humid district of high mountains and deep heavily-forested valleys, and instead of dust, cactus and adobe huts, there were thatched roofs and huts ablaze with the passionate purple of bougainvillea. But apart from burned huts and scorched walls and the ever-circling vultures, there was no immediate sign of war.

The rebellion here seemed less well organized than in the north. It was a lazier area with a gentler climate where there was never the same fierce struggle to survive. Instead of desert there were flowers and heavy trees and the humidity of the tropics. Perhaps because of it the people seemed to feel that, with the Madero régime likely to collapse at any time, it wasn't worth risking lives to destroy something that was busily destroying itself. There were no government troops about, and no rebels, just a lot of half-clothed men sitting in queer old saddles on broken-down horses, carrying grotesque and obsolete weapons.

For three days the newspapermen tried to get an interview with Zapata but he was lying low and was not in Anencuilco. Eventually a market stallholder in Cuautla offered to make contact but by this time the Americans had given up trying. They had made a point of going often to the telegraph office because there was a strong freemasonry between the telegraphists who were always tapping out the latest news to each other, and hearing that things were starting to move again in the north, the Americans had decided they were in entirely the wrong place. Harley was just on the point of following them back to the hotel when the telegraphist burst from his office. He had just picked up an unexpected item of news and was wild-eyed with excitement.

'The government's sending a new army against the rebels,' he said. 'General Salas, the War Minister himself, is leading it.'

Campo's intelligence had been good. 'What else?'

'General Blanquet and General Aubert are going with him to command the columns guarding the flanks. They expect to meet the rebels near Torreón.'

Bolting back to the hotel, Harley found the Americans had somehow also heard and were busy packing their bags. To take a train to the capital, it was necessary to reach Cuernavaca but it was a long drive and the only taxi available was ancient, its broken springs bound together with rope which had been soaked in water to tauten it. The contraption seemed the only connection between the tonneau and the wheels, and they had gone only a quarter of a mile when the engine exploded. They managed to hire another car but it picked up two punctures, and the steering was so bad that outside Cuernavaca they subsided into a drainage ditch where the driver finally mutinied and refused to go any further.

Humping their luggage, they finally found an elderly victoria and had just climbed aboard when a ragged wild-eyed band of men rode past, firing their rifles into the air. Dogs, children and women ran for the side of the road and the ponies pulling the victoria bucked and almost bolted. It wasn't hard to find out what had happened. The Government troops in the area had been withdrawn for Salas' campaign in the north and the ragged armies of Zapata had not been slow to notice.

The train to the capital was held up several times, due to the nervousness of the crew who imagined trees laid across the line at the end of every cutting. It seemed ages before they steamed into Mexico City to learn that Salas's reinforcements were ready to leave and were occupying three trains at the Buenavista station. Grabbing a taxi, they reached the platform to fall, sleepless, dirty and unshaven, into one of the carriages of the headquarters train just as it began to pull out.

5

Just as Campo had suggested, the train was carrying General González Salas, Madero's War Minister. With him were Generals Aubert and Blanquet, all three dressed in smart uniforms of blue heavily decorated with gold and looking as if they were going to a levée rather than to a battle. The platform as the train drew out was filled with fashionable men and women waving goodbye.

As they halted near Bermajillo on a spur line to draw water from a battered water tank and to allow the troops to cook their rations, the newspapermen managed to buttonhole the headquarters group for an interview.

'I shall move directly up the track' Salas said. 'General Blanquet and General Aubert will command the flanking columns moving up on the right and left and we shall defeat the Orozquistas at Torreón.'

'Watch your step, General,' one of the Americans advised. 'They know you're coming. They said so.'

Salas smiled. 'It won't stop us wiping them off the face of the earth,' he promised. 'I have trained troops. They're nothing but a rabble.'

Before they set off again, there was a lot of juggling with the trains. Until then, the train carrying the generals and their staffs had been leading; now it was transferred to the rear. Harley and the Americans stood by the track watching as the engine lurched across the points to the blast of a whistle, to roll clanking to a spot further up the line. As it passed, the driver leaned from the cab and grinned at them, then the carriages, old wooden structures which looked as if they might have been bought as a job lot from the Americans after the Civil War, began to rumble past, the brake shoes grinding as the train slowed to a halt once more.

As the soldiers scrambled back aboard the box cars, the trains set off again, jerking into motion then settling down in a monotonous rhythm. The track consisted of a single set of rails, for the most part dead straight as they headed through the mesquite-scattered desert, but here and there swinging in a wide loop to skirt a rise. Harley was watching from the window, wary and uneasy. Campo's threat had not been an idle one, he felt sure.

Ahead of the generals' train in which he was travelling with the Americans, he could see the other two trains on a slow curve, long ribbons of smoke streaming back from the locomotives as they chugged up a slight gradient to the northern plateau. Night came and he fell asleep to the grinding of the wheels, swaying and jolting in his place, his backside sore with the shift and movement of the hard seat. In the morning, they halted again to take on water and to allow the soldiers to make their coffee. Fires were built from scrub and they squatted down alongside the track.

The newspapermen were invited to join Salas's staff for breakfast and they ate fresh rolls and drank chocolate. Salas and the other generals had changed now into field service dress and were strung about like Christmas trees with swords, pistols, binoculars and map cases.

'Soon,' Salas said, 'the Orozquistas will know we've arrived.'

Bored with the unchanging scenery, they dozed during the day as the trains rumbled on. The dust kept wafting in through the slatted shutters at the windows to fill the compartment with grit and leave them feeling dirty and unwashed. Later in the morning Harley and one of the Americans went to the observation platform at the rear of the carriage. Salas and his staff were drinking brandy in the dining saloon and poring over maps. Nobody was offering any information and it was clear they were going to have to wait until the action started.

Accepting a cigarette from the American, Harley looked up as he lit it and stared along the track. It swept to the right in a long slow curve and ahead of the headquarters train the two troop trains chugged steadily northward, their funnels filling the sky with drifting puffs of dark smoke as they climbed. Then Harley's head lifted.

'What's that?'

Ahead of the leading train, hidden by a rise in the ground, there was what was clearly another locomotive. It was still out of sight but he could see streaming smoke that indicated it was travelling fast.

'That's a train!' The American stared. 'On a spur line? At that speed?'

'There isn't a spur line there!' Harley stared again. 'It's on *this* line. And, by God, it's coming towards us!'

Then, abruptly, bursting into sight, they saw a locomotive pulling two box cars appear from behind the rise. Moving steadily towards the leading troop train as it chugged laboriously up the incline, it had smoke rolling back over the tender in a long coiling black ribbon. Lifting his binoculars, Harley saw two figures jump from the cab.

'For God's sake,' he said. 'That's the crew!'

Heading down the incline, the oncoming train was gathering speed all the time, rocking and swaying wildly as it approached. Then, Harley realized that all round the boiler, in the tender and on the cowcatcher, wooden boxes had been lashed, and it finally dawned on him just what was happening.

'That's dynamite!' he yelled. 'And they've jammed the throttle wide open!'

'Kee-rist!' Turning abruptly, the American ran from the observation platform to inform Salas.

The first of the troop trains began to spurt steam, the wheels shrouded as the crew tried to halt it. Behind it, the second train was also spurting steam. Then Salas' train jerked and shuddered as the brakes were applied. There was a crash of glass from inside the saloon and, as locked wheels slid along the track, Harley was flung against the rails of the observation platform with a force that knocked the breath out of him.

As the leading troop train came to a halt, it was flung forward as the train immediately behind, sparks flying from the brake shoes, ran into the rear end. The last coach was lifted from the track and dust and stones were flung up as the rails buckled. Then soldiers began to jump from the box cars, hatless, coatless, weaponless, and began to run. They had seen what Harley had seen and they were scattering into the desert, small hurrying figures among the cactus and mesquite.

The American newspaperman was back now, accompanied by his colleague. Then Salas and several of his officers appeared. Their faces registered shock, amazement and horror. As they watched, the oncoming locomotive, travelling now at a tremendous speed as it reached the bottom of the slope, ploughed into the leading train. There was a thunderous iron crash and the engine of the halted troop train leapt into the air, roaring steam. As the train buckled, box cars were lifted into the air and a whole row of them were flung on to their sides in a huge cloud of dust.

Then, with the maverick locomotive still driving forward into the wreckage under its own momentum, flinging the stationary train aside as if it were a writhing, living thing, the whole horizon seemed to split apart in an orange-coloured flame. There was a terrific jolt that shook the carriage where they stood, and a tremendous hurricane of air. The earth seemed to shake and Harley caught a glimpse of running men tumbling and staggering as the ground rose skywards in a column of mushrooming dense black smoke in which gushed several separate flashes of orange.

The long roar of the explosions blended and reverberated into one long blast and the sheet of flame clawed upwards in a tremendous wave of noise that beat at the ears. It was like staring into the muzzle of a blow lamp, and, his nostrils full of the smell of explosive, Harley was flung aside again, this time back against the door of the saloon.

As he picked himself up, he saw great steel wheels hurtling through the air like bombs, with fragments of wood and metal and human flesh, then they came showering down, thudding as they struck the ground to send up clouds of dust. Planks descended like leaves in autumn, flicking backwards and forwards as they slid down across the air.

'Holy Mother of God!' Salas breathed, his face white.

Ahead of them there was a tremendous pile-up round the crater caused by the explosion. The thundering locomotive's speed had driven the leading cars of the approaching troop train off the track before the explosion and they lay on their sides now among the smoke, splintered, wrecked, torn apart by the blast that seemed to have reduced both locomotives to scrap iron.

The men who had bolted into the desert were beginning to recover their wits now and had turned back to drag their injured comrades from the wreckage. Axes began to bite into wood and there was a chorus of panic-stricken voices. Salas and the other two generals seemed to be petrified by what had happened and were still standing by the headquarters train, staring ahead while regimental and company officers directed the rescue work.

Moving along the track through the wreathing smoke to the point of the explosion, Harley heard the first bullet thud home into one of the carriages. As he looked up, he saw more splintered holes appear and, swinging round again to face the north, he became aware of men on horses wearing sombreros and red shirts appearing from behind the rise that had hidden the oncoming locomotive. They came into view in a rush, yelling and screaming curses as they waved rifles, revolvers, swords and machetes. Behind them came more men, hundreds of them, running on foot, and then he heard the crackling of shots.

The government troops had dropped their axes now and were frantically searching for lost weapons among the debris. But they had scattered across the desert to get away from the coming explosion and they were hatless, even shoeless, and for the most part had nothing with which to defend themselves. Officers ran among them, whacking them with the flat of their swords and cuffing them with their fists. But the shock of the explosion had shattered their morale and they were too widely dispersed to have any coherence in what they were trying to do. Some fired off scattered shots, while a few officers managed to get groups of them lying behind clumps of cactus or rocks or in the hollows to fire back, but the Orozquistas were among them before they were properly organized, shooting and swinging at them with their weapons.

Standing among the wreckage, Harley watched as the melée developed. Then a group of Federal soldiers broke and began to run, and almost at once others followed, first in ones and twos, then in groups, until the whole of Salas's army seemed to be running, with the Orozquistas roaring after them, shooting at anything that moved.

A soldier running alongside the wrecked trains was spotted by a horseman carrying a cavalry sabre who went clattering after him, swinging his weapon. The soldier's head was snicked off as neatly as if it were a joint in a butcher's shop and the body, still running, went on for a few more steps before it crumpled against the wheels of a box car. Some of the raiders had forgotten the chase now and were climbing into the cars and officers' carriages, flinging out blankets, clothes, weapons, food, but the rest swept down on the running groups of Federals, giving no quarter.

A screech from the whistle of the headquarters train made Harley swing round. As he did so, the train jerked, shuddered, jerked again, then began to move in reverse. There was no sign of Salas or the other two generals and all he could see was one of the American newsmen on the observation platform, trying to make up his mind to jump but finally deciding that the train was already moving too fast. The Orozquista horsemen swooped down, galloping alongside, firing with everything they possessed; a window fell in and Harley saw splinters flying from the woodwork. But the train was picking up speed now and, as it vanished southwards, one last foolhardy rider tried to leap aboard, missed his grasp and fell beneath the wheels to be carved into bloody pulp while his horse trotted away, stirrups swinging, its tail high in the air. His thwarted comrades sawed at the mouths of their mounts and swung them round, foam-flecked and staggering, to complete the butchery of the scattered and fleeing units of Madero's army.

Surrounded by drifting smoke, splintered wood, scorched scrap iron and bleeding human beings, Harley and the remaining American looked up as the Orozquista cavalry thundered down on them. The machetes were flashing and screaming men were dropping to the dust with hideous wounds. Then, just when they were wondering when their turn was coming, they saw Campo himself, riding towards them, followed by a man carrying a red banner. All about them Federal soldiers were being rounded up in groups to be mown down by rifle fire.

Seeing the newspapermen, Campo galloped towards them and hauled on his reins so that the horse slid to a standstill, lathered and snorting with excitement.

'Ha,' he grinned. 'Buenos días, gentlemen! You will want to write this for your papers, eh? I think we have taught Salas and Madero a lesson, no?' He gestured to where the headquarters train was disappearing into the distance. 'I think we have shown the War Minister a lesson in how to run a war. The chocolateros in Mexico City will be trembling in their shoes now. And we did it with nothing else but a handy hill and a locomotive packed with dynamite. What do you think of my travelling bomb?'

6

It took Harley and the American three days to make their way back to a civilized town of any size where, without equipment or anything beyond what they stood up in, they caught the train south. At Zacatecas, they learned that Salas, having bolted at full speed southwards with his train, destroying the bridges behind him while his demoralized army had been cut to pieces, had capped his failure by committing suicide.

Eventually, they found a hotel among the narrow streets where they could rest, buy clothes and luxuriate in a bath to wash away the grime, the blood, the dust and the memory of the butchery. Then, seeking news at the station, Harley picked up the latest information from the conductor of a northbound train.

'General Huerta's coming,' he was told. 'He's taken Salas' place and he's coming to take over.'

In retirement since Madero had removed him from his command against Zapata, Huerta had been appointed to bring order to the northern armies. By the following day, the story had been expanded. Huerta had promised to defeat the rebels and Villa had been ordered north to act with him. The peón and the Científico, Harley thought. The crude and the unpredictable hand in hand with the cunning and the skilful.

After the massacre at Rellano, the Orozquistas had retired north towards Jiménez and their base at Chihuahua and, following them in one of the troop trains moving up from Mexico City, at Torreón Harley found the newspapers were wildly condemning Madero. The north was buzzing with rumours and it was obvious to the newsmen long before Huerta arrived that something was going to happen because of the growing nervousness of the surrounding districts and the build-up of equipment. Passing through the barren lands of scrubby mesquite and dwarf cactus that stretched to the quivering skyline, they kept seeing armed camps, in one place grouped round a battered water tank destroyed by Orozco's guns, in another around a demolished railway station among a group of adobe dwellings. The bitter parching wind spiralled the yellow dust in twisters across the desert.

Orozco's army, known as the Colorados or Red Flaggers, had imposed a reign of terror on the north, burning, pillaging, robbing, murdering and torturing. Plundering the American Mormon colonies to which Orozco had promised neutrality, they stole crops, cattle and weapons, and left a trail of homeless people carrying everything they possessed heading towards El Paso. Behind them, taking advantage of the growing anarchy, came the bands of the lawless, claiming they belonged to one or other of the armies. Murders had once again become commonplace and bodies hung from telegraph poles as one side or the other wreaked vengeance on stragglers.

After their success against Salas, the Orozquistas had halted just short of Torreón and, called to a conference, Villa had arrived to join Huerta. The first meeting was held in public to indicate to the world the unity of Madero's forces, and the newsmen crowded round a table set under a group of eucalyptus trees that were black against a crimson sky. What would Huerta, the product of the Chapultepec military school, make of Villa? And what would Villa, the product of the bare plains of Chihuahua, make of Huerta?

In full dress uniform, the general peered through his spectacles at the guerrilla, who, after trying to emulate some of the snap of the young Colegio Militar officers, stood awkwardly, his hands hanging loosely, his toes turned in like a small boy's. In deference to Huerta, he had removed his hat, hanging it by its chin-cord over the handle of the pistol at his belt. He looked clumsy and ill-at-ease and Harley saw one of Huerta's officers grin and whisper behind his hand to his neighbour.

Huerta's reputation as a brandy drinker had been well-earned and he was clearly far from sober. Reaching out, he gave Villa an abrazo, praising him for his efforts and prophesying what great things they would do together. Villa, who never touched alcohol, clearly distrusted him and didn't enjoy being pawed by him. Yet, even if Huerta wasn't entirely sober, he was careful to praise Villa's guerrillas, although, suspicious and hard-eyed, he went on to point out that he expected smartness in his commanders and, above all, absolute obedience. Then, with everybody listening, he discussed supplies and inspections for a while, Villa always one jump ahead of the questions. Everything Huerta demanded he had already thought of and it was easy to see the regular officer didn't like it and was beginning to realize that Villa was no longer just a rough and ready guerrillero.

'General Villa will assume command of all non-regular units,' he announced. 'He will move ahead of the main body to provide security at the front and on the flanks. There will be an aggressive policy, with mounted combat patrols probing the northern routes and clearing the railroad.'

The two of them posed for the photographers, then the rest of the conference was held in private. But the journalists didn't disperse, hoping to pick up some crumb of news, and as Villa appeared, he saw Harley among them and spoke out of the corner of his mouth. 'He's trying to teach me my job,' he growled.

Columns of guns, lorries, waggons, horses and men kept arriving and daily more trains appeared, piling up on the line south. With Huerta's arrival the situation had begun to brighten for the government, and moving to Torreón, he started to amass supplies along the railway line. Villa brought up his men and the Orozquistas were forced to retreat, ripping up the railroad as they went. Despite his brandy drinking, Huerta knew what soldiering meant and work on the track went on non-stop. At night, with the sky blazing with stars, lanterns and flares gave light for the men bending over the rails with sledges, spikes, nails and ties. Alongside, fires had been lit and conical-hatted men trailing rifles gathered round to warm themselves as they watched.

All the time more trains kept arriving, studied by amused newsmen used to the disciplined transport of troops in

Europe. Villa's trains were swarming with women and children and on one a family was even living on the cowcatcher of the engine, where they had hung out a line of washing and were baking tortillas on a little fire of mesquite twigs, indifferent to the noisy roar of the boiler.

Johnny Cox turned up again. In spite of his drinking, he had an instinct for news. He seemed faintly embarrassed and was full of excuses for deserting Harley. 'It's safer up here,' he admitted. 'Nobody's trying to kill my cartoons and, better still, nobody's trying to kill *me* because of 'em. Besides – ' he grinned ' – Angelica's up here. We ought to be able to see her.'

'Sooner than you think – ' Tamsy had appeared like a shadow at Harley's elbow and his words reached Harley's ear in a low murmur ' – San Gabriel's been burned down.'

As the Stutz roared along the dusty corrugated road, the sky ahead was dark with a hanging pall of smoke. Of the Mormon settlement there was nothing but charred timbers, collapsed adobe walls and twisted corrugated iron sheets. The Mormons were packing their children and what remained of their possessions into ramshackle carts and were preparing to head for the railway line.

San Gabriel was not destroyed but it hadn't escaped unscathed. Animals, horses and crops had been taken and one end of the house had been set on fire. A stark chimney groped towards the sky above blackened walls and Angelica was trying to round up the remainder of her stock with what was left of her staff. Several of her men had been snatched up by the raiders and forced to join their army, and she reappeared in a hurry, her hair tied back, her eyes blazing and close to tears with anger, despair and frustration.

'The bastards even cleared out my soup kitchen in Chihuahua,' she said. 'I was hoping to start one in Mexico City before long but now I've got to get this one going again before I can go down there.'

'Who did it?' Harley asked.

'Orozquistas. They had a red flag with 'Reform, Liberty and Country' painted on it. They emptied the place of all we've got.' She kicked at a stone. 'Goddam war!' She glared at Harley. 'And don't remind me, you goddam Limey, that there was once a time when I was all for it. I still am. I'm all for destroying vermin like these who won't let people live in peace. Politicians! This country's got too damn' many politicians.'

Eventually her anger disssipated and she managed a weak smile. 'Oh, come on in,' she said. 'We can feed and water you, I guess. At least we're alive and that's something.'

The following morning they took her into Chihuahua to replace the things that had been stolen. It wasn't easy, because before moving south the Orozquistas had raided the big stores and they had to search the backstreets for what she required. As they did so, Tamsy brought news from the telegraph office that Huerta had reached Rellano and that a battle was building up.

As they began to throw their equipment into the Stutz, Angelica watched them bleakly, her face pale and set, her eyes bright and unexpectedly moist.

'I'll be all right, goddammit!' she said defiantly. 'I've looked after myself before. I can again.'

In her bearing was all the courage of those American pioneers who had pushed westwards, southwards, northwards from the coast, driving into the wilderness to make themselves new homes, braving the harsh winters and the dry, baking summers, the wild animals, the Indians, the fact that they had nothing but what their hands could make, never thinking of themselves as brave, but enduring year after year what at times seemed impossible odds.

Harley touched her hand and her head turned quickly so that she stared at him proudly, daring him to be sympathetic. She was still watching as the car roared away.

For three weeks, while Huerta didn't move, Villa conducted a lone campaign against daunting odds, capturing small towns he was never strong enough to hold, scattering Orozco's rearguard as he opened the road to the plains of Conejos. But he was a difficult subordinate with a casual attitude to discipline, rank and uniform, and Huerta's officers regarded the rough and ready guerrillas with contempt and never hesitated to poke fun at Villa's honorary rank.

'They don't greet me when I arrive,' Villa grumbled. 'I'm

just a peón and when I'm dusty and tired they don't bother to offer me food or drink and they look at me as if I stink.'

Cox had informed him of the raid on the Ojarra hacienda in the hope of picking up a story and Villa had promised vengeance. They were camped by this time in a small town called Fillipo de Mayos, built round a hacienda that had been sacked and burned in Madero's revolution. The streets were blurred by the banks of brown dust blown by the wind against the walls, and from the interior of the church, windowless and with three enormous bells hanging on the rack in the tower, a cloud of incense came as the women camp followers prayed for victory. Guns were stacked in corners and saddles piled in the dust, and the bare little houses were crowded with soldiers, their women, and the chickens and pigs they had looted from the surrounding countryside.

Being guerrilleros, they received no uniform and, operating far from Huerta's main army, little in the way of supplies. In rags and almost starving, they squatted round their little fires to boil corn husks and meat. Then an old violinist in a tattered sarape who could play only one tune, *O Sole Mio*, started sawing at his instrument and a few men grabbed for girls and started pirouetting and toe-pointing. Someone found a pianola in the ruined hacienda and pushed it on to the patio. The soldiers took turns playing it and started to stick candles into bottles around the burned and blackened walls and among the riot of wild vines that grew among the roof beams. Before long the patio was crowded with blanketed men, even now a little uneasy to be in one of the great houses they had never been allowed to enter, but an orchestra was raised and the pianola took over when they tired. A barrel of wine was rolled out and one of the young men started teaching the others the Turkey Trot, which he'd picked up in El Paso, and soon they were all at it.

Already far from sober, Johnny Cox was dancing with a girl in a sugar pink dress that seemed to scream out loud and somebody pushed a stout middle-aged matron at Harley.

'Vamonos a bailar,' he yelled.

They danced several times then, as the violinist remembered a long-forgotten waltz, Harley saw that Angelica had arrived from San Gabriel and was standing near one of the fires, her expression lost and lonely. Johnny Cox was already divesting himself of the girl in the pink dress but Harley beat him to it and took Angelica in his arms. She said nothing, moulding herself to him, holding him tighter than necessary.

'You shouldn't be here,' Harley said as they turned. 'There's going to be a battle.'

'And a battle's no place for a dame?' Angelica retorted sarcastically. 'For God's sake, can't you understand? I've *got* to be here.'

'Why?'

'Because I – ' she stared at him, her eyes sparkling unexpectedly, then her expression changed. 'Because my goddam place is with the army!'

At once they were at each other's throats again and as they argued the music changed. The dancing grew wilder and finally one of the men hit the girl in the sugar pink dress over the head with his pistol for spending too much time with Cox. Cox was drunk enough to feel constrained to defend her and, as they faced each other, there was a subdued clicking of revolvers among the crowd and mutterings to the younger men. 'Ananacio, go get my rifle!' 'Luís, my shotgun, quickly!'

Harley drew Angelica out of the line of fire and they joined the spectators gleefully watching the proceedings from behind trees and carts. Anticipation grew as the two men faced each other and, with the Mexican loath to shoot an unarmed man, Cox was drunkenly bleating for someone to lend him a weapon when Villa arrived. Swinging his powerful arms, using his boots and fists, he pushed the would-be duellists aside.

'To your horses!' he yelled. 'We've better things to do than kill each other! The Red Flaggers are north of Corral Yermo.'

With Harley and Tamsy riding close behind the flag, wrapped to the eyes in their sarapes against the wind, they entered the desert again, moving over a series of sandy rolling plains covered with black mesquite. Lining the road were the little wooden crosses the country people erected on the spots where a violent death had occurred, to indicate the fighting that had taken place there the year before. They were just riding up the slope into Corral when they saw conical hats behind an adobe wall and on the roofs of the scattered houses, and horses were wrenched round as they realized they had ridden into a trap.

The check as the column saw the danger was only momentary, however. There was no question of organizing their force or deploying into line, no chance to bring up guns. Villa raised his arm and pointed forward, spurring his horse at once into a gallop.

'Viva Villa!'

Roaring their battlecry, the men behind him raked their mounts' flanks with their enormous spurs, then, waving swords, rifles, pistols, whips, and yelling like madmen, they swept after him into a headlong charge.

'Holy Jesus Christ!' Seeing what was sweeping down on him from behind, Tamsy kicked his horse into a gallop to avoid being ridden down. There was no chance to get out of the way. It was a case of going with them or being crushed underfoot as the horde of screaming men thundered down on them.

It was still early, and yellow clouds like brush strokes swept across the sky, the golden light that was flooding the heavens touching the hills with ochre and tinting the stunted trees and cactus and the ends of the mesquite. Despite the ragged clothing of the riders and the total lack of order, there was a terrible majesty about them as they swept up the slope. Merged into the movement, Harley and Tamsy found themselves carried along, absorbed tightly into the mass of bone and muscle as the other riders swept round them.

On the high plain, the air was clear as crystal, magnifying everything, and, startled by the pounding hooves and the yelling of the riders, crows burst into the air. A few rifles and pistols were discharged as the flag rippled red, green and white. Nostrils distended, the horses were now in a thundering gallop, eyes bulging, manes and tails flying, dust and stones lifting under the pounding hooves.

As the rifle fire began to ripple out and a machine gun started its slow clack-clack, one of the Villistas, his sombrero over his face, slumped from the saddle and several mounts went down with a crash and the jingle of equipment, their riders rolling under the hooves of the following horses. Villa was riding as if he were part of his mount. Alongside Harley,

Tamsy, his head down, was alternately swearing and praying in a flat monotone.

'Holy Biddy, the Lord Jesus Christ take care of me now and for evermore!'

From the corner of his eye, Harley saw more horses go down, but he was almost unaware of being shot at. Then, as he saw the man in front of him fall from the saddle clutching his face, he heaved at the revolver he wore at his belt, deciding he had better have it in his hand for safety.

As they reached the top of the rise, they realized that in front of them, between them and the Red Flaggers, a ditch had been dug behind a low line of brush. Villa saw it in time and leapt it magnificently, but several of the following riders were too late and their mounts slammed stiff-legged into the opposite bank, the snaps as their forelegs broke clear above the firing. Screaming, the horses fell back then scrambled up again, wild-eyed and crippled, trying to fight their way out of the ditch, their broken legs swinging. As they did so they were knocked flying by the following riders, until the ditch became a yelling confusion of men and animals.

Avoiding the tangle, Harley leapt the ditch and saw that others had also made it safely. As they reached the machine guns, he saw Villa's arm flash down and the gunner fell away, screaming, his face covered with blood. A man rose in front of him, dressed in overalls, a frock coat and boater, and swathed in ammunition belts. As his rifle came up, Harley smashed him over the head with his revolver, but the next moment a second man came at him, his rifle pointing, and this time there was no choice but to fire. Dropping his weapon, the man went over backwards like a felled tree.

Riderless horses were running in all directions but the Villistas had reached the Red Flaggers' lines now and were among them, yelling, swinging swords, machetes, pistols, rifles. The very speed of Villa's reaction had startled the Orozquistas and one of the two machine guns they possessed had jammed after only a few rounds. One of the Villistas kicked it on to its side and the other gun was overwhelmed by frenzied, screaming men. Then, as the riders hauled in their ponies, their heads tossing bloody froth from the cruel curbs, the Orozquistas broke. Flung back by the sheer impetus of the charge, they began to run, scattering across the plain, those Villistas who could still drive their jaded mounts forward slashing at them with their weapons. But the horses were worn out now and as they stumbled to a halt the riders slid from the saddle and started firing at the Red Flaggers from the ground. Most of them were toppled but one was surrounded and caught unwounded. His captors snatched away his rifle, an excellent Winchester, and, stripping him naked, made him run through the brush and cactus, shooting at him as he went until finally he was rolled over into the dust. The man who shot him claimed the Winchester.

With the Orozquista forces smashed, they began rounding up the prisoners. One of them said he was from the Ojarra hacienda but, as he began to point out the men who had taken part in the raid on San Gabriel, Villa gestured.

'Get rid of them all,' he snapped. 'Then we'll not miss any.'

They were shot or hanged in groups from the trees in the square of Corral Yermo while a band played lively marches in the bandstand. Harley watched unemotionally, aware of the enormous capacity for cruelty that existed in every man. Villa's face was grim.

'He pagado mis impuestas,' he growled. 'I've paid my debt to Dona Angelica.'

As the Orozquistas were pushed relentlessly northwards, it became obvious to the newspapermen that Huerta wasn't enjoying the fact that his troops idolized Villa. It was Villa who was doing the hard work and keeping the fighting well away from them, and it was significant that the songs they sang – *The Killing of Reza* and *Pancho Villa's Wedding* – glorified the guerrilla leader, not the professional soldier.

Villa's horsemen were quartering the plains now, searching the villages and the arroyos, dragging out the hiding Orozquistas to hang them or shoot them – in lines of three so that one bullet could do for the lot and save ammunition. As the Orozquista retreat became a rout and the desert was filled with fleeing men, Huerta hurled his troops once more against the Red Flaggers. Villa, outnumbered three to one but employing the guerrilla tactics that were second nature to his peón army, ambushed a force coming to their rescue and wiped it out in the hills.

As they drew breath, more trains puffed up from the south to discharge men, guns, ammunition and horses. Stragglers caught up and patrols went out to find supplies and fodder. The horde of pressmen and hangers-on increased, trying to egg someone on to do something, arrogantly sure that these representatives of a backward, primitive country would happily allow themselves to be butchered so that more sophisticated societies could read comfortably of their sufferings with their breakfast coffee.

Huerta still appeared to be full of energy. Every pressman in his camp knew he was fuming at Villa's indifference to the orders he kept sending him. Then someone said he'd seen Villa in the camp and they began to expect action – if nothing else, a blazing row that would make a good copy. But Villa seemed to have disappeared again and soon afterwards Tamsy Flood arrived with the news that something funny was happening.

'What sort of funny?' Johnny Cox looked up from the camera he was repairing.

'Goddam funny sort of funny,' Tamsy said. 'Villa just rode in between General Navarrete and General Hidalgo and he was surrounded by a squad of guys with fixed bayonets. It looked to me as if he'd been arrested.'

7

There was an immediate dash to find out what had happened.

As they besieged Huerta's headquarters, Tamsy's news turned out to be true. Villa had been arrested on charges of persistent insubordination and refusing to return stolen horses. Navarrete confirmed what they'd heard.

'He was ordered to report to headquarters,' he said. 'But he claimed he was tired, and that he'd appear as soon as he'd recovered. Unfortunately that isn't the way Huerta works. Villa was turned out of bed in the middle of the night, told to hand over his weapons and taken to Huerta's office. There was a guard lining the walls on three sides; the other wall was lined by Huerta's personal staff. It was a court martial.'

'In the middle of the night?'

'He offered little defence.' Navarrete shrugged. 'That was about all. Huerta addressed him as Honorary General Francisco Villa and said he'd been found guilty of insubordination and banditry and that he was to be shot.'

'Shot, for God's sake! When?'

'In the morning. Four o'clock.' Navarrete frowned. 'I think Villa believes Huerta's just trying to frighten him and he's ordered his men to stay out of town in case they start something. But he's wrong, gentlemen. Huerta means what he says.'

'*With Villa*?'

Navarrete shrugged again. 'Captain Hernandez has charge of the firing squad. Villa's brigade is to be broken up.'

'Shouldn't we inform Madero? It's surely a joke.'

It was hard to believe it could be anything else. Thanks to the press corps' stories, Villa had become a household name not only in Mexico but in the States. The people who read the newspapers knew nothing of his spasms of engulfing rage or of the women he had married, only that he won battles. For the newspaper-reading public he provided the whiff of excitement they loved as they went about their lives, the little man that the little men loved; the man who, despite his disadvantages, had proved himself equal to every challenge, taking on generals schooled in war and wiping the floor with them.

But the story was so incredible it needed confirmation. While a few newsmen bolted to their quarters to write their copy, the more careful sought out Huerta's staff for the details. Villa's crimes were fully enumerated for them – disobedience, insubordination and robbery. When Harley enquired further, it turned out that he had been charged with ignoring a lawful order in time of war, attempting to subvert the forces under his command, and appropriating 260,000 pesos while looting. The horses with which he had originally been charged had been forgotten, and it seemed the truth was that the bankers of Parral had complained about the money Villa had requisitioned, and that Huerta, disliking the publicity the uneducated, untutored peón had been receiving, was allowing his jealousy to get the better of him.

Seeking out Madero's brother, Raúl, who was a colonel with Huerta's army, they found he was already heading with Navarrete for the telegraph office. As they hurried to the Stutz to shoot off in pursuit, Angelica appeared, wearing a heavy coat against the wind and with a shawl round her head.

'I heard they'd arrested Villa,' she said.

'Damn right they did,' Cox replied.

'Holy Mother of God, Villa and Zapata are the only honest men in the bunch of crooks trying to seize power in this rotten country!'

Arriving at the telegraph station just behind Madero, they found him arguing with the telegraphist.

'My orders forbid me to use the line,' the telegraphist was

saying. 'General Huerta's express wish. He wants it kept open for his own use.'

'Damn your orders!' Madero thundered. 'Send this message at once. "*To the President. General Huerta orders Pancho Villa shot at four a.m. Wire reprieve.*" '

The telegraphist gave him a startled look. 'But the line's blocked at Torreón, Don Raúl,' he said. 'And all outgoing messages have to be checked. I'd need your orders in writing.'

Madero snatched up a pencil and as he began to write the key began to click.

'Inform the telegraphist in Mexico City that he's charged personally with seeing the message reaches the President's home.' Madero turned to Navarrete. 'For God's sake, go and see Huerta! Get a stay of execution until we can hold a full investigation. If they shoot Villa we'll lose half the army at a stroke.'

A keen wind was moaning softly at the door, sifting the sandy soil against the walls and into the cracks. Madero looked round desperately and Cox fished into the long ulster he was wearing and offered him a cigarette. He nodded gratefully and, lighting it, crushed it out almost immediately as the key started clicking. They all whirled at the sound, their eyes following the operator's pencil.

'*President is out of town –* '

'Jeeze!' Cox said. 'That's put the cat among the pigeons!'

' *– I am relaying your message to him.*' The message was signed by Madero's secretary.

Raúl Madero slammed his fist into the palm of his other hand. 'Warn him the President will hold him personally responsible if Villa's shot,' he snapped.

As the minutes ticked by and nothing happened, Navarrete returned. 'A temporary stay of execution only,' he said. 'One hour.'

Madero thumped on the desk. 'Why in God's name does my brother have to be out of the capital at this of all moments?' He swung to the telegraphist. 'Call them again! Insist they move fast.'

The sky was growing pale and no sign of a reply had come. Harley nudged Cox. 'I think our place isn't here,' he said, 'but back in the square to see what's happening.'

When they reached the centre of the town, bugles were

already cutting the stillness. Government troops were lining the barrack square, watched by an officer who directed the newsmen where to stand. As he watched, it occurred to Harley that if there were to be a reprieve it must surely have arrived by this time and he headed for Huerta's headquarters to find out. There was only one other newspaperman who had thought to interview the general and together they found him preparing to head for the railroad. He was stuffing a bottle of brandy into his briefcase and his desk, littered with glasses, looked as if he'd been sitting up all night. Huerta himself seemed sober and full of life.

For a few minutes he answered their questions but he was evasive and unforthcoming. Returning to the barrack square they found the newsmen who had turned up for the execution being pushed by an officer into a group to one side of the firing squad.

'No photographs,' he warned. 'There are to be no cameras.'

There was a battery of machine guns at the gate and a mound of earth by the wall where a grave had been dug. Nearby a crowd had begun to gather to watch the killing, among them Angelica, still wearing the coat and shawl, her hand to her throat, an expression of utter disbelief on her face.

All about them the windows were shuttered and the streets were silent. Then they saw a carriage appear and stop. Immediately the drums began to sound in a steady menacing roll and somewhere out of sight someone began to whistle the Dead March to the beat. Finally they heard the rhythmic shuffling of sandals as a squad of men with rifles appeared through the misty greyness of the early morning. In the middle of them was Villa, looking puzzled and angry, as if he might suddenly explode into action and send his escort flying. He was dressed in the civilian suit which had become his undress uniform, his watch chain across his stomach, knee-high leggings and an American campaign hat tilted as usual to the back of his head where it clung in a rakish angle as if it were nailed there.

As the squad came to a halt, the drums stopped and there was utter silence as Villa shuffled to a stop among them. The sergeant in command strode to the wall and made a large cross on it with a mattock and ordered him to stand in front of it. Harley was looking about him by this time. The farce was going on too long. If there had been a reprieve, why wasn't it being applied?

Villa's anger burst out at last in a shout. 'Why?' he demanded. 'Why are they going to shoot me? Por dios, if I'm to die, I have a right to know why! I've served Madero faithfully.' He stopped, choking with indignation, his eyes wet with tears.

Again the sergeant told him to stand at the foot of the cross he had made and again, the tears streaming down his cheeks now, Villa demanded an explanation. As the sergeant tried to force him to the wall, he knelt on the ground, begging for mercy. But it wasn't fear that was in his eyes, only cunning and rage, and it was obvious he was playing for time, putting off the execution to the last second in the hope of some change in circumstances. As he rose, the sergeant stepped forward.

'I'm to offer you a blindfold, mi general.'

'Damn the blindfold!'

'Then I'm to offer you a last reasonable request.'

'Very well then,' Villa roared. 'Grant me this: Tell me why you're doing this. I've had no trial! This is murder!'

The stolid expression on the Indian face of the sergeant didn't change and Villa turned and stared at the grave that had been dug. There was stilll no sign of a reprieve and, glancing back towards the headquarters building, Harley could see officers strolling about indifferent to the drama being enacted only a hundred yards away. One of them was actually stifling a yawn.

As the firing squad lined up facing Villa, an officer appeared, walking briskly towards them. Halting, he drew his sword. The first rays of the sun flashed on the polished blade as he lifted it. Villa still looked bewildered but he seemed suddenly to accept that he really was to die and to have become reconciled to it. Gathering himself to meet it, he tilted his hat forward against the yellow sun shining in his eyes and took off his watch and chain and fished money from his pocket.

'I am permitted to reward the soldiers?' he asked. 'To ask them to aim straight for the heart?'

The officer agreed and about-turned to take up a position to the right of the firing squad. As he did so, Harley saw and orderly approaching from headquarters carrying a sealed envelope. He didn't seem to be hurrying, but neither did the officer in command of the firing squad, and he realized it was all part of a cruel game – the vengeance of Huerta and his staff of military college men, who were dragging out the tension as long as they dared to torment the untutored guerrilla leader who had so often showed them how to fight.

The orderly suddenly seemed to think he was drawing it out *too* far and broke into a hurried trot. Reaching the officer of the firing squad, who was fiddling elaborately with the hilt of his sword to waste time, he handed him the envelope. The officer tore it open, spent a full minute reading it over and over again, then pocketed it with a nod.

As the officer spoke, the squad straightened and a long drum roll started. Turning immediately on the drummer, the officer told him to stop.

'Ground arms!'

Replacing his sword in its scabbard, the officer turned and, swinging round, Harley saw that Cox had moved to the left of the line of the firing squad and was buttoning the front of the long ulster.

As the firing squad was marched away, Villa sagged against the wall, leaning against the bricks, breathing heavily, his mouth hanging open, his great chest rising and falling. He had accepted that he was a dead man and was finding it difficult to realize that he was not.

Then Raúl Madero and Navarrete appeared, pushing through the crowd towards him in long strides. 'You're reprieved, Don Pancho,' Madero was saying. 'I gave them the President's message ten minutes ago. You're to be sent to Mexico City under guard.'

The pressmen tried to push close and questions were shot at Villa.

'What was it like, Pancho?' Cox asked. 'What were you thinking?'

'I knew he wouldn't dare.' Through stiff lips, Villa struggled to speak. 'I knew he was only trying to frighten me.'

'What's going to happen now?'

'I know this.' Villa's brows came down. 'I'll never allow

myself to be unarmed and helpless again, my friend.' He made an effort to pull himself together and even managed a smile. 'I'll be all right when I get to Mexico City. The President will make things right. He knows who his friends are.' He looked at Harley. 'Have you spoken to Huerta? What did he say when he learned about the reprieve?'

Harley shrugged. 'Nothing,' he said. 'That old Indian never says anything much. Just "It was an affair of honour." That's all.'

As Villa was led away, still protesting his innocence and his faithfulness to the revolutionary cause, Cox appeared alongside Harley. He was smiling and, edging closer, he opened the front of the long ulster. Hanging on his chest from a strap round his neck was a camera.

'Boy, this'll bring me a fortune,' he said. 'I got a picture of the only man ever to stand before a Mexican firing squad and survive.'

The press corps was waiting on the station as Villa, under a heavy guard, was thrust into a third-class compartment for the journey south. Huerta was already moving his army north for the next clash with Orozco.

As they watched, Angelica Ojarra arrived like an angry whirlwind.

'I'm going to Mexico city,' she said. 'I'll make sure he gets a good lawyer.'

There was a stiff breeze stirring the dust and, as the passengers headed towards their reservations, Villa was at the window of his compartment. He seemed cheerful and confident and was eating an orange and spitting the pips to the platform.

'It'll be all right, compadre,' he said to Harley. 'The President will fix it.'

'How about a picture, Pancho?' Cox asked. 'Big smile to show everybody you're not worried.'

Villa gestured his agreement but an officer appeared. 'No photographs,' he snapped. 'This man is regarded as a criminal.'

Cox said nothing but Harley noticed he was still wearing the long ulster and had no doubt that the picture had been taken.

The news of the arrest had got around and a squad of soldiers had been mustered to hold back the crowd of peóns, beggars, girls and children that had gathered.'It'll be the same all the way south,' Angelica said angrily. She gestured at the crowd. '*They* know who's for them and who's for themselves. The poor, the hungry, the tired, the angry, the exploited, and the cheated – *they*'ll see him safe.'

Harley very much doubted it. Despite the revolution, the hungry, the exploited, and the cheated still weren't getting what they had asked for.

The train had to leave before time to avoid a riot and as it steamed slowly from the station, Villa had his head out, waving to people along the platform. There were the familiar cries of 'Viva Villa' and an old woman threw a bunch of flowers.

'Heaven and Our Lady of Guadalupe go with you, Don Pancho!'

Standing on the platform, Harley watched Angelica pass, sitting at a window, rigid with self-righteousness. Her outbursts, sometimes irrational and irresponsible, always threatened to soar into an indignant scream, but her emotions were warm and honest and she made no attempt to hide them, so that her rantings could have an immense dignity.

It was only as he turned away to leave the platform that Harley realized that Cox had disappeared and it dawned on him that he had slipped aboard the train and was heading for Mexico City with Angelica.

8

Among the businessmen and bankers of the north with a lot to lose, Huerta was rapidly becoming a national hero. While Villa waited in Mexico City for his trial, Harley followed the general as he smashed Orozco's army at Bachimba then, moving ahead in a wide sweep, he stumbled across Orozco's troops pinned against the border at Ojinaga. Some of them were already crossing into the States while Orozco, still not admitting defeat, raged up and down, slashing at the defecting soldiers with his crop and urging them to remain to fight. All round them were riderless horses wandering free, their reins dangling, railway trucks deserted on the lines, and all the scattered equipment and abandoned weapons of a shattered army.

The Orozquistas were hungry and in no mood to stand and fight, and the houses were full of moaning wounded, lying close together, sometimes several of them sharing the same blanket. Orozco's rebellion had reached its end. There was nothing more and they were cursing Orozco for dragging them into it. Huerta was still pushing northwards and now there was nowhere else to flee. However a last attempt to stand was made. Trenches were dug and guns were brought up and Orozco put on a show of confidence. But the fiction could not last and at the first sign of Huerta's approach the demoralized rebel army began again to crumble.

With no semblance of order, the road to the frontier became crowded with men shuffling northwards, interspersed with groups of horsemen on animals stumbling with weariness. Behind them was a trail of broken weapons and, standing by the roadside with a crowd of gaping peóns, Harley saw Orozco himself, his mean, handsome face taut with fury. The next day, they heard that he had fled to the United States, and the last sign of resistance vanished. The defeated army simply waited in huddled groups round their fires for Huerta to round them up.

The newpapers containing the news of the victory also carried the story of Villa's transfer in handcuffs to the Federal Penitentiary. Nobody was listening to his plea that he had used the money he was accused of stealing to pay his troops, and that the men he was accused of subverting were men he had recruited himself and were the last people in the world to be turned against Madero.

Harley's final despatch from El Paso brought a letter from Isobel Hartnell asking why had had disappeared so soon from her side. There was also a telegram from Sproat with a suggestion that he would soon be needed in Europe, but there were rumours of new uprisings against Madero so he hung on, deliberately sending extensive reports of the pursuit of the last of the rebels. With Huerta in Chihuahua City, however, Orozco's rebellion was over and, reluctantly, Harley began to pack his bags. but instead of going north to New York, he decided to visit the capital again to check up on the situation there. If all was quiet, he would pick up a ship home from the south.

As he was preparing to leave his hotel the half-expected telegram arrived from Knowles.

'Rising in Veracruz. Government troops on way.'

Another telegram arrived at the same time from Sproat, 'Come home. Uprising over,' to which Harley telegraphed back 'Staying here. Another one just started.'

He picked up his information as he sped south. The man behind the latest trouble was Felix Díaz, a nephew of the deposed dictator, who had been chief of police in Mexico City during his uncle's rule and was now commander of the garrison in Veracruz.

Stopping in Mexico City to pick up fresh clothes, Harley tried to contact Angelica. He had her address in the Calle Bolivar near the Ciudadela, the city barracks and arsenal, but there was no reply as he hammered on the door. It was a big house in a neighbourhood of big houses and no one knew or even seemed to care where she was. They were wealthy people who found no joy in the repeated rebellions and hoped that eventually Madero's weak government would be replaced by a strong man who would make Mexico stable again. They knew of Angelica and a few had even called on her, but she had refused their invitations and they all considered her a little mad. Perhaps she was, Harley decided, but it was an impulsive warm-hearted madness.

The line to Veracruz had been built by the French in the days of Maximilian and the train passed through tropical jungle, groves of mangoes, bananas and giant coconut palms surrounded by pink and yellow bushes of begonia and orchids, bomba and colorines lighting the trees with bursts of vivid hues above mysterious rivers and lily-covered pools hidden beneath moss and fern. The drop from Mexico City was over seven thousand feet in a mere two hundred and fifty miles, and the crisp atmosphere of the highlands gave way to a sultry humidity as the train reached the marshes and sand dunes of the coast.

With its pools and canals, its mosquitoes, its diseases, its backward sanitation, its lethargic inhabitants and the vast flock of vultures that attended to its garbage, the City of the True Cross was stiflingly claustrophobic. The train was stopped at a small halt on the outskirts and an officer and several policemen walked along the carriages, checking the credentials of the passengers.

Staring at Harley's papers, the officer gave a cold smile. 'You're too late, señor,' he said. 'It's all over.'

Several men were removed from the train to the rear of a whitewashed building and soon afterwards the sound of shots occurred as executions took place. As the shooting stopped, the train was allowed to proceed at slow speed but as it came into the station at Veracruz, it was immediately surrounded by more soldiers who watched as the passengers alighted, prodding at packs and asking to see into luggage.

Outside the station there was no sign of fighting and Harley learned that the rising had fizzled out. There had been no support for the rebels and they were now in one of the city hotels trying to decide what to do next.

Hiring a cab, he found the place surrounded by rebel soldiers and policemen, all of them confused and aimless. He tried repeatedly to get inside to obtain an interview but every time he was faced by a man with a rifle pointed at his chest. In the end he slipped in through the kitchen entrance and found his way to the suite of rooms Díaz and his staff had occupied, only to find it empty apart from scattered chairs, the lingering smell of cigar smoke, dropped papers and a pair of white gloves lying on a chair. The manager appeared, looking bewildered.

'I think it's over, señor,' he said. 'Nobody seems to want it. General Beltrán has surrounded the city and the navy has blockaded it from the sea.'

There was a buzz of excitement running through the city as Harley left to find someone who could tell him what had happened. Alongside the wharves in the dock area there were two warships, old and out-of-date, secondhand equipment from wealthier nations, their crews standing in groups on the quayside chattering. There were government sentries on all the public buildings, along the breakwater, outside the vast edifice that housed the lighthouse, even by the statues of George Washington and Benito Juárez. More soldiers waited on every corner, shabby, dark-faced men recruited in the area, sweating in their shapeless khaki, the iced drink vendors doing a roaring trade among them round the bazaars and under the arcades.

There seemed remarkably little sign of the rebellion and an officer he found drinking chocolate in a café made clear what had happened.

'No other group fell in behind Díaz,' he said. 'And those who backed him were quick to withdraw their support when they saw the odds against them.'

'And now?'

'Díaz has been arrested. He and twenty-six of his officers are to be shot.'

'Names?'

The officer produced a list.

'All army,' Harley said, scanning it. 'What about the políticos?'

The officer grinned. 'There are always some of those, señor.' He produced a second list and among the names

Harley saw that of Féderico Toral. 'They'll not be rounded up,' the officer said with a shrug. 'Because they are only guesswork. Nobody can be certain and the President prefers to trust them.'

Learning that the arrested officers were to be entrained for Mexico City, Harley headed for the station. There seemed a great deal of apathy, as though Veracruz was indifferent to who ran the place. It was still swarming with soldiers, their ranks threaded through by urchins begging for coins or cigarettes, the fringes haunted by prostitutes, and ice cream and lemonade vendors. Down the street a squad of vultures lurched about, their black wings spread, picking at the body of a dead dog lying in the gutter.

Eventually a whistle shrilled and the soldiers fell into some sort of order. Then several carriages, swarming with soldiers, appeared. In the first of them, Harley recognized Felix Díaz, a good-looking youngish man with wavy hair and a moustache whom he'd seen often about the capital. He was in full dress uniform but wore no sash or weapon. There were at least half a dozen heavily-armed officers guarding him. The other carriages bore the men who had been in rebellion with him, all in uniform, all without weapons, armed squads of soldiers marching alongside.

As the convoy halted, Díaz rose in his carriage and tried to address the crowd that had gathered. There were peóns, labourers, fashionable men and women and they showed no surprise or interest as he spoke.

'The army's honour has been trampled on,' he said in a loud voice.

Nobody seemed to know what he meant and he was dragged down to his seat. Soon afterwards the whole group was lined up and, with Díaz at their head, were marched towards a waiting train. Newspapermen had arrived in dozens now, all of them too late to see anything, and all they could do was follow and watch as the defeated rebels were thrust into compartments with their guards. Then the train lurched, buffers clashed, and it began to move out of the station. It was clearly all over and, apart from sending a long despatch to Sproat with the facts, there was no point in remaining in Veracruz.

By the time Harley returned to Mexico city, Huerta had also returned from the north. He was facing an unexpected charge of plundering his campaign funds but, cleverer than Villa, he had taken the confident view that Madero would never dare dispute anything with the hero of the hour and had merely claimed that he was no bookkeeper. He had guessed right and, instead of being charged like Villa, had been promoted major-general.

'They retired him all the same,' Knowles said. 'Letters have been found that implicate him in plots.'

With the new rebellion over, Sproat promptly started making urgent noises again but once more Harley ignored his telegrams, convinced that somewhere beneath the urbane surface of Mexico City dark forces were stirring.

Felix Díaz had managed somehow to wriggle out of the death sentence imposed on him. Knowles knew of powerful friends who had arranged a stay of execution, while the Supreme Court, also loaded with Porfiristas, had claimed that since he had left the army to start his insurrection, he could not be court-martialled and could only be imprisoned to await trial. It confirmed Harley's suspicions that there was more to come.

No sooner had the story appeared when Angelica arrived at Harley's flat. In a furious temper, she stormed in, trailed by Johnny Cox, who had the look of a cat that had been at the cream.

'Has Madero gone mad?' she demanded at once. 'While Villa's in prison accused of appropriating money he used to pay his troops, Huerta gets away with the same thing without an explanation and Díaz gets no more than a prison sentence. No wonder Villa's puzzled.'

'You've seen him?'

'Sure, we've seen him,' Cox said. 'Several times. Katie got permission.'

Katie, it had become, Harley noticed, not Kathleen, and certainly not what it had been in the north, Angelica.

'Where is he?'

'Military prison at Santiago Tlalelolco, poor bastard!'

'He's not exactly suffering,' Angelica said, sharply realistic. 'Food's sent in and he has his cell cleaned for him. But he still can't understand why a pardon doesn't come.'

It was obvious why. Madero was afraid. Of plotters. Of Zapata, who still refused to recognize his government. Of all the people waiting to thrust a knife in his back. Even of Huerta who, because he had saved the government, couldn't be touched.

'He tries to understand that it isn't easy for a president,' Angelica went on. 'He has a girl in there sometimes. He says she's a great comfort.' The old electric grin came unexpectedly. 'He asked *me* to stay. He said he'd like to keep things proper and was willing to marry me.' The grin came again. 'He's learning to read. I found someone to teach him. Hell, it's painful to watch but he's doing it.'

Harley's press pass took him into the prison. The warden was not at first willing to admit him but a hundred peso note persuaded him that the visitor meant well. Villa, who was in the garden, his head bent over a slate and a child's spelling book, looked up as Harley approached, then he grinned and jumped up to meet him with an abrazo.

'Mi amigo,' he said. 'You have come to tell the world the truth?'

'As near as I can, Don Pancho.'

'But not a pardon?' Villa's brows wrinkled. 'Who told you I was here?'

'Dona Angelica.'

'A good one, that. If I were free and she would have me I would marry her.'

'I thought you were married already.'

Villa grinned, his eyes mischievous. 'Marriages don't mean much,' he said. 'But you must never do violence to women and you must always lead them to the altar. I've got several wives who are legitimate in the sight of God, but they're not shamed or embarrassed, because any slip there was, was mine.'

'What if the priest objects?'

Villa shrugged. 'You just threaten to put a bullet in him and he comes round soon enough.' He paused, frowning. 'They tell me I'm kept here because, if I'm not, Huerta will lead his troops in open revolt.'

Harley pushed a package forward. 'I brought you some books, Don Pancho.'

Villa looked at them and with great difficulty mouthed the

titles. '*Campaigns of Napoleon*. This is the Napoleon I have heard about across the sea.' He stared at the print. 'I am learning to read, but it is a slow process and I doubt if I can manage these.'

'Look at the maps in them. They'll be enough to show you how he fought his battles.'

Villa managed a smile. 'I've learned many things, compadre, since I came here. Do you know the stars are millions of miles away?' He looked awed. 'And I can now sign my name. Watch.' Hissing between his teeth, his tongue following the movement of his awkward fingers, he wrote his name on a sheet of paper. It already contained dozens of them, all surrounded by extravagant flourishes. It was a long time before he passed over the paper. 'Keep it, amigo. Fifty years from now your sons will be able to sell it for a fortune.'

He sat back, frowning, watching Harley closely. 'I've also learned that Zapata didn't betray the Cause. He ditched Orozco immediately he realized the Científicos were behind him. But he says Madero does nothing but make promises and he refuses to give up what he's gained.' Villa's face tautened. 'But Zapata's still free, my friend. In his own hills. *I* planted sweet wheat and harvested bitter weeds. They know I never turned my men against the President and that the money I took in Parral was used to pay them.'

Though Harley had no difficulty believing Villa would never try to subvert men from Madero's side, he had to take with a pinch of salt the information that all the money he had acquired had gone to pay his troops. Villa liked the good things of life and, like Huerta, had been brought up in the Mexican tradition of helping yourself. He had been a bandit for too many years for a little of it not to have stuck to his fingers.

Villa's smile had gone now and his eyes were ablaze. 'I don't like it here,' he growled. 'It stinks of treachery. There are plots and counter-plots. Bernardo Reyes is here.'

Every newsman in Mexico knew General Reyes. He was a pompous bearded sycophant who wore bells on his spurs to make them ring more clearly and relished being photographed in full military regalia. He also enjoyed raising rebellions but, with nobody interested in his aspirations to power, he had finally been forced to surrender to the authorities.

'Huerta visits him,' Villa went on quietly. 'He says that they're old comrades. I hear they're also bringing Díaz from Veracruz.' He paused, vibrant and powerful as an animal. 'They should have shot them. All they think of is power. Everybody in here knew about that rising in Veracruz before it happened. It was probably even planned here and Reyes was probably part of it.' He leaned closer. 'There is also one other, compadre. One *you* know – Féderico Toral.'

9

The capital was on edge. Three rebellions had been put down but Zapata was still under arms in Morelos. Ever since 1910 there had been constant turmoil, looting and destruction, and hard-faced businessmen were using the situation to get the last peso of compensation from the government. Madero's tax on the profits of foreign oil companies had brought American and British financiers, among them Lord Cowdray and Lord Morne, to Mexico to dispose of the nonsense, and Wilson, the American ambassador, eager to see a return to the strong-arm rule backed by capital which would suit his businessmen friends better, was involved in pushing every claim for damaged property he could find in an effort to embarrass the government.

Sproat's reply to Harley's despatches indicated his bewilderment. 'If Madero unacceptable to entrenched business and unacceptable to masses, who supports him?'

It was a good question. With every day it was becoming clearer that even the support which had pushed Madero into power was dwindling as the simple needs of the peasants – land, water, food, schools – were not being met. Madero had promised, but could not provide. Knowles could not answer the question any more than Harley, and half the press corps of America and Europe were setting themselves up in Mexico City for the next heartbreaking event.

Villa was not deluded. Passionate, emotional, always blindly loyal to Madero and the ideals of the revolution, he could see the trouble coming even if the educated correctos could not. 'Everything he's done,' he told Harley, 'has come to nothing. And yet, mi amigo, if he pardoned me and got me out of here, I should still be his friend.'

What Harley had been told on his way to Mexico – 'The more you try to understand Mexico, the less you'll ever know' – seemed true. Madero's government seemed apathetic, one day indifferent, the next full of promises it could never keep. Madero himself swung wildly from being a stern avenger of Zapata's brigandage in Morelos to being an apostle of peace, pleading for the poor, apologizing for the bandits who plagued his rule, claiming it was the conditions he had inherited that had created them. Even his wife was unsatisfactory. Small and brittle-looking, wearing inappropriate gowns, she was a keen spiritualist to whose advice Madero liked to listen. But, while Madero seemed blind to the dangers, Villa knew even in prison of the plots against him.

'They tried to involve me in them,' he said. 'One of Reyes' lawyers approached me. He said if I gave my word to help I'd be free within days.'

Harley listened in silence while Villa kept his head down and pretended to form his letters as he talked, a volatile man, trying to express long-buried thoughts in the simple words that were all he knew. Aware of his painful inadequacies, he was struggling with his slate and his pencil and his maps of Napoleon's campaigns, to reach towards the light he had been denied all his life in order to help the one man he believed in.

'He must be warned, mi amigo,' he insisted. 'I've tried to get messages to him but they're all intercepted. There's only one man who has his ear and that's Abraham González, the governor of Chihuahua. He knows me. He recruited me to the cause and he's an honest man. Madero will listen to him. But first I must get out of here. Are you interested, mi amigo?'

Harley smiled. 'I'd want exclusive rights to the story.'

Villa smiled back. 'The guards don't look twice at me any more,' he said. 'And they wouldn't look at anyone coming to help me. There's a boy who works here. A clerk called Jauregui, He's employed by the military courts. He could help. I want someone to contact him. Will you?'

Jauregui was a pale young man whose lean frame and frayed

clothes spoke eloquently of the pittance he earned. To pick up a few extra pesos, he returned late every evening and worked as a clerk to those prisoners who were unable to form their own letters or to the lawyers constantly passing in and out of the place.

Angelica, who had used him to take books, pens and paper to Villa, pointed him out. 'He's desperate for money,' she said.

Cox's eyes flickered in alarm from one to the other. 'Do you mean you're goin' to get involved in this?' he said.

'Of course!' Restless, eager to prove herself, committed by compassion and her implacable hatred of treachery, Angelica was afire.

Cox looked uneasy. 'If they find out they'll kick us straight out of the country,' he said. 'You just leave me out.'

'I left you out from the start,' Angelica snapped. 'You'd never stay sober.'

'I've not been drunk for months.'

'You will be. Eventually.'

As Cox started to collect his belongings, she didn't even turn her head but as he rose to leave she swung round. 'Write anything about this,' she said, 'and I'll kill you! Personally! I'm a dead shot.'

'Can you trust him?' Harley asked as Cox disappeared. 'I never could.'

'He's safe. He's got money in his pocket because he's persuaded some publisher in New York to produce an album of his pictures and drawings. It's when he runs short that he's dangerous. Think we can persuade Jauregui to help?'

'Not "us",' Harley said. ' "Me." Keep out of it, Angelica.'

'I'm in this as much as anyone!'

'I don't want someone with half-baked ideas of romance and daring getting in my hair,' Harley said sharply. 'The way you look now's enough to tell everybody within a mile that you're up to something. I'll do it on my own.'

That night as Jauregui left the prison, Harley was waiting for him.

'I'm a friend of General Villa,' he said quietly.

Suggesting a drink, he sat with Jauregui at a table on the sidewalk.

'You look as though you could probably do with a good meal,' he continued. 'Will you join me?'

As they tucked away the frijoles, Jauregui talked. 'I know General Villa well,' he said. 'The corridor where the cells are situated is separated from the administrative section where I work only by an iron grill. His cell is at the end. The others are empty at the moment. I often see him.'

'I think he'd be glad of your help. He's still very slow with his letter-writing and he'd like to talk to you.'

As they rose, Harley pressed a large denomination note into the boy's hand. 'I'll meet you tomorrow to hear how things went.'

The following night, unable to contain her curiosity, Angelica insisted on being present when Jauregui appeared. He was smiling and his dark face looked pleased.

'I saw him,' he said. 'He asked me to copy a letter for him.' He fished in his pocket and flourished a sheet of paper. 'I'm to deliver it tomorrow at the same time.'

The next time Jauregui appeared, he looked dazed. 'He gave me a hundred-peso bill,' he managed to gasp. 'He asked about me and when I told him that most of the time I was hungry, he slipped something into my hand and said he hoped things would change for the better. When I looked at it, I couldn't believe it. I must be there tomorrow to thank him.'

As Christmas approached, they began to wonder when Villa intended to make his move. Harley couldn't put off Sproat's demands that he return much longer and Madero suddenly seemed to have got a grasp on events, despite the hositility of Wilson, the American ambassador.

It had become Harley's habit to wait for Jauregui in a café near the prison and when he next appeared Angelica was waiting for him defiantly. For some time, thwarted in her attempts to be part of the plot she had been planning escape routes and building up a stock of false moustaches, dark glasses, uniforms, cloaks and huge sombreros. This time, however, she had come to warn him.

'Faithful Fred came to see me,' she said. 'He was suddenly very concerned for my welfare. Was I okay for money? Was there anything I needed? It was all a lot of baloney. He's heard of you hanging round here and he's wondering what you're up to. He got himself appointed Deputy to the Minister at the Police Secretariat. Perhaps he thinks he ought to earn his salary.' She paused, frowning. 'He wanted me to go to one of the President's receptions. To show loyalty, he said. To Madero? I didn't believe him. And he's not interested in me any more. I discovered his spread was mortgaged to the hilt and when he found my money was tied up in trusts so he couldn't touch it he cooled off. No, there's more to it than that. Why's he sending up the big balloon about loyalty? And why did he ask about Villa?'

'What *did* he ask about Villa?'

'Was he loyal to Madero? Was he ever likely, in view of his imprisonment, to go against him? Why did he want to know that?'

When Jauregui arrived, he looked startled. 'Villa wants me to buy a hacksaw and black wax,' he announced in a shaken voice. 'He wants me to cut the bars of the grill that separates my office from the cells. He's given me money. Where shall I obtain a hacksaw?'

'I'll find one for you,' Angelica said briskly. '*And* the wax.'

Jauregui looked scared. 'He asked if I'd do him a favour and I said yes. Then he asked if I was brave. I said I thought so. He told me his imprisonment was a put-up job and I agreed. I think he trapped me a little. He wants me to start sawing tomorrow and showed me where to cut. He wants some of the bars of the grill sawn through and the cuts filled with wax so it can be removed with a good pull.'

'Are you going to do it?'

'I wonder if I have the courage, señor.'

The following day Jauregui nervously announced that he had started work. 'I filled the cuts with the wax. You can't see them unless you search.' He looked pleased with himself. 'I sawed through two bars. I can do the lot in four goes.'

That evening there was a knock at the door of Harley's apartment and as he opened it he found himself facing a man in a brown suit and bowler hat who had policeman written all over him. His heart jumped and he saw Angelica, who was also there, give him a nervous look.

The detective presented his credentials gravely. His name was Alemán, and he had come to complain about an article Harley had written for the *Courier*.

'It is hostile to Mexico, señor,' he explained.

'In my country.' Harley pointed out, 'the government puts no restrictions on newspapers.'

'You are not in your country, señor. You are in Mexico.'

The detective fished in his pocket and produced a cutting from an envelope. 'It was seen by the Mexican Minister in London and forwarded to us.'

'Do you check on all newspapermen who write critical despatches on your country?'

'Some more than others.'

'Even your large and powerful neighbour to the north?'

Alemán coughed. 'The United States is a special case, señor.'

The interview ended with no more than a warning and, as the door closed, Angelica flung herself at Harley and hugged him delightedly.

'I thought he'd found out about Jauregui,' she said. 'But he hadn't. It's okay. It's okay.'

Harley didn't release her. 'I'd go further than that,' he said. 'I'd say it's a pity we don't do it more often.'

Immediately she frowned and pushed him away. 'Cut that out,' she snapped. 'This is serious.'

The following day was Christmas Day and they agreed to have dinner together in the city, but when they met Jauregui he was bubbling with excitement and shaking with nerves.

'They know something's on,' he said. 'But they don't know what. The Deputy to the Minister, Señor Toral, came yesterday asking questions, but he knows nothing and it's almost finished. The file makes a noise but I saw hard whenever a team of horses or a troop of cavalry comes past. On Sunday a municipal band played so I got a lot done. General Villa sits in his cell practicing on a typewriting machine he's rented as if nothing was happening and the guards never look at either of us. He comes out tomorrow.'

Harley and Angelica exchanged glances. 'Christmas Day?'

'He says everybody will be celebrating the birth of the Blessed Niño. The churches will be full. People will be at home on holiday. The prison staff will be depleted. Some might even be drunk. I have only the last two bars to saw through. It will take no more than a few minutes.'

'Won't the guards be suspicious if they see you there on Christmas Day?'

'There's always an occasional lawyer. Even on Christmas Day. They've been busy lately, too. One or two will be going in to see General Reyes. His lawyer for one. He's always there. And the Deputy to the Minister. General Villa says we can't put it off and that we have to succeed.'

10

Every newspaper in Mexico City carried roughly the same headline. 'NATIONWIDE SEARCH FOR GENERAL VILLA. DARING ESCAPE FROM PRISON.' The police, out in force, searching for Jauregui, were promising an early apprehension of the fugitive.

Harley had been waiting near the prison when Villa had appeared. He was wearing a bowler hat and a long cloak worn flung over his shoulder to conceal his features. Under one arm was a leather despatch case, the lawyer's badge of office, and he was holding a handkerchief to his face as if he had a cold.

Angelica had organized a taxi and Villa and Jauregui had been driven to Tacubaya where Villa had pretended that the man he had come to see was not at home and had bribed the taxi driver to take him on to Toluca. At Manzanillo they had taken the train to Mazatlán, and via Guaymas, to Hermosillo and the United States.

All known friends of Villa were being investigated. The police were everywere, checking bars and stopping cabs and carriages. The taxi driver who had taken him to Toluca had not been uncovered, but he had doubtless read the headlines and was lying low. There had also been a lot of activity at the Ministry of Police and Tamsy had reported seeing Toral standing outside.

'With that guy Alemán who came,' he said.

When a telegram from Villa arrived from Tucson in Arizona, Harley sent off his story at once to London and, to hide his involvement, he also handed it to a few of his more responsible colleagues. It was a good story and he expected a little praise, but all it brought was a dry reply from Sproat. 'Better people have escaped from better prisons.'

For several days he waited for something to happen, expecting all the time to hear that Reyes and Díaz had been shot and Toral and Huerta imprisoned. By this time he was certain that Villa had warned Abraham González and González had surely warned Madero. But nothing happened. The capital seemed calm and there was no news of any sudden spate of arrests.

Then, early in the morning, while Harley was still in his dressing gown, Angelica appeared in his flat, looking scared.

'The police came to see me yesterday evening,' she said. 'That guy Alemán. He wanted to search the house but I daren't let him. I had to claim I was an American citizen.'

She was still in Harley's flat when the police arrived. It was Alemán again, full of early morning enthusiasm, and he eyed her suspiciously.

'Señora Ojarra,' he said. 'What are you doing here? You were here the last time I called.'

Harley smiled enigmatically. 'What do you think a lady's doing in a gentleman's flat at this time of the morning?' he asked.

Alemán frowned and explained the reason for his visit. 'We've checked the newspaper stories, señor,' he said. 'You seem to know a great deal about General Villa's escape.'

Harley shrugged. 'Most of it made up. With your editor a long way away, if you don't know the facts you invent them. A foreign correspondent's world is one of inventions, misrepresentations, even lies. The Messina earthquake was written up in London, and many a headline-winner about shattered cities has been drafted on green lawns back home.'

The detective was puzzled. 'But you gave the escape route, señor. Exactly. Tacubaya and Mazatlán.'

'One of the American papers gave Veracruz and Guatamala.'

'Yours was the correct one.'

'An inspired guess. No more.'

As the door closed behind the detective, Angelica looked

nervously at Harley. 'You bastard,' she said. 'He'll go back with the news that Angelica Ojarra's your mistress.'

Harley smiled. 'Newspapermen will do anything for a story.'

Deciding that the government agents were growing too inquisitive for comfort, they decided they would be well advised to leave Mexico City for a while and they headed north for the border. In El Paso the first person they saw was Johnny Cox. He smelled of whisky and was bewailing the absence of worth-while pictures.

'Nobody just wants to see Mexico,' he said. 'The *Tucson Globe* says it wants soldiers and a few stiffs in the gutter.'

Since the carnival days of the Madero revolution, the gaudy saloons of the stockyard district had become quieter and there was no wild shooting at night. There were still hundreds of Mexicans about, however, most of them unable to return home, and they had all drifted together into Little Chihuahua which was where Harley was headed.

Hiring a car, he set off with Tamsy at the wheel. Almost immediately, he became aware that they were being followed by a Ford driven by Johnny Cox. Never blessed with an excess of energy and always willing to pick up his stories by any means available, fair or foul, he had guessed that Harley was in contact with Villa, and was watching him like a hawk.

'Keep driving, Tamsy,' Harley said. 'And keep your eyes front.'

For two days every move they made was followed and Cox even booked into the same hotel, his car always parked nearby. It was going to require a major operation to shake him off and on the third day, Harley let himself be seen making a telephone call before heading to a shabby downtown address. There, with Cox lurking not far behind, he talked earnestly to a couple of Mexicans, especially recruited for the occasion. Late that afternoon, he drove with Tamsy to the cable office just before it closed for the day and filed a message for England. 'By telephone from El Paso: Villa and five associates shot Presidio Friday. Details following soonest.'

Addressing it to a mythical newspaper, he handed it in. As he left the cable office he noticed Cox's Ford waiting just down the road and as he drove off, he saw it start up and begin to move forward. Seconds later it halted by the cable office and Cox disappeared inside.

That evening Cox was conspicuous by his absence but he arrived late, in a riotous mood and a good way towards being drunk. While he was busy celebrating at the bar, Harley slipped out of the back door of the hotel and picked up a taxi to Little Chihuahua.

There were few cars and the smell of horse manure was strong from the droppings in the street. At the La Roma Hotel, the address he'd been given, the reception clerk, an old man with an Indian face, shook his head at his enquiry. 'He's not here, señor,' he insisted. 'Try the Elite Confectionery. He likes ice cream.'

Tucking into a large sundae, Villa was wearing a suit, spurs, a stetson and the long strapped leggings he favoured. He was flanked by the grinning Jauregui and the small shape of Urbina. As Harley appeared he leapt to his feet at once.

'Mi amigo,' he said. 'You know Urbina and Jauregui? Fierro's here, too, and a few of my old bodyguard. What news have you from Mexico City?'

'No news, Don Pancho.'

'Nothing?' Villa's face fell. 'You mean they haven't arrested Huerta? I told González and wrote to Governor Maytorena in Sonora. I told them to impress on the President the need for quick decisive measures. Why doesn't he do something?'

He was puzzled by the indifference. 'Surely he wouldn't ignore my warning,' he said, his whole bulky being on edge with frustrated energy. 'Why can't I do something?' he went on. 'Madero needs me and it's a lifeless existence here with nothing to do but make plans I can't use.' His face twisted in a scowl. 'Because I *can't*, mi amigo. González advised me not to return, so until the time comes for me to go back, I have to show the gringos I'm not plotting anything.'

He was depressed and bored, longing to use some of his primeval vigour on behalf of his country, but United States agents were watching him all the time, trying to catch him in some breach of the neutrality laws.

'You can't go round the corner without stumbling over a plot of some sort,' he said. 'I even had a German agent to see me. He was offering money and weapons, and support if I went back into the field. What are they after, Inglés? I thought they were expecting a war over there.'

'That's what I heard, too.'

'I also had one of Huerta's friends. That old Indian had the nerve to ask me to join *him*. Me! The man he wanted executed! I should have shot his damned agent! In Mexico I would have. But at least I know now what to expect of these gold-laced generals. I threw him down the stairs.'

He was heavily distrustful and contemptuous of the tangled by-ways of Mexican politics, then he grinned suddenly. 'There was even a man who wanted me to compaign for president. *Me*! He actually thought I would *like* to be president.' He laughed, too instinctive to know how to be devious. 'I've managed to learn a lot about my country, mi amigo. Some of it good. Some of it bad. A lot of it treacherous and bloody. But I have no ambition to be the man to put things right.'

Frustrated, he started talking again about Mexico's need for good governement. His ideas were of a República de los Indios, but the only way he could think of his country was as a group of small farmers and industries owned by the people, a busy, prosperous Mexico that contrived somehow to be the leisurely graceful country he had always wanted.

'The way to do it,' he insisted, 'is to use the gringo methods. Their machinery. Tractors. Threshers. Binders. Machines that do the work so that a man doesn't wear himself out. And schools. That's what we need! So that every child can read and write and know what's going on.'

After his tirade he calmed down, and returned to his own plight. His face was heavy.

'America is okay,' he said, gesturing at the melting sundae in front of him. 'I meet a few old friends and a few who remember I helped to put a president in power and might well do so again. But – ' his voice rose in a fierce angry pride ' – but it's not *my* country, amigo! It's not mine!'

Part Three

1

Just beginning to stir, Harley was brought abruptly to life next morning by Tamsy Flood hammering on his door.

'Boss,' he grinned. 'Villa's been assassinated. In Presidio. I just got a telegram from a buddy of mine. The *Tucson Globe* says he was shot with five of his officers in a gun battle with Mex government agents. Cox swallowed it hook, line and sinker. He was into that telegraph office after we left like a rat up a drain. He even improved on it, and we left it so late they couldn't check up on his story. They went ahead and published. Boy, will he be sore.'

Harley grinned up at him, then Tamsy's smile died. 'There was another as well, Boss. For you.'

It was from Sproat. 'IN STATES. NEED TO TALK. MEET IMMEDIATE HALFWAY. SUGGEST SHERRY'S PARK HOTEL WASHINGTON.'

Washington was a funny half-way stage but that was Sproat all over. He was the editor and believed in claiming his privileges.

Cox was by the reception desk as Harley arrived to send a reply. His expression was considerably less friendly than it had been the night before. 'You tricked me, you bastard,' he said at once. 'I told Tucson that Villa had been shot when he hadn't.'

Harley smiled. 'I wonder where you could have picked that up.'

Cox's face grew red. 'You know goddam well where I picked it up! I paid the telegraph clerk to let me have a look at it. You goddam knew I would. You fixed it. You wrote that telegram especially for me. There's no goddam *Princes Risborough Times*! I checked.' His anger faded quickly as it always did and he looked reproachful. 'That was a shitty thing to do to a guy, Harl'. The *Tucson Globe* won't trust me none after this.'

Harley caught the first northbound train. He knew what Sproat was after. He wanted action. He was keeping a man in Mexico and nothing was happening. But even in El Paso the air was full of rumours and Knowles in the capital had stories of increased anarchy that put flesh on the bones. Landless peasants were expecting overnight miracles, but, while the land Zapata had seized had been immediately and ruthlessly declared forfeit, the great estates Madero had promised to carve up remained untouched. He was trying to apply legality to something that couldn't be achieved legally and the delegations of sombreroed men waited in vain. And, instead of trying to win over Wilson, the hostile American ambassador, Madero could think of nothing except to send General Angeles, head of the Military Academy, to take command against Zapata and, in a city grim with suppressed hatred, became shrill in his accusations of Amercian interference.

Sproat's hotel apartment had all the splendour of a throne room but he was in a hostile mood.

'Drink?' he said.

'Thanks.'

'Sir.'

Harley smiled and said nothing and Sproat glowered and changed the subject. 'Your hanging story,' he went on. 'Pity they didn't carry it out. I'd have been rid of you for good and all.' He handed over the drink. 'I'm here on business. Newspapers are becoming more international and we want to know what's happening in America because what happens here today invariably happens in Europe tomorrow. Came on the *Lusitania*. Sick all the way.' He gestured. 'There's also a little matter I want to talk about.'

'Such as?'

Sproat took a swallow of his drink and went into the attack. 'You're for the high jump.'

'Which particular high jump?'

'You ever been fired? Because you're damn near it at the moment! Lord Morne wants to know why we spend so much time writing about Villa, whom he considers to be just a cheap bandit, and about this Madero chap, who he says doesn't yet know that the sharp end of a pencil is the one that writes. He and Cowdray are indignant about the way he wants to collar their profits.'

'So he wants to get rid of Madero?'

'Not in so many words.'

'How many?'

'He feels we're slanting our reporting too much. He thinks – '

'*He* thinks?' Harley's voice was icy.

Sproat frowned. '*I* think – that the line the American Ambassador's taking is the right one.'

'The American ambassador is a dangerous meddler. He's got a lot to answer for.' Harley tried to explain. 'Madero came to the presidency with the good will of eighty per cent of the people. Unfortunately, he knows nothing of the machinery of government. He's an apostle of peace and goodwill, but peace and goodwill don't work in Mexico. If he had a little of the toughness of Porfirio Díaz, Mexico would be content.'

'We decided in London that with his election the revolution was over.'

'It might be over in London. It's far from over in Mexico.'

'Is he a good man?'

'It's not a good man they want. No President of Mexico can afford to commute the death sentence on as many plotters as Madero has. Díaz would have shot them. Instead, they're in comfortable prisons and allowed regular visitors. Lawyers. Army men. Other plotters.'

'Your countrymen seem a bloody treacherous lot.'

'Treachery's a basic commodity in Mexico.'

'All right. Point taken. What about this blasted General Villa?'

Harley tried again to explain. 'Bandit-turned-revolutionary. Non-smoker. Non-drinker. Likes ice cream and women and thrives on battle.'

'But still a bloody bandit!'

'Bandits in Mexico are different. Politicians are regarded with cynicism because they're all involved in graft. Bandits are admired because they're usually campesinos or peóns who've been forced into it by oppression.'

'I heard he shoots prisoners.'

'In Mexico everybody shoots prisoners. He's no different from anyone else. But if anything exceeds his ruthlessness, it's his patriotism. And the people idolize him because he robbed the rich to feed the poor. It's true his temper's usually on a short fuse but it's a cruel country where life's cheap. Mexico's dominated by death. They even have a Day of the Dead when the children eat candy skulls and skeletons as ours eat hot cross buns at Easter. Mexico's history is red with blood. But a lot that's been written about Villa is pure fiction. Some of the people in Mexico posing as newspapermen ought to be writing novels. They say that before he came out for Madero he was a famous bandit with Ignacio Parra, another great bandit. But Parra was just a desperado whose army consisted of a few men who were satisfied to steal a few mules.'

'So how are we supposed to present this paragon of virtue?'

'Take your pick. Whatever else he is, he's a Mexican. Not some other country's lackey. I got to know him well. I helped him escape. It's a pity you thought fit not to publish the story I filed.'

Sproat managed to look sheepish. 'It was a decision we made. You'd better tell me more about him.'

'Basically he's a savage, but with a lot more heart than some of the people who're trying to grab power. And there are more people who bless him than curse him. He's been a thief and a murderer, but he's also a surprising sentimentalist and, as it happens, a man of unimpeachable idealism and a bit of a genius at war into the bargain. Whatever they tell you about his army, it's one of the most disciplined in Mexico and, like Zapata, he's one of the few who's never changed his coat.'

'I thought Mexican generals all coveted the presidency.'

'Not this one. His place is the saddle and he knows it. If Madero would listen to him he wouldn't be in danger. And if anything happens to Madero – and I think it will – then

Villa will be the first to shout "Revenge" and do something about it.'

Sproat rose, took Harley's glass and filled it again. 'You know, you're supposed to be on the outside looking in. Reporting events, not taking part in them.'

'Mexico isn't like England. You don't vote for a party to represent you in Parliament. You have to stake your soul on your beliefs and if you're wrong, you're a dead man. There must be hundreds who're dead simply because they chose the wrong side. Sometimes, they didn't have much option. They were *obliged* to take the wrong side, because they were conscripted, or tricked, or swindled into it, or because they'd sworn an oath to defend the government and were honourable enough to stick to it. Mexico makes no distinctions.'

Sproat thought for a moment. 'You'd better write this Villa up. We'll make it a feature. Let's have a story.'

'You've had one.'

Sproat was unperturbed. 'Let's have another. People like folk heroes. How about photographs?'

Harley fished in his brief case for a few of Cox's prints.

Sproat stared at the ragged dusty sombreroed figures swathed in ammunition bandoliers. 'Are these what they call soldiers?'

'They can ride and shoot and they're brave. They've defeated government troops again and again. Whatever they might think in the marble halls of Westminster, this is as big as the French Revolution.'

'Unfortunately,' Sproat said dryly, 'it's also three thousand miles from our readers.' There was a long silence as he poured himself another drink. 'I was going to fire you, Harley,' he admitted. 'At the very least I was going to cut off your expenses so you couldn't afford to stay. Now I'm not so sure. Certainly, we've had good coverage. We've beaten *The Times* and the *Mail*'s been hopping mad more than once. But sometimes I think you're too damn Mexican. Still, you show more understanding of the place than most people. What's going to happen? Knowles says something will. What do *you* think?'

Harley shrugged. 'Madero has a remarkable penchant for doing the wrong thing. He'll do the wrong thing again.'

'And?'

'Immediately he's deposed the masses will realize that, even if he was wrong, he was trying to help them – which is more than anybody else is doing or ever will do. They'll rise.'

Sproat stared. 'Another bloody rising?'

Harley shrugged. 'That's the way it happens in Mexico.'

2

The train south was full of newspapermen. Every city in the United States seemed to have sent its quota, and in addition there were whole groups from the border towns of Douglas, El Paso and Laredo, and the big New York magazines and news agencies.

Laden with equipment Johnny Cox seemed to have forgotten his humiliation in El Paso. 'I got me the pictures of Villa in the end,' he said. 'In the Elite Confectionery. I've sold dozens in Little Chihuahua and Juárez. They stick 'em up on the wall with the picture of the Madonna and the suffering Christ. Those guys want him back. But he wouldn't talk for publication. He had four bodyguards, two revolvers and a knife to make sure I got the message.'

He had been busy since returning to Mexico and his cartoons appeared regularly in the columns of *El Independiente*. He had even added his mite to the obscenities scrawled on the walls outside bars and cafés, with caricatures of Americans, Mexican generals and politicians. They were scurrilous, merciless and hit out in every direction; at Madero himself, at Huerta and, above all, at Féderico Toral – Angelica's Faithful Fred – who was wanting to resign the position he had accepted in the government on the grounds of pressing business.

On every platform at the Buena Vista station, you could fall over newspaper correspondents surrounded by mountains of baggage, guns, cameras, typewriters, suitcases and assistants, and the hotels were turning away those who hadn't booked ahead. Among them were even a few female reporters anxious to find out how the revolution was affecting womanhood in Mexico, and one ardent suffragette from London keen to see Mexican women get the vote. They were all aware that something was in the wind and were out scavenging for anything they could get.

'There's one thing,' the *Mail* correspondent observed. 'We don't have to please the military, because it isn't *our* military. Lord Roberts approved of the press so long as they approved of *him* and he manipulated them to puff up his career. Here it doesn't matter. If the press tends to be compromised in war, it doesn't in *somebody else's* war.'

In the bars and cafés of the teeming turbulent back streets, the opinion seemed to be that Madero had deceived them, that he did not have the energy to do his work, and that he had devoted himself only to telling everybody what a good democrat he was.

'Which is true enough,' Knowles agreed. 'But it's not a democrat this country needs.'

Johnny Cox was watching the President like a hawk, feeling that he was the key to anything that was likely to happen. In the belief that he might also somehow be involved, he was also watching Huerta, who was usually to be found drinking at the El Globo café, polishing off brandy from a cup and saucer.

'If I watch that old bastard,' he said, 'I can't go wrong.'

But he could. And he did.

Like everybody else, the police were taking the view that Madero couldn't last much longer. Having dropped their enquiries about Villa's escape, they were sitting on the fence, no longer interested in anti-Maderistas, and Angelica decided to risk a visit to the capital. She turned up at her house near the Ciudadela, and predictably Cox, who had always been interested in her, arrived on the doorstep a few hours later. But he had been drinking and she turned him away, and he was asleep on the sofa in Harley's flat when the first hard news of trouble arrived. Knowles had had the ear of the president's brother, Gustavo, for some time and he burst in with information of a plot.

'It was given to Gustavo Madero by an army captain I

know called Ayguadé,' he announced. 'He's having to feign sickness in case the game's given away. Gustavo passed it on to me.'

'Who's behind it?'

'Felix Díaz. He was transferred to the Ciudadela, the barracks here, but he's been in touch with Reyes at Santiago Tlalelolco. Madero must be mad to allow those two within reach of each other. Reyes has been plotting for years.'

He had ferreted out a complete list of the conspirators. 'Twenty-two of them,' he said. 'Among them Felix Díaz. Bernardo Reyes. Reyes' son, Rodolfo, General Mondragón, General Blanquet, General Beltrán and Huerta.' He paused. 'There's some doubt about Huerta.'

'I'll bet it's true,' Harley said. 'That's why he tried to have Villa shot, up there in Torreón. He was already beginning to get ideas and knew he'd never swing him to his side. Who else is there?'

'Ministry of Police. They're essential.'

'Féderico Toral?'

'So I heard.'

'So did I. Go on.'

'Quintero of the Ministry of War. Arellano from the Ministry of the Interior. They're a formidable lot. Toral handles the daily running of the police and Quintero and Arellano control communications and movement orders. Blanquet commands four thousand men at Toluca forty miles away, Beltrán commands the infantry at Tacubaya, and behind them are several Científicos.'

'Where did your Captain Ayguadé get this list? Plotters aren't usually obliging enough to provide names.'

'It came from Santiago Tlalelolco. Only General Angeles seems not to have fallen in with them, but he's out of the city anyway, coping with Zapata. And perhaps Villar, commander of the city garrison. But he's ill. If Madero has any sense he'll shoot the lot.'

'He's not arrested anybody yet.'

'He will. He's at the palace at Chapultepec. Gustavo's gone to warn him.'

They spent the next two hours trying to telephone a Mexican stringer of Knowles at Chapultepec. Eventually, with Harley glued to the extension, they found the man they were after. He had heard of Gustavo Madero's visit and had been watching the presidential palace.

'There were half a dozen other reporters there,' he said, 'and we managed to get hold of one of Gustavo's staff. He told us the president laughed at Gustavo and said Blanquet and Beltrán had proved their loyalty by putting down Díaz's rebellion in Veracruz.'

'What about Huerta?'

'He said the question mark against his name proved the list was false, because Huerta was retired over the money that went missing during the Orozco rebellion and has neither authority nor troops.'

'Huerta's the one man who could mould this lot into something dangerous,' Knowles said.

'The President says he drinks too much to be dangerous.'

'It doesn't stop him always being up bright and early in the morning, looking as if he's never heard of brandy. Doesn't Madero believe *anything*?'

'Only that he's been democratically elected and that the people of Mexico will respect that.'

'Vázquez Gómez didn't respect it,' Harley snapped. 'Orozco didn't respect it. Reyes didn't respect it. Díaz didn't respect it. Neither will this lot.

Knowles' informant didn't dispute the fact. 'All I know is that he thinks there isn't a plot.'

Knowles slammed down the telephone and looked at Harley.

'I'll dare bet there is,' he said. 'Let's go and see Ayguadé. He lives at Toluca.'

They tried for ten minutes to rouse Cox but he fought them off and buried his head in the cushions, so they told the Indian woman who cleaned the flat to make black coffee for him and, hiring a cab, shot off between the double row of trees in the Paseo de la Reforma. In the distance they could see Chapultepec Castle, the summer residence of the President, above a sea of gigantic branches, their tops a copper filigree in the sunshine. It was a Saturday and half the capital was heading south to enjoy the Park, which had been made from the fabled gardens of Montezuma and the grottoes and follies of the eighteenth century Spanish viceroys. As they passed the entrance, they had to stop the car to allow three men on horses to enter. One of them was an enormously fat man in the uniform of a general.

'Ruíz,' Knowles said. 'He has the cavalry at Tacubaya.'

'The other one's Navarrete, the artilleryman. I met him in Torreón.'

'He has the batteries at Tacubaya. The one trailing behind has the guard at the National Palace.' Knowles looked puzzled. 'What are they doing together? I thought Navarrete couldn't stand Ruíz and that the chap behind didn't know either of them.'

They found Ayguadé's house without difficulty because there was a squad of newspapermen and two photographers outside. It was an old residence in a side street, with a courtyard full of plants and a small fountain playing in the sunshine, but it looked like a fortress. The back of the courtyard consisted of a high wall and on either side were the high windowless gables of the neighbouring houses. Two of Ayguadé's friends were holding guns, one watching the wall, one the gate, and there were others surveying the street from upstairs windows. Inside the house in cool rooms bright with reflected sunlight, worried-looking women were waiting nervously for what might happen.

After a lot of arguing and solemn promises not to reveal his identity or his address, Ayguadé agreed to receive a deputation of newsmen, one from each interested country, and in the end there were two Americans, one claiming he was really a Canadian, Harley, a Frenchman and a German. They were ushered into a back room where chairs had been set out and Ayguadé, who was writing at a desk, rose as they entered.

'I'm putting everything I know down on paper,' he said. 'In case anything happens to me.'

He insisted that not only was the plot real but that it was about to be put into effect. 'Reyes is to take over as provisional president,' he said. 'Then Felix Díaz will be elected constitutionally for what remains of the six-year term begun by his uncle Porfirio.'

'How can it be constitutional,' Harley asked sharply, 'when they know the result already?'

Ayguadé shrugged. 'That's Mexico, señor. General Mondragón's to be Minister of War, Reyes' son Minister of Justice and Huerta commander-in-chief of the army.'

'The list you saw?' One of the Americans leaned forward. 'Why did Huerta's name have a question mark against it?'

'Because he doesn't think Reyes or Díaz are presidential material.'

'Who does he think is?'

Ayguadé smiled. 'Who do you think, señor? If he's coming into the plot, he wants the main prize.'

'When's it to start?'

'March 16th.'s the date I heard.'

'Where from?' Harley asked. 'The prison at Santiago Tlalelolco?'

'Yes, señor. The commander there is involved but one of his staff saw the list and copied it. He passed it on to Colonel Mayol, at the Ciudadela, who showed it to me. He then passed it on to Gustavo Madero because he felt something should be done. Has something *been* done, señor?'

Harley shook his head. 'No,' he said. 'Nothing's been done.'

'Then I think they'll push it forward. It'll probably be this week-end when government offices are closed and officers are on leave and the president is out of the capital.'

It was obvious that their place was in Mexico City. There was still no sign of trouble in the capital, however, beyond the fact that the trolley cars heading into the city were ominously full of cadets coming in from Tlalpán. Johnny Cox, heavily hung over, appeared, announcing that he didn't believe there would be trouble because he had been taking pictures of Madero waving his top hat to the crowd as he and his cabinet attended ceremonies in front on the statue of Juárez.

It was now almost midnight but, hiring a cab, they headed for the military academy at Tlalpán to see what was happening. Though the gates were closed, it was obvious the neighbourhood was aware of something going on because small groups of people were congregating in the cafés. Inside the academy they could hear shouted orders then, as they waited, the gates opened and a column of aspirantes were seen lining up, led by an officer on a white horse. Harley counted the cadets as they passed.

'That's not enough to overthrow the régime,' Knowles snorted. 'There are ten times that number of loyal troops in the city.'

It was Angelica who, with a rare insight into what was happening, gave them the clue that the uprising was on. She had been busy with the poor of the capital. She had been trying – without much success – to recruit a band of welfare workers for her scheme to provide meals, but had managed only to acquire a few women from the back streets whom she was having to pay out of her own purse. It was one of these who had brought the information.

'They've cancelled leave for the army,' she said. 'One of my women was expecting her husband home but he sent a message that all leave's been stopped.'

It didn't take long to confirm the fact and to learn that the plotters were relying chiefly on the cadets from the Military Academy, practically all of them from families opposed to Madero. But there was nevertheless a considerable movement of troops inside the city, presumably being pushed into position to halt the rebellion. Again it was Angelica who gave them the truth. His leave stopped, her helper's husband had informed his wife that he was being temporarily moved *out* of the capital.

Harley stared at Knowles. '*Out*?' he said. 'They'll do no damn good there!'

A few telephone calls confirmed that the officers of the newly-moved troops were all loyal to Madero, and that most of the men left in the capital were commanded by officers involved with the plot. General Mondragón, who appeared to be in command of the rising, had been able to raise another eight hundred men, mostly cavalry, to add to his cadets.

'Why doesn't somebody warn the President?' Angelica demanded angrily.

'Someone has,' Harley said. 'He takes no notice.'

Driving back to Tlalpán, he was joined by Knowles. At the junction of the road from Tacubaya and the road from Chapultepec, a column of troops was waiting, wearing the simple white of a line regiment, their medical orderlies carrying baskets marked with red crosses strapped to their heads. Among them were several squadrons of horsemen, their iron-shod hooves clattering on the cobblestones, at their head the fat general they had seen at Chapultepec. He was in full dress and wearing a bicorne hat.

'Ruíz.' Knowles frowned. 'Is *he* involved? If he is, Navarrete will be, too.'

'It's only six bloody months since *he* was fighting for Madero!'

'Counts for nothing in Mexico,' Knowles said. 'And if those two are in it, then doubtless the commander at the Palace is, too.'

The cadets had halted and Ruíz had moved to the side of the road to watch his men pass. With jingling equipment, the clatter of hooves and the flutter of lance pennants, the cavalry swept ahead, followed by infantrymen in full battle equipment. As the last files passed, the cadets were set in motion again.

'They're heading for Santiago prison,' Knowles pointed out. 'That can mean only one thing. They're going to free Reyes.'

3

Despite the hour, the tramp of feet, the shouts and the clatter of hooves had brought men and women from the streets around to watch, and there were already crowds lining the pavements and standing in shop doorways and bars. A few small boys had shinned up lamp standards for a better view and, despite the officers' attempts to keep them at a distance, the civilians were mingling with the soldiers.

The first streaks of light had begun to appear over the rooftops as the column swung in front of the Ciudadela and halted. Mayol, the officer in command, appeared and one of Ruíz's officers rode up to him.

'We're here to give Mexico her freedom from the maniac Madero,' he shouted. 'We demand the prisoner, General Díaz.'

Mayol refused and the officer was joined by Ruíz, his huge body overflowing the saddle. He gestured, and a squad of soldiers surrounded Mayol. As he was marched away, the guard joined the rebel column. Soon afterwards Díaz appeared, wearing undress uniform, but someone brought a horse forward and offered him a sword which he buckled round his waist.

The rebellion was increasing in tempo. Telephoning Santiago Tlalelolco from a nearby café, Harley discovered that the officer in command there had been found unreliable and been replaced by a loyal officer. Rebel forces were expected at any time.

Yelling for Tamsy and the Stutz, they roared out to the

prison and as they slithered to a stop they found they had run straight into a new drama. Officers of both sides were facing each other by the gates of the prison.

'That's Villareal,' Knowles said, indicating the officer in command of the prison guard. 'He'll not go over.'

As he spoke, the officer turned to address the men of his command but as he did so one of the opposing soldiers drew his revolver and shot him in the back. Thrown forward by the impact of the bullet, Villareal collapsed on his face and, while his men were still uncertain, the rebel force swept forward. There was no more shooting and they hurried inside the prison. Within minutes, Bernardo Reyes appeared. His hair and imperial beard had been carefully combed and his head was high as if he were posing for a photographer. Somebody led a horse forward and handed him a sword, and he climbed into the saddle.

At the National Palace, Gustavo Madero had arrived to take control of the situation. His pince-nez glasses shining, his hat thrust back, he was standing on the seat of his car, haranguing a squad of soldiers, theatrical, reckless, the one member of the Madero family who seemed prepared to do something practical.

'Are you going to give up what the President has given you?' he was shouting. 'In return for what the rebel generals will give you? What did *they* ever give you?'

The soldiers were caught by uncertainty. An officer they recognized as the commander of the guard appeared shouting for the arrest of Gustavo, but the soldiers, who could always be shot by their own officers if they didn't do as they were told and by the other side if they did, suddenly decided to take matters into their own hands. One of them snatched away the officer's revolver and another his sword. Other officers who had appeared were rounded up and marched away.

Gustavo climbed down from the car, and, removing his hat, began to mop his brow. As he lit a cigar, the newsmen who had chased their quarry to the Palace began to call out to him.

'How about a story, Gustavo? What's happening?'

For the first time, Gustavo became aware that his

impromptu speech had been witnessed by outsiders. Tall, plump, the very essence of a businessman-politician with his black jacket, striped trousers and wing collar, he suddenly seemed to dissolve into a frightened human being. An uncertain smile played across his face as he waved the pressmen forward.

'They were waiting to admit the rebels,' he said. 'I got here just in time. When they arrive now, we'll have someone in command here we can trust. They'll get more than they expect.'

In spite of the success, it was obvious there was more to come. The rebel generals could not stop now, and the pressmen taking up points of vantage outside the Palace, saw a car bearing a uniformed officer swing into the Zócalo. Knowles identified him.

'General Villar,' he said. 'Commander of the city garrison. He'll not go over.'

Sensing business, cafés were unlocking their doors early and, posting Tamsy Flood at the corner of the Zócalo, Harley tried to snatch something to eat. There were several other newsmen in the café, all eyeing each other warily, each wondering what the others were up to and what provisions had been made to get stories away. Knowles had dug his messenger out of bed and he was waiting to hurry off with the story being written over coffee and rolls.

With the daylight, people began to appear for early Mass. Seeing the crowds gathered in the Zócalo and the mass of soldiers, they stopped to watch. Emerging from the café, driven out by some sixth sense, Harley saw Angelica just going into the Cathedral. She was dressed for church, in blue with a black lace mantilla on her head.

The high vaulted interior was curtained with silence, and at the altar, in the lamplit dimness of early morning, a priest was intoning. The ritual monotony of the chanted words came down the silent building, quiet, laden with mystery. All round in an atmosphere of mercy and pity and peace, people knelt with bent heads.

His eyes searching, Harley automatically dipped his fingers in the holy water and crossed himself, aware that it was something he hadn't done for years. Then he saw Angelica. As he touched her arm her head turned. Her face was calm and absorbed with her devotions but as she saw him her eyes narrowed with irritation.

'What do you want?' she demanded. 'Here?'

'You shouldn't be here. There'll probably be shooting.'

The anger vanished at once and the old eager anxiety to be in at the death filled her eyes. 'I'll be ready,' she said.

'I didn't tell you so you could be ready,' he retorted. 'But so you could protect that silly neck of yours, and the necks of all the other people you might risk.'

Her eyes flared, then her face became expressionless again. 'I'll be ready when I'm needed,' she repeated, and turned away to kneel down.

For a moment, he was tempted to drag her away forcibly, but the place was full of people absorbed in their prayers and it was no time to cause a commotion. For a moment longer he stared at her, then he turned on his heel and headed for the door.

As he returned to the café, he could see men on the palace roof, setting up machine guns and crouching behind the turrets and the central tower that held the bell which Díaz had rung every September as he celebrated Mexico's independence from Spain. The flat-fronted building, as much a fortress as a palace, was silent.

Knowles had just finished his despatch when Tamsy appeared.

'Troops, Boss! They look as if they're from Santiago Tlalelolco.'

There was a rush for the door. Harley was in the lead and as he reached the Zócalo he saw a column approaching up the Calzada de Tlalpán. Reyes had changed into full uniform and was riding at the head, a splendid figure in blue and gold, a sword at his side. Despite the urgency of the occasion, he was riding with his head turned slightly to the right so that the newspaper photographers on the sidewalk could see his splendid moustachios and thick imperial beard.

An American reporter running alongside him yelled up to him. 'What's going on, General?' he asked.

Reyes didn't slow down and the reporter had to jot down his notes as he trotted close to his stirrup.

'I shall occupy the presidential office,' Reyes said,

'proclaim myself provisional president and announce the bloodless overthrow of the maniac, Madero.'

'Listen, General, the guard has changed!' The American tried to warn him. 'General Villar's in command now.'

For the first time, Reyes looked down at his informer then he gestured. 'General Villar is an old comrade-in-arms,' he said stiffly. 'He'll not oppose me.'

The crowd watched uncomprehendingly as the leading files swung into the Zócalo and headed across the square to the National Palace, where the gates were still closed. As the column pressed forward, a sharp challenge came from the palace and as Reyes' hand went up, Ruíz, huge and unwieldy on his horse, trotted up to him with his staff. The group of officers talked for a moment before one of them spurred forward.

'Open the gates! Open to admit the provisional president of Mexico!'

There was a long silence and the officers began to grow impatient. There was a lot of hurried conferring. Horses pawed impatiently at the ground. The troops leaned stoically on their arms, the cavalry, which had also swarmed into the square after Ruíz, forming a menacing half-circle behind, their eyes fixed on the palace gates.

'They're opening!'

The cry went up and the crowd gave a great sigh, as if the drama were almost too much to bear, and pressed forward to see better. Trusting neither Mexican politics nor the mercurial Mexican temperament, Harley found a position behind a tree. He noticed the *Daily Mail* correspondent huddled behind the next one.

As the gate opened, the figure which appeared was that of General Villar. His face looked grey and ill but it was firm and set. 'This is the presidential palace,' he said. 'My orders are to guard it.'

'Stand aside,' Reyes shouted. 'We intend to enter!'

It was a moment of opera bouffe as Reyes postured wildly, his head up, then, as though he couldn't believe that Villar would order his men to fire, he stood in the stirrups and motioned the column forward. As the cavalrymen behind him gathered their reins and the orders rang out for the cadets to move, Reyes drew his sword and pointed it at the palace.

Immediately there was a shout from the roof and Harley took cover. Glancing across at the *Mail* man, he saw him rigid behind his shelter as the volley crashed out. Men dropped and Reyes, still in front of his column, his arm raised, slowly began to crumple. The sword dropped from his hand, then his body folded and finally rolled from the saddle to sprawl on the ground while his horse trotted away riderless, showing the whites of its eyes, its tail in the air.

The column had scattered immediately, running in every direction, diving in ones and twos and groups down the narrow streets or into shop doorways. Officers brandishing swords and blazing away with revolvers shouted orders above the screaming of women and children from the direction of the Cathedral. As the return fire started, Harley saw Villar in the gateway of the Palace stagger and fall. Two officers dragged him out of sight, then the machine guns opened up from the Palace roof.

There were so many troops in the Zócalo that every bullet found its mark. Riders toppled from their saddles and horses crashed to the ground with a jangle of equipment, among them that of General Ruíz, who lay alongside it, one leg trapped by the weight of the dead animal. A wail lifted from the crowd near the Cathedral as the sweep of the machine guns caught them. Women screamed and, despite the best clothing they were wearing for Mass, everybody flung themselves to the ground, hugging the pavement and trying to snatch shelter behind barrows, chairs, benches, trees or the metal stands of the shoeshine boys.

For a moment there was a lull as the rebel column milled about in disorder, then the gates of the Palace opened and troops surged out, yelling. Díaz, at the head of the Tlalpán cadets, was trying to turn his forces out of the withering fire. Reyes' men, panicked by the volley, scattered backwards among them, disordering their ranks, and began to withdraw across the south-west corner of the Zócalo towards the Ciudadela.

Ruíz was on his feet now, his sword gone, his hat trampled underfoot. But he was too fat to run and as the palace troops caught up with him an officer swung him round, snatched the revolver from the holster on his belt, and surrounded him with men. The Zócalo was emptying rapidly as the machine guns played over it, but in addition to the sprawled figures of soldiers, cadets and senior officers, there were also civilians, including women and children, who had been caught in front of the cathedral by the scythe-like sweep of the guns. As the troops melted away, wailing women clustered around dead and dying relations lying near the steps and under the trees.

As Harley began to run from the Zócalo, he saw Angelica bending over a young soldier sprawled under the trees, his dark face grey with pain.

'What the hell are you doing here?' he shouted. 'I told you there'd be shooting!'

'I'm needed,' she snapped back. 'Mexico needs politicians and newspapermen like it needs a hole in the head, but it sure as hell needs people who're not going to latch on to it to fill their own goddam coffers!'

Ignoring Harley, she gestured at a group of women who promptly headed towards her.

'Are those your people?'

'I came expecting trouble. It seems we've got it.'

A vast spreading stain of red coloured the soldier's uniform and one of the women bent to offer him a drink from his canteen. As she stooped, Harley snatched the canteen away.

'He's been hit in the stomach,' he said, slamming the canteen into Angelica's hands. 'A drink's the worst thing you can do for him. When you set yourself up in business as a Red Cross ambulance, you might take the trouble to find out something about first aid instead of trying to dazzle everybody with your flashy heroics.'

Angelica's hand came up from her waist in a round-arm swipe. As it struck his cheek, he staggered back but, as he stalked away, he noticed that she was fiercely preventing her helper from offering the canteen again.

4

Extra editions of the newspapers were on the streets even before the bodies had been cleared away.

'REVOLTING GARRISON FREES FELIX DIAZ AND GENERAL BERNARDO REYES.' 'GENERAL REYES KILLED IN ATTACK ON PALACE.' 'INSURGENTS SEIZE ARSENAL.'

Angry at Angelica, angrier still at the butchery in the Zócalo, Harley found Knowles with a group of pressmen in Gustavo Madero's office. Gustavo was in high spirits, smiling and confident at the outcome of the battle.

'I'm going to see the president now,' he announced. 'To tell him the rebellion has been crushed. I've been in touch. He's full of fight. A thing like this brings out the best in him. Then I shall go and have some breakfast. It's been a long night.'

It had been a long night for the press corps too. They had been living on coffee and brandy ever since the previous lunch time, but with the despatches sent and still red-eyed with sleeplessness, they were near the Alameda gardens awaiting the President's arrival from Chapultepec.

Ever since the dispersal of the rebel troops, cars containing cabinet ministers had been arriving one after the other to sweep through the gates of the Palace, and Madero himself finally appeared, riding a grey horse at the head of a huge column of mounted police and loyal cavalry. Waiting for him with a general's escort was Huerta, his blank Indian face expressionless, his spectacles gleaming in the sun. As

Madero appeared, he rode up to him and saluted. For a fraction of a second, Madero hesitated then he accepted the proferred hand.

As the column got under way again, it was halted again near the Alameda Park by troops searching for dissident officers who were still roaming the narrow streets. As Madero waved his hat at the crowd and began to head for the palace, a shot rang out from the scaffolding round the half-built Palace of Fine Arts. The crowd, which had lined the pavements to watch his arrival, began to scatter, and as Harley dived with Knowles behind a tree they were almost knocked over by cavalrymen hurtling forward to make an arrest.

As Madero rode into the Zócalo, carts appeared to remove the dead. Ambulances were still taking away the wounded and Angelica was standing among the helpers, her skirt blood-splashed, looking a lot less confident than she had. The carcasses of horses still lay in front of the Palace and the sight seemed to stir Madero. Within an hour, a bulletin was issued to state that a specially convened meeting of the cabinet had passed sentence of death, with immediate execution, on General Ruíz and the commander of the Palace Guard.

'By God,' Knowles said, drawing his breath in sharply. 'The little man can show speed and ruthlessness when he wishes to. For a change, I think he's got the situation under control.'

They decided to divide the coverage of the city and, with Knowles watching the Palace for bulletins, Harley set off with Tamsy for the Ciudadela where the rebels, now under the command of General Mondragón, were holed up. The city was in a ferment. Cars containing staff officers roared along the great avenues towards the Palace and the police and army barracks. From time to time a squad of fully-armed, fully-equipped troops tramped past. Occasionally, somewhere out of sight, a shot rang out or a burst of fire came from the direction of the Ciudadela. Facing it, loyal troops were occupying every street corner and window, and machine gun posts had been set up behind barricades of logs.

The flat-fronted one-storey barracks, low and ugly and standing alone in a wide square surrounded by narrow streets, was silent, its windows shuttered. With the aid of binoculars it was possible to see they had been barricaded and that several of the shutters, hit by rifle fire, hung crookedly. An officer informed them that the artillery from Tacubaya was inside with the rebel force.

'They're working the guns up to the roof,' he said.

Snatching a hurried meal of tortillas and beans at a nearby café, they headed back to the Zócalo. The cabinet was still in session but an announcement was expected at any moment.

Knowles was jubilant. 'Madero's got the city in the palm of his hand,' he said cheerfully. 'That lot in the Ciudadela are outnumbered five to one and troops have been called in from the outlying districts.'

By lunchtime the promised bulletin appeared. It announced that General Angeles was to be called back from his campaign against Zapata in Morelos while the troops in the capital had been given to General Huerta.

Knowles stared at Harley. 'Huerta?' he said. 'It can't be true! That old buzzard's implicated in the plot.'

All movement had ceased. The city was paralyzed. Except for the troops and police and occasional ambulances searching the residential districts for wounded rebels, the main streets were deserted. Government offices were still functioning but nobody was taking any chances, clerks and officials making their way to their desks through roads well away from the main avenues, moving cautiously from doorway to doorway in case of an outbreak of firing, because Díaz had stationed men with quick-firing guns on all the high buildings near the Cuidadela.

The newspapers were still functioning, however, and with the cable office open, Knowles' messenger brought a telegram from Sproat suggesting that Harley should return home after all. 'Europe erupting,' he said. 'Mexico second team.' It was with considerable pleasure that Harley sent his reply. 'Revolt against Madero,' he announced. 'Fighting continues. Expect increase in salary.'

Newspapermen and photographers haunted the cafés, among them Johnny Cox, waiting with his camera and sketch book, a wide grin on his face.

'I got one of the whole cabinet,' he boasted. 'They allowed

us in. One of the American ambassador, too, going to see Madero. Stars and Stripes flying from the car and everything.'

During the day artillery was seen arriving and rumours spread that the bombardment of the Ciudadela was to start the following morning. News also arrived that, with the attempt against Madero, men were flocking to the flag of Zapata who had pledged his support to the President. Somehow Harley found it hard to believe.

In those areas of the capital near the Ciudadela cafés had shooed out their customers and put up their shutters as a precaution, but the revolt seemed to have quietened down. Both sides were strengthening their defences and neither seemed prepared to move first. Troubled by his own anger and the despair in Angelica's face when he had left her in the Zócalo, Harley sought her out.

The house was quiet with the shutters in place and she was living in the back rooms away from the street with a couple of servants. An American woman who had just arrived from Veracruz was growing hysterical in the tense atmosphere, and two or three more women with their children were sitting well away from the window because of the occasional burst of machine gun and sniper fire.

As Harley was ushered in, Angelica's face set in an expression of hostility.

'Come for a story?' she asked. 'About the half-baked American charmed by the trappings of militancy?'

'I came to apologize,' Harley admitted. 'What I said to you was unforgivable.'

Her face went pink with pleasure and her anger melted at once. 'Honest?' she said. 'You don't think I'm just an interfering screwball dame?'

He shook his head and she gestured at a room off the hall. 'Come in here. We've just made tea. I'm setting up a little hospital just in case,' she said, a trace defensively, as she poured. 'But I've done it properly this time. I've got nurses. Genuine ones. Two of them Americans who've offered to help. I've also got a doctor.' She managed a smile. 'I did it wrong. I won't again.' She gestured to the window. 'What's happening? I haven't been out since the shooting started.'

'It looks as though Madero's pulled it off. It only requires a determined attack and they'll have to throw their hands in. Huerta's in command.'

'I heard he was in the plot himself.'

'Madero seems to think he isn't. Angeles is being brought back to the capital. The press are tying themselves in knots trying to be in two places at once. Johnny Cox is making money from the troubles.'

She gave him that wide electric grin of hers. 'He asked me to marry him.'

'He's a good-looking chap.'

'I'm not after good looks.' She grinned again. 'Faithful Fred turned up too.'

'Again? Who's side's he on now?'

'His own. I heard he'd been seen with Huerta. At the moment he's trying to find out who's drawing those cartoons in *El Independiente*'.

'I thought everybody knew it was Johnny Cox.'

The grin came again. 'If he finds out, it'll be a good idea for Johnny C. to make himself scarce. Wealthy men, generals and politicians in Mexico don't take kindly to being made fools of, and those cartoons are good. Madero on a donkey as Christ. Faithful Fred as Judas. Boy, that was nasty! Huerta as Pontius Pilate. What about you?'

'My paper thinks there's going to be trouble in Europe and to the great British sporting public that's nearer home. What's happening here might be in China or even on the moon.'

As they talked Tamsy appeared. 'Things are starting, Boss,' he said. 'They're going to set up an attack on the Ciudadela. I got the car right outside. Huerta's got his batteries in the streets. But it ain't goin' to be a walkover because the rebels have got *their* guns in the park in front of the Ciudadela.'

As they climbed into the car, their heads were lifted by the sound of a gun. The city was silent, almost as if it were waiting, and the crash of the explosion shattered the stillness. Immediately, another explosion from the direction of the Ciudadela showed where the shell had landed. Tamsy looked at Harley as he cranked the engine. 'That's it, Boss,' he said. 'It's started. 'Now only the Lord Jesus Christ knows when it'll finish.'

5

'Oh, boy! This sure is some country!'

Watching from the doorway of a café near the National Palace where at least a dozen newspapermen were sheltering, Johnny Cox spoke the thoughts of all of them.

The bombardment, going on now for over three hours, had already killed several people not even remotely connected with the rebellion or the attempts to put it down. It had started with shots from Huerta's guns stationed near San Diego Street, but after he had been seen inspecting his positions at dawn, Huerta himself had disappeared and all attempts to find out what was happening had ended in failure.

They had been in the café ever since the first shells had been fired. Now, it seemed unlikely that they would be able to get away before dark because machine gunners were spraying the streets with bullets.

As they watched, a Federal battery appeared on the corner a few hundred yards away and swung into a nearby garden. As the teams clattered away again, the gunners heaved the spade tails round and, squatting behind them, began to turn the training handles.

As the first shot roared out, filling the air with the acrid smell of explosive, a gun at the other side of the city replied. The shell landed by a nearby tree, slicing it in half, and the café window fell in from the blast. Desperately, to the screams of the women behind the serving hatch, the owner pushed tables and chairs into the entrance to make a barricade. The newspapermen scrambled out across them and began to run in a crouch along the wall. But no other shell landed nearby and, left alone with Tamsy in the café, Harley noticed that the shells coming from the Cuidadela were landing nowhere near the battery.

'Tamsy,' he said, 'there's something bloody odd happening around here.'

'Sure is, boss,' Tamsy agreed. 'People are killin' each other.'

'Not that, Tamsy. That battery out there's been in full view for half an hour now and nobody's fired at it yet.' Harley stuck his head out to watch one of the guns fire another shot. The shell seemed to fall very wide of the Ciudadela and the return fire went nowhere near the National Palace.

'They seem to be landing in the residential areas, Tamsy. I wonder if the bastards are in league with each other. Let's get nearer.'

As they ducked out of the café, a shell removed a decorative turret on a nearby house. Bricks and tiles cascaded into the street and they could hear women screaming. Bent double, Harley followed Tamsy then, as a machine gun opened up, he began to run on all fours. Heavy firing came from the west, and a gun went off nearby with a crack like a clap of thunder. A shell crashed into the street, flinging up stones and dirt and filling the air with a smell like a photographer's magnesium flare. The noise sounded like a skyscraper coming down. Running figures fell and Harley saw a man sprawled headless in a pool of blood.

The British Embassy was several blocks away near the Paseo de la Reforma. It was a large square building in its own grounds. A window on the staircase had been broken by a shell fragment and wooden shutters had been smashed and splintered. The opinion of the staff was roughly the same as Harley's.

'They seem to be firing at random into the city because the Ciudadela's not being hit.'

The embassy was virtually marooned and they were concentrating all their energies on caring for the refugees who had claimed their attention. They were a mixture of British and Americans who had not been able to reach their own embassy, and had no means of communication with the outside world because the telephone lines had been cut by the shelling.

By evening the streets were littered with debris, and the city was going through spasms of despair, hope, exhilaration and despondency. Incoherent, confused stories from the newspapermen tried to keep track of the struggle but remarkably little was known because no one on either side was offering information and the journalists were thrown back on their own resources. Every government office out of the line of fire where a responsible official might be found was besieged by newsmen loudly demanding to be told what was happening. Finally they learned that Madero had gone to Cuernavaca.

'Why? Has he resigned?'

Nobody was quite sure and several of the invading journalists bolted off to try to get the information away. Immediately rumours started that Madero had fled, but it turned out instead that he had gone personally to confer with the Governor of Morelos and General Angeles in an effort to persuade Zapata to support him. He had left Huerta in command in the capital.

Sensing that the drama had moved to Cuernavaca, Harley told Tamsy to drive him there in the Stutz. It was only an afternoon's journey and as they left the capital they met a string of cars and taxis, then the first of the troops from the south marching towards them. They were hot and dusty and followed by heavily-laden carts. Between two of the regiments, riding a horse, they recognized General Angeles. He was tall, thin, handsome, moustached and ascetic-looking, his cap drawn down so that the visor covered his eyes. He was considered to be a brilliant soldier and one of the few honest men in the army.

He told them that he wasn't happy at leaving Morelos to Zapata and asked what was happening in the capital. When they told him Huerta had been left in command he frowned.

'I need to be there,' he said at once. 'The President has returned already and I think he needs friends around him.'

Remounting, he signalled for the column to start again and they stood by the Stutz to watch the soldiers trudge by.

'Tamsy,' Harley said. 'Get us to Cuernavaca. Let's see what's happening.

They scrambled back into the Stutz and Tamsy gave an exhibition of muscular co-ordination and split-second timing, whipping round waggons and carts and oncoming mules, slipping through narrowing gaps in a way that almost gave Harley heart failure.

'Close enough to that guy,' Tamsy said cheerfully as they shot between the rear of a cart and a man hauling a barrow, 'to remove the snot from his nose.'

Cuernavaca, with its famed Borda Gardens, had been one of the favourite haunts of the Emperor Maximilian, a place of heavy foliage, crumbling verandahs, statues, lily pools, fountains overgrown with roses and tangled groves of oranges and mangoes. There was no sign of any soldiers but a great sense of alarm. As they arrived in the square, there were several other cars packed with suitcases and people who looked as if they were about to leave.

Then, just as they were drawing to a halt, the whole place erupted into violence. Into the square hurtled a whole army of heavily-sombreroed men on horses, shouting and waving rifles which they fired into the air. Frantically the people by the waiting cars started to scramble aboard. A shot was fired and a man trying to crank the engine of one of them crumpled against the bonnet and lay draped across the mudguard as the car was surrounded by yelling horsemen. Slipping from the saddle they began to drag the people from inside and women screamed as suitcases were prised open and garments began to fly. A soldier wearing a woman's shawl, pranced away, grinning, in a mock fandango, and another hopped on one leg as he tried to drag a pair of women's frilly drawers up over his trousers. A girl was hauled away, shrieking, her dress torn open from her shoulders to her waist, and a chauffeur who tried to protect her fell backwards as a man in a sombrero swung his rifle by the barrel.

'For Christ's sake, Tamsy,' Harley yelled. 'Get us out of this or we'll be caught up in it too!'

Tamsy had kept the engine running and now he swung the Stutz round, the engine screaming, the wheels shuddering against the cobblestones. The soldiers saw what was happening and several of them ran towards them and hooves clattered on the paving as horses were wrenched round. There was a narrow gap between the back of a huge hay cart and a fruit barrow and Tamsy headed for it at full speed. As he reached it, a child stepped out from behind the cart and he yelled in fright. With a flick of his wrist, he swung the Stutz off course and the mudguard hit the fruit barrow. Oranges, lemons, mangoes and other fruit flew into the air as the barrow was spun round and fell on its side. A shot starred the windscreen high in the corner, then they were thundering out of the town. As they left another group of horsemen, also bent on pillage, came round a corner and, as they saw the huge car with its glaring headlamps roaring down on them, they hauled on their reins, the whole group flung into disorder. A horse reared above Harley, its front feet threshing the air, and another went down spectacularly on to a stall laden with trinkets, bringing the rush matting roof about its head.

The bent mudguard was scraping against a smoking tyre but they dared not stop until they were clear of the town; then they halted and the two of them put their strength against it and heaved the twisted steel clear so they could limp back to Mexico City. When they arrived the firing was still going on and while they had been away the rumours had grown wilder: Madero's absence had been noted and it was being said that Gustavo Madero had been named president in his place. Madero himself had gone mad and it had been he who had ordered the bombardment of the city. A British ship was waiting at Veracruz to take him into exile.

Unable to find any transport to replace the damaged Stutz, Harley and Tamsy moved on foot through the poorer quarter of the city where barefoot Indian women in colourful skirts and blouses crouched on the pavement over calabashes of vegetables or a single piece of old newspaper covered with the few beans they hoped to sell. The rebels had opened the Balom Prison and pulled the freed convicts into their ranks, and had gained control of the main market and those slums nearest the Cuidadela to maintain the flow of recruits. Their agents were busy in the crowded streets and men were arguing loudly outside the cafés and bars.

They turned up on Angelica's doorstep just as it grew dark. She gave them a meal and they decided to sleep on the floor of the kitchen. As darkness came the firing died down. Nobody knew how many had been killed but it seemed that the casualty list already ran into three figures, few of them the soldiers who were doing the fighting.

Angelica didn't believe that Madero had fled. At first Harley put it down to an excess of idealism and revolutionary spirit, but once again she had facts. One of the women in the house had learned from her husband that there was to be a meeting.

'Who between?'

Angelica shrugged. 'Madero and Huerta, I suppose. They'd hardly meet the rebels, would they?'

'When?'

'I don't know.'

'Where?'

'National Palace, I expect. But if Huerta's included, it'll probably be in a café where he can get his brandy.'

When daylight came the following morning there was no sign of Angelica and the other women and they found them eventually in one of the attics standing on chairs to peer out of the window. It gave a view of the area in front of Ciudadela and the Morelos Gardens where the rebels had set up their batteries.

'Something's happening,' Angelica said.

Men in Rurale uniform were just emerging from the streets on the north side of the fortress. As they deployed into line and began to move slowly forward, machine guns began to hammer at them and under the blind ferocity of the firing the line dissolved and bolted for shelter, leaving prostrate figures sprawled on the paving. Almost immediately, they reappeared, reformed and supported by reserves, but the same thing happened again, the survivors scattering for the nearby streets. A third time it happened, this time the uniforms those of Federal troops, and yet again the butchery occurred until the whole area in front of the Ciudadela was covered with dead.

'They're sending those men across open ground,' Harley said as the firing died down and white flags appeared to allow the wounded to be removed. 'There isn't a scrap of shelter. What in God's name are they trying to do?'

'I'll tell you what they're doing,' Angelica said, her eyes

wet. 'This is Mexico and those are troops loyal to Madero. Huerta's getting rid of them so he can come to some arrangement with Díaz.'

'He wouldn't dare,' Harley said.

She turned on him bitterly. 'You don't know a goddam thing,' she snapped. 'That old Aztec would dare anything.'

6

When Knowles appeared, he looked tired.

'Madero's back,' he announced. 'I've seen him. He's brought Angeles and his troops from Cuernavaca. He says he obtained a promise from Zapata that he wouldn't take advantage of what's happening here.'

'Do you believe it?' Harley asked.

'Why not?'

'Because it's not Zapata's way.' Harley described what he had seen in Cuernavaca. 'I think the stories are all wrong. There's no such thing as a deal between them. There was no armistice. The Zapatistas simply held their hand until Angeles had withdrawn, then they moved in. All that's happened is that Zapata's gained ground.'

With the city ominously silent, they decided to check with the American Embassy. Part of the building had been turned into a relief station for families rescued from the danger zone by volunteers. The American ambassador, a lean, moustached, energetic man, was doing the organizing and as the refugees came in he was sending them to houses in what were considered to be safe districts. The American drivers and messengers were braving the firing again and again and a hospital had been set up where both combatants and non-combatants were being treated, irrespective of their nationality.

For a while it seemed as if the firing had ceased, then, as the sun appeared, the first gun of the day started, to be answered at once by another. A machine gun joined in, the echoes coming down the long avenues. Apart from the cannonade, however, remarkably little had been done since Madero's return to overcome the force in the Ciudadela. Rubbish was piling up along the streets and here and there gutted buildings, set on fire by the shelling, reared like skeletons against the sky. The only movement came from women carrying white flags trying to buy food for their families. In every doorway, groups of them waited, before making a hurried rush to the other side of the road. But all the shops in the area near the fighting were closed and everybody who could had moved out to the suburbs, while politicians and officials had taken shelter in the embassies and legations.

Trying to reach his own flat through a jungle of hanging wires, Harley passed a wrecked shop where plaster models with pink legs were spilled on the pavement. Among them was a real man, but *his* legs were missing. Just down the street an old woman was clearing broken glass from her front door. Every morning they had heard this same strange and terrible sound of people sweeping their front steps free of debris.

By lunchtime they heard General Angeles had been posted to the outer suburbs, officially to watch for any rebel infiltration from the south. As everybody watched helplessly the firing continued. Trenches were now being dug in the streets and every home was in state of siege. The worst of the shelling seemed to have hit the areas where the influential voters lived, and they looked empty and forlorn, with smashed windows and flayed trees, the street lighting poles down, here and there a burned-out car. The café where Harley and Angelica had met Jauregui was a tangle of smashed chairs, and there was a shell hole in the road by the door.

Dead soldiers and civilians had been dragged into heaps under the trees where police were drenching them with gasolene and setting them on fire in an effort to prevent disease. Little heaps of charred matter with a scorched but unburned and easily recognizable hand or foot still remained while passers-by hurried along with their handkerchieves to their noses against the smell.

The following morning, the American ambassador agreed to

meet the press. His was the only embassy still functioning properly. The British ambassador was pinned in his cellar because the rebels had erected machine guns and cannon in front of his Legation and the firing they attracted was pockmarking the walls with holes.

To reach the American embassy Harley and Tamsy had to pass the YMCA building which was being taken over by Díaz troops. There, foreign students, clutching what few belonging they had been able to salvage, were standing in groups in the street, wondering what had hit them. Even as they talked to the newspapermen, a volley from the upper windows lifted their heads, then a shell screamed into the top storey to send bricks, tiles and glass flying.

As everybody scattered, one of the students fell to the pavement with blood pouring from his head. Lifting him into the Stutz, Harley and Tamsy drove him through the littered streets to the embassy. The place was crowded and the ambassador had just returned from a trip across the city to persuade the warring factions to allow him to establish a neutral zone.

'It's time this goddam fighting was over.' An elderly man grabbed at Harley's arm. 'My business is being ruined by these damned greasers. You tell 'em, young feller, in those newspapers of yours. Tell 'em we need a stable government here in Mexico. Revolutions are bad for business.'

Despite the introduction of censorship, the cable office was still functioning but it was necessary to make a wide detour by the Alameda gardens to reach it. Uninvolved, untouched by the tragedy, the newspapermen were treating the journey as a game. They had started a censorship derby in which several of them would mount horse-drawn carriages and set off to get their messages properly stamped and bring back the timed receipt from the cable office. With the shelling and the chances of having their horses shot, it was reckoned that three hours was a fast time for the course. Yet all the time a steady relay of drivers was getting through with official and private cables, and Harley was able to bribe one of the Mexican employees to include his own despatches among those going from the embassy.

To an orchestration of bangs and the clattering of machine guns from the streets outside, Ambassador Wilson appeared, full of energy and determination. 'I have wired Washington,' he announced, 'That practically all local state authorities, police and Rurales have aligned themselves with Díaz.'

'Are you sure that's true, Mr. Ambassador?' one of the American journalists asked. 'I saw battalions of loyal troops butchered in front of the Ciudadela this morning. It looked to me as if *they* hadn't gone over to Díaz, even if the guy who was ordering them forward had.'

Wilson seemed to resent the remark. 'Public opinion, both native and foreign, is overwhelmingly in favour of Díaz. I have taken a direct hand in affairs. Together with the German and Spanish Minister, I have been to the National Palace.'

'Were you fired on, Mr. Ambassador?'

'That I was. By both sides. But we saw the President. He blamed the destruction of American property on General Díaz but he agreed to a cease-fire so that we could talk to the rebels. General Díaz, on the other hand, blamed the government. I have General Huerta's assurances that the rebels will soon be defeated and I have also been in touch with Catholic leaders and aides of General Huerta. They all promised to do what they could to bring about a cease-fire.'

'American nationals *I*'ve spoken to, Mr. Ambassador – ' the American newspaperman was insistent ' – aren't satisfied that everything is being done to destroy the rebellion. What's Huerta up to, sir? A member of the Japanese Legation told me he could guarantee to raise enough men to get into the Ciudadela and destroy the entire rebel force in twenty-four hours. If they can, why can't Huerta?'

While Wilson was still pondering his reply, another American journalist jumped up. 'I'll tell you what I think, sir,' he said loudly. 'There are people here who want to be rid of Madero and this is their way of doing it. We all know how many foreigners have interests here. What about the Guggenheims, Lord Cowdray, Lord Morne and Mr. Doheny? William Randolph Hearst owns land in Mexico as big as Maryland and Delaware combined and there are seventy-five thousand Americans living here. US investment is more than all the capital stock owned by the Mexicans themselves. I reckon those guys are influencing what's being done.'

'That is outside the sphere of my influence,' Wilson snapped. 'And I did not come to listen to a political speech.'

It brought the conference to an abrupt halt.

With the continuing bombardment, it had become difficult to obtain food, and now whenever the newspapermen went out they stuffed their pockets with biscuits, cheese and bottles of mineral water and brandy. Angelica promised another meal and as the Stutz arrived outside her house she was letting out two men carrying suitcases. Harley eyed them suspiciously.

She waved away his fears. 'It's nothing,' she said. 'I gave them permission to use the cellar. They're printers who've lost their premises in the shelling and they're using a duplicator in place of their press.'

She was in no doubt about what was affecting the American ambassador's attitude. 'He's working for big business interests,' she said. 'It doesn't suit them to have Madero in power.'

She fished in a drawer and produced a pamphlet urging support for Díaz. 'They say it's produced in the cellar of the embassy,' she insisted.

'Does the ambassador know?'

'I bet he does.' Her face cracked in that wild grin of hers. 'But he's not the only one who can get into the printing business. There are others at it, too.'

She produced another pamphlet. Across the top in large letters was the message. 'Support Madero!!! Only *Madero* has the True Interests of Mexico at Heart.' Below in smaller type, the message continued. 'General Huerta Is A Traitor!!! He Is Known To Have *Met Díaz Aides* At El Globo. There are to be more meetings!!! They are in league with each other and *Díaz Is to Replace Madero*!!!' Beneath, there was a long screed suggesting what everybody had felt for a long time but had never said – that there was something very odd about a battle which destroyed only troops loyal to Madero, which kept Angeles – the only really reliable general – out of the way where he couldn't intervene, and which smashed civilian property but did remarkably little damage to the headquarters of the warring factions. 'The Ciudadela has been hit only *once*,' it concluded. 'And the National Palace only *twice*!!!'

'What do you think of it?' she asked.

Harley frowned. 'Angelica, this is dynamite. Where did you get this information about this meeting at the Globo?'

'One of the waiters. His wife was sheltering with me. She told me about it.'

'Are you sure?'

'Huerta's well-known there. The café was closed to normal custom and a room was set aside for the meeting.'

'Do you know what was discussed?'

'I can guess. It's obvious what they're up to. They want to destroy everybody's appetite for a voice in their own government. Huerta's thinking of defecting and they're working out how to get rid of Madero.'

Harley studied the pamphlet again. 'Angelica,' he said quietly. 'You wrote this.'

'No, I didn't.'

'It's your style, Angelica. What are you going to do with it?'

She frowned sulkily. 'They were to be passed round. Instead of newspapers.'

The implication of what she said struck him at once 'Is that what those bloody men were doing in your cellar?'

She didn't deny it and looked scared but defiant.

'Angelica, if there's anything mad and dangerous you can do, you'll do it. Don't you realize, there's a real danger Madero *will* be overthrown? The American ambassador's even trying to engineer it. And if he is, they'll try to find out who was responsible for these. They'll be looking for anybody involved with it. Don't you realize you've put your head in a noose?'

Her chin rose. 'They won't touch me.'

'They'll shoot the men who did it. And you'd be responsible for their deaths. They might even shoot *you*. In the meantime, thanks for the tip. I'm going to the Globo to watch it. Back *and* front.'

That evening with Knowles watching the back of the café and Harley and Tamsy watching the front, they saw a large black car arrive, its windows shadowed by drawn curtains.

The gunfire that had been echoing round the city for days seemed to have died, as if the rebels were in collusion and were allowing the car a safe passage. As the vehicle slowed to a stop, through binoculars Harley saw the square shape of Huerta climb out and hurry into the café. He was in civilian clothes with a soft felt hat low over his spectacles.

For two hours he was inside the restaurant then, when they had begun to think nothing was going to happen, the black car drew up again and he reappeared and climbed inside. A man standing in the doorway lifted his hand in a gesture of salute as the car drew away. As if to a signal the guns started again.

They had arranged to meet Knowles in a back-street bar out of the line of firing. It was full of men trying to get a drink, and a few women, venturing out during the lull and caught by the renewed bombardment, were also sheltering there, chattering like sparrows in a corner by the door. Knowles had tried to check by telephone with the Globo what had been going on, but nobody had been willing to talk. They decided to wait until it closed and waylay one of the waiters as he left for home.

The man they chose was scared and backed up against the wall as they stopped him, but a hundred-peso note persuaded him to say who had been present at the meeting.

'General Huerta, señor.'

'You're sure?'

'There's only one man who drinks brandy like that, señor.'

'Who was the other man?'

'I think he came from General Díaz.'

'What did they talk about?'

'I was never close enough to hear, señor. But I've seen them before.'

'Together?'

'More than once.'

They decided to try their discovery on the American ambassador. One or two other newspapermen had a copy of the pamphlet Harley had seen and they agreed to act together.

Once more the bombardment was in full swing and water and electricity supplies had been cut off. In the teeming backstreets beyond the reach of the food lorries trying to get into the city, people were on the verge of starvation, and there were now nearly two thousand people crowded into the American embassy. In the neutral zone a shell had struck the corner of the American library, bringing it down with a roar of falling bricks and tiles, and all round the area, buildings were pockmarked and holed by bullets and shell fragments.

As they entered the embassy, Wilson, the ambassador, was preparing to throw his weight behind a demand that Madero should resign. 'It cannot go on like this,' he announced. 'I intend to call a meeting of the diplomatic corps and I hope other foreign representatives will be able to come. It's the only way peace can be regained.'

'Why not,' Harley asked, 'find out first why General Huerta met one of General Díaz's agents at the Café Globo last night?'

They gathered again at the embassy to learn what had happened at the meeting of the heads of the diplomatic corps.

Significantly, Wilson didn't turn up and a statement was read out by his deputy. 'The ambassador,' he said, 'convinced the meeting that they should urge the president to resign and place his powers in the hands of Congress. The President denied the rights of foreign diplomats to interfere.'

Despite Madero's objections, it looked very much as though the city was ready to accept anything that would guarantee a halt to the destruction and the killing. Angeles was still in the southern suburbs where he couldn't bring his batteries to bear, the Madero home had been set on fire and Madero's family had fled to the Japanese Embassy. Madero himself was still in the Palace. Another armistice was arranged to allow food to enter the stricken city and it was significant that several waggonloads were seen heading for the Ciudadela. It began to look as though the pointless battle would never stop. The dead numbered in the region of two thousand and the small charred and stinking heaps lay everywhere about the city centre and graves were appearing in the public parks.

The story of Huerta's meeting with Díaz's agent appeared to be common knowledge now and they heard that Gustavo Madero had had him arrested. But Huerta had protested his loyalty and had been set free by the President. Almost immediately, they heard that the American ambassador had been warned to expect Madero's overthrow. It seemed very much as though Huerta had realized that if he didn't do something soon it would be too late.

The following day, with the guns still thudding away, Madero agreed to the conference the press had been demanding for days. The strain showed in his face, the round cheeks had grown hollow, there were dark circles under his eyes, and he seemed to jump at the sound of every explosion. He had not lost his courage, however.

'The rumours of my resignation,' he said firmly, 'have no foundation. I have never for a moment entertained the idea. I was elected president by the free, untrammelled and bona fide vote of the Mexican people – ' he was reciting the words they had all heard before as if they were a Creed ' – and I intend to be faithful to the trust committed to me. Even though it costs me my life. My place – ' he lifted his hands and struck the arm of his chair with his clenched fists ' – is here! Here!'

As they left, Knowles sighed, his normal dignity slipping. 'God help the poor stubborn little bugger,' he said.

7

The story of the meeting between Huerta and the Díaz agent had been passed on by someone to those newpapers which were still publishing and Angelica was scared.

'It wasn't intended to be in the newspapers,' she said.

But by this time, the press censorship was being rigorously applied, and every newspaperman in the city was bending his mind to methods of getting his despatches away through the firing. Some were being smuggled by rail via Puebla to the coast for a ship to Europe or the States. Others were being driven out of the city to Tula. A few, among them Harley and Knowles, had arranged secret routes via the diplomatic bags and for longer despatches Tamsy was roaring north in the Stutz to a wayside halt south of Querétaro where they were put aboard a train for the border.

The bombardment had not stopped and there were constant bursts of sporadic machine gun fire. One of the American correspondents had been hit in the head by a stray bullet as he watched from his balcony and was now fighting for his life, and one of the French newspapermen had been killed by a sniper by mistake.

The gunfire seemed more erratic than ever now and the pavements were strewn with broken glass, stones, paper and blowing chaff. Here and there a street was blocked by a fallen wall or tree. Near the Ciudadela a column of smoke rose where a building had been set on fire. Shutters hung askew over splintered windows, and corpses lay like flattened bundles in the street. Others lay propped up in doorways where they had been dragged to die and the air was foul with the stink of uncollected rubbish. The city was dead, symbolized by a crumpled house, a bath still hanging in mid-air by its plumbing, and it was becoming more difficult to move about as supplies of gasolene ran out. Tamsy had to drive regularly out of the city to fill the car, going further every time as others discovered his source of fuel.

Trying to reach his flat, Harley found himself in an area of shops, where he saw two children struggling with a grill across a door. At first he thought they were looting, then he saw they were trying to free an imprisoned dog. Just down the street a queue of women in black was waiting stoically to buy bread. They were talking among themselves, bewailing the difficulties of obtaining food, and many of them clutched white flags made of sheets. As he passed, a funeral went by, led by a violinist playing *The Blue Danube Waltz*, and they all solemnly crossed themselves. A child was lying in an open box-like coffin painted in broad stripes of blue, pink and white, its feet bare, its hands crossed under a wreath of paper flowers, and it was followed by a small procession of weeping, stumbling relatives. Then a single shot rang out and sent a cloud of magpies clattering from the jacarandas growing round the bandstand in a nearby square. As if it had been a signal, a machine gun started up.

For a moment nobody moved, then bullets clinked against the stonework above their heads, bringing down plaster and stone chips before whining away into the distance. One of the women screamed and they had just started to scatter for shelter when the machine gun caught them. The queue crumpled and blundered, panic-stricken, into the side streets, leaving several of the women on the ground, covered with blood and squirming like fish in a basket. As the machine gun swept back, more of the running figures fell and the air was filled with wailing.

The gun stopped, as if the man behind it had lost interest, and people began to appear nervously from doorways. As Harley helped to pull the living clear, there were blotches of scarlet staining the surface of the road. A woman clutched a dead baby to her with one hand, while the other tore agonizedly at her hair. Next to her, the child's grandmother, tears streaming down her face, shook her fist against the murderers.

It was a long time before the street was cleared. Exhausted and hungry, and realizing that Angelica's house was nearby Harley began to head for it with dragging feet. She was nervous as she opened the door. She was alone because her Indian maid had disappeared on a shopping expedition and she thought she might have been killed by the firing.

'She probably was,' Harley said and told her what he had just seen.

She gave him a shocked look and glanced about her as if wondering what to do, what to say. Her hospital had come to nothing because the firing had stopped anybody reaching it, and the women who had been sheltering with her had vanished during one of the truces.

A nearby gun kept pounding away in monotonous crashes that shook the rooms and set the chandeliers tinkling. Then there was a rattle of musketry, the crunch of broken glass beneath running feet and the rumble of wheels as a cart clattered past trying to collect the dead.

Harley was unshaven, his eyes bloodshot, his trousers stained with blood, his jacket crumpled from sleeping in it. Angelica eyed him critically.

'You look like hell,' she said.

In a garden across the street several bodies sprawled on the grass. A dead horse lay in the shafts of an overturned cart surrounded by a nightmare of cracked asphalt and uprooted paving stones by a shell hole. Then they heard the tramp of feet as a long column of men were marched towards the National Palace.

'Madero has brought the 29th Regiment into the city,' Harley said. 'To take over the defence of the Palace.'

Angelica was worried because she had noticed police agents in the street asking questions and she had a feeling they suspected her of producing the pamphlets.

'And don't say I told you so,' she said angrily. 'Or I'll hit you with something.'

As she spoke the gun fired again. The crash of the shell seemed nearer this time and Angelica's head jerked up.

'That was at the end of the street,' she pointed out. 'At the other side of the house.'

The words were barely out of her mouth when they heard the slow clack-clack of a Maxim gun and suddenly, unexpectedly, the windows fell in.

'Oh, my God,' Angelica screamed.

They bolted for the kitchen but there was no other sound and they crept back to inspect the damage. The bullets had brought down chunks of plaster and the chandelier had shed several of its crystal drops. A picture had fallen from the wall and a tall blue and yellow vase had collapsed into shattered shards.

'I'm scared, Harley,' Angelica whimpered. 'And I'm tired. I'm tired of the killing.'

Harley poured brandy into a dusty glass and was just crossing the room to hand it to her when there was a crash outside and they heard shell splinters thud into the ceiling. Angelica was still staring at the damage with horrified eyes when the machine gun started again and the wall above her head sprouted spurts of dust and plaster. Pulling her to the floor, he dragged her into the corner just as the ceiling came down with the chandelier.

'Oh, God,' she moaned. 'When will it all end?'

There was another crash and the room was filled with smoke, only a solitary candle remaining alight. Angelica's fingers clawed at Harley's arms in spasmodic twitches and she seemed to be trying to bury herself in his chest, her face in the angle of his neck. All her spirit seemed to have gone and, realizing that she was not as tough as she had pretended, he put his arms round her and began to stroke her hair.

'Stay still, Angelica. Stay still.'

Eventually they crawled on hands and knees under the arch formed by the stairs, Harley carrying the brandy bottle. As he reached her side there was another crash and she flung herself at him.

'It's all right, Angelica. We're safe here!'

'I don't feel so goddam safe.'

He lifted her chin and as he kissed her he found she was kissing him back fiercely.

'Steady on,' he said.

'I don't want to steady on.'

There was another crash and a roar of tiles sliding off the roof and the alcove beneath the stairs filled with acrid smoke.

Pushing her down, Harley flung himself across her in case the stairs came down on them. As the din subsided, he saw her staring up at him in the light of the solitary candle, her lips parted, her eyes bright.

'Stop pretending, Harley.'

'Stop pretending what?'

'You know goddam what! I'm frightened. Stay here. Sleep here. With me. I've spent too much of my goddam life alone. For God's sake, I want you to, and if they blow us up I could go to my Maker without you ever knowing.'

She grabbed him clumsily and, choked with emotion, sought his lips.

'Oh, Harley!' There was something plaintive in her voice, the plea of a woman who felt she had missed too much of life and was desperate to catch up with it before it was too late. 'There are girls prettier than me,' she went on in a shaking voice as he stroked her hair. 'God knows why you should be so concerned.'

He smiled. 'Most girls don't have your courage.'

She wasn't so sure. At that moment her thoughts seemed to be exactly the same as any other woman's.

'It's gone quiet,' she murmured. Her nerves were tingling, her stomach full of butterflies, but her eyes were steady on Harley's face.

'The back bedroom's safe,' she whispered.

Harley woke slowly. The breeze coming through the shutters stirred the curtains. Outside he could see the palms in the garden and could smell smoke.

He turned his head to find Angelica sitting up, holding the sheet to her throat to hide her nakedness. She was still puzzled by her actions. She had thought she was dedicated exclusively to Mexico but it hadn't stopped her ending up in bed with a man.

Harley crossed to the window, trying to see out. After ten days of bombardment the city was silent. 'Something's happened,' he said.

She wasn't interested and obviously felt the need to excuse her behaviour.

'Perhaps we've all grown a little desperate for love,' she said falteringly. 'There's so little of it in Mexico these days.'

She looked at him frankly. 'With all the dying around us, perhaps it makes more sense for the rest of us to go on living.'

He was dressing quickly and she felt a twinge of alarm that he was about to leave her.

'Where are you going?' she demanded.

'To find out what's happened. Something has. When I've finished I'll come back.'

'That's what you always say: You'll be back.'

He reached for his jacket then he bent over her, kissing her throat as she turned her head away. She didn't smile.

'Don't go, Harley,' she said with sudden misery. 'Don't go away from me!'

He was heading down the stairs when he heard a thunderous knocking on the door. Wrenching it open, he saw Tamsy there, the Stutz in the road behind him. Tamsy stared at him then his eyes lifted and, turning, Harley saw that Angelica had appeared on the landing. She was round the corner where she couldn't be seen from the door, but there was a large mirror opposite the stairs and although it was cracked all the way across, it showed her, in two jaggedly separated halves, clutching the sheet to her.

Tamsy's eyes lifted to Harley's then he seemed to come to life. 'Knowles said to get you, Boss. General Blanquet arrested Madero.'

'Blanquet? How? He was in the plot.'

'Sure. Huerta asked him to change sides with the 29th. Regiment and Madero felt it was safe because he helped put Maximilian in front of a firing squad. Instead he used the opportunity to grab the President. There's to be a statement. Knowles has got it all.'

Knowles was banging away at a typewriter. 'It's over,' he said. 'Where were you?'

'Sheltering from the firing.'

Knowles stared at him then glanced at Tamsy and Harley knew that they had both guessed where he had been.

'Madero's a prisoner,' Knowles went on. 'His guards shot one of Blanquet's officers and Blanquet's men fired back and killed Madero's cousin. The Vice-President has also been arrested and they've both been charged with treason. They've also got General Angeles and Gustavo Madero. I think we should get over to the American embassy. Nobody seems to know anything except Wilson.' He gave Harley a long look. 'Pity you weren't here.'

The United States ambassador had a smug look on his face as he fronted the newspapermen.

'General Huerta,' he announced, 'sent me a message announcing the overthrow of the government and asking me to inform the rest of the diplomatic corps. This I have done. Messages have also gone to General Díaz in the Ciudadela.'

'Why, Mr Ambassador?' one of the Americans asked. 'If General Huerta was fighting General Díaz to stop him usurping power, why inform *him*?'

'To stop the fighting.' Wilson waved a hand dismissively. 'I've invited General Huerta and General Díaz to this embassy for talks to bring about a cease-fire.'

That afternoon, Huerta and Blanquet, the men who had betrayed Madero, appeared together on the balcony of the Palace to be cheered by the huge crowd which had gathered to express their relief that the fighting was over. It was difficult to see which way things were going. Supporters of the dead General Reyes seemed reluctant to see Huerta take power but, as the newsmen gathered at the American Embassy for the projected meeting between the warring factions, the Reyes supporters were also there, cynical and hard-faced, to see what they could get out of the deal. Behind them among the politicians and army men, Harley noticed Féderico Toral. He nodded at Harley, smiling broadly as if certain of the security of his position.

The two battling generals appeared in civilian evening dress, escorted by cars carrying American flags. As Díaz entered the reception room the American ambassador led the clapping. Like all the other diplomats he was in evening dress, so that the occasion seemed less like the death of a democracy than the celebration of a victory.

Studying the line of men in immaculate clothes lining up with the American ambassador for an official photograph in front of Johnny Cox and other cameramen, Harley was appalled at the combined treachery and heartlessness they had shown. They all – Toral included – had changed sides so often it was dazzling. Between them, these men, concerned only with ambition and the acquisition of power and the wealth that came from hand-outs and corruption, had caused the streets and lanes of Mexico to flow with the blood of hundreds of innocent people. The whole land was bathed in blood and they had allowed it, caused it even, for their own ends. Then he remembered that his own father had been a general in this same army, probably knew these men, and that he had had to flee the country for his part in the rising against Porfirio Díaz. Had he, too, been involved in such cruel perfidy? Was it in his own character waiting to come out? It was an uncomfortable heritage to live with.

Unable to work out how it was that both sides seemed to have won, the foreign diplomats looked bewildered but followed Wilson's lead. The newsmen were regarding the whole affair with a great deal of cynicism, but it wasn't *their* business and there was champagne to launch whatever agreement was made. When the interested parties reappeared from the conference table it was to announce that peace had been agreed and that the agreement was to be known as the Compact of the Ciudadela.

'More like – ' Johnny Cox had been busy at the champagne table and his voice was loud ' – the Compact of the American Embassy.'

Huerta was to become provisional president but Díaz was free to pursue his candidacy for president, while the army had united for the salvation of the country.

'A wicked despotism has fallen,' Wilson beamed.

Johnny Cox's voice came again, loud and aggressive. 'Who's running this goddam country? Madero? Huerta? Díaz? Or Ambassador Wilson? I reckon the bastards were all in league with each other.'

With the cease-fire, the cable office was packed with newsmen all clamouring for their despatches to be sent off first. Leaving Tamsy to see his own safely away, Harley headed for Angelica's house. Men were working outside, replacing tiles and clearing up debris, and a man in overalls was bricking up a hole in the wall. Angelica looked strained and tired as she opened the door.

'I haven't got any goddam servants,' she said. 'They're scared to come back. What's happening?'

He told her what he knew. 'Madero's under guard at the National Palace. We're waiting now for the announcement of Huerta's cabinet.' He gave her the names. 'Madero's cabinet will resign. All except the Foreign Minister who's next after the vice-president in succession to Madero. He's not being forced, so that when Madero and his vice-president resign, he'll succeed to the presidency, appoint Huerta Minister of the Interior and resign himself. Huerta, who'll then be next in line, will become provisional president. All very constitutional. Madero goes into exile.'

Like every other newsman in Mexico City, Harley was red-eyed with lack of sleep. But things were happening so fast that none of them dared disappear from the centre of the whirlwind. Within twenty-four hours there had been three presidents and they all knew it wasn't finished yet.

They hung round the National Palace all night, trying to find out what arrangements had been made for the departure of Madero and his vice-president. A special train for Veracruz was waiting in the Buenavista Station with their wives and families on board, but in the early hours of the morning an announcement was made that the departure order had been cancelled because Huerta had learned that the commander of the Veracruz garrison was a Madero supporter who planned to free him as soon as he arrived.

Huerta appeared to be making sure of his position. He had already removed those officers in Veracruz who had opposed Felix Díaz's rising and replaced them with his own men; it seemed to indicate that he had more ominous reasons for halting the exodus to the coast.

Tamsy was deeply suspicious for another reason. 'When I took the Stutz to the Garaje Holquín for gas,' he said, 'there were a coupla army officers there hirin' cars. I got their names. I saw the paper they signed. Captain Cardenas and Lieutenant Pimiento. They hired 'em for the 22nd. Why, Boss?'

'Why not, Tamsy?'

'Boss – ' Tamsy's hard-bitten face was heavy with suspicion ' – when a mobster wants to get rid of a guy, he don't use his own auto. He steals one or hires one.'

Convinced that Huerta's promises were worthless, they waited for the next tragic development. When dawn came, Harley was dozing in a chair in Knowles' office. As the telephone rang, Knowles snatched it up.

'What!' he yelled. 'When?'

Slamming down the telephone, he reached for his coat. 'Gustavo Madero's been murdered,' he said. 'His body's been found on the outskirts of the city. He's been shot.'

It was obvious that another round of treachery was starting. When they arrived at the Cuidadela where the murder was said to have taken place, a crowd of newsmen was already there baying for information. Wild rumours were on the streets. Gustavo had been tortured. Officers at the Ciudadela had emptied their revolvers into him. He had been lynched in the courtyard by drunken soldiers. He had made a break for freedom and, according to the ley fuga, had been shot down. A statement told them nothing.

For three whole days, the newsmen, all of them concerned now for the safety of Gustavo's brother, the ex-president, kept the death watch at the Palace, haunting the cafés round the Zócalo, taking it in turns to watch events, agreeing even to share information. Aware of the date that Tamsy had heard mentioned at the Garaje Holquín, Harley was waiting with the group at the Palace late in the evening when he saw the great doors swing open and two cars emerge.

'Boss!' Tamsy's voice by his ear was urgent and excited. 'Those are the cars from the Garaje Holquín. They got Holquín drivers behind the wheels.'

Pressing forward, Harley was just able to make out Madero's face through the window, surrounded by a heavy guard of soldiers.

'It's the president!' one of the waiting American journalists yelled. 'And that's the vice-president in the second car! What the hell's going on?'

They began to run after the cars at once but they were quickly outdistanced and, as the cars swung out of the Zócalo and vanished from sight, they stood huddled together for a moment, then the group splintered as some rushed off to find a telephone, others to find cars or taxis. As they vanished, Tamsy Flood appeared alongside Harley with the Stutz.

'I thought you might need me. The guys commanding the escort in those cars are the guys who hired 'em – Cardenas and Pimiento.'

It was some time before they picked up the two cars again. They were moving slowly but steadily towards the north of the city, keeping off the main boulevards and making turns as if to shake off anyone who might try to follow.

'They're heading for the penitentiary,' Tamsy said.

As they neared the prison, a late-night string of carts coming from the north with garden produce for the city markets got in their way and they lost sight of the two hired cars. Tamsy was almost jumping in his seat with impatience as Harley leapt from the Stutz and grabbed the head of the mule pulling one of the carts. The driver started to shriek abuse but Harley dragged the animal's head round until its hooves were clattering on the pavement and the cart was broadside on to the road, halting the whole convoy so that Tamsy could squeeze past.

There was no sign of the other cars now and Tamsy was pounding the steering wheel with fury. As they braked to a stop near the prison, the commander of the guard moved forward, waving them away.

'Two cars,' Harley said. 'Have they gone in?'

'No cars have entered here, señor?' the officer said. 'And I must ask you to leave.'

'Why? Are you expecting them?'

'We're expecting nothing.'

He was obviously agitated and Harley was immediately suspicious. He jerked a hand. 'We'll wait over there, Tamsy.' he said. 'Something's obviously brewing.'

As Tamsy slowly moved the Stutz from the prison gates, there was a flurry of shots from the streets behind the prison and Harley swung round on the Mexican.

'What's that?'

The officer shrugged. 'I heard nothing, señor.'

'You must be deaf. *I* heard shooting.'

The officer's face was blank and stony. 'Not here, señor. We have no trouble here. It would never be permitted near the prison. Perhaps someone fooling about at the other side.

Some family quarrel. They often occur. This isn't the most salubrious part of the city.'

Followed by Tamsy, Harley headed for the dark streets beyond the high walls and as he made his way along the rear face of the prison he saw the two hired cars standing in the road among a group of men. Immediately, a policeman ran towards him, trying to push him away. A representative of the *New York World*, who had managed to grab a taxi, had joined them now and as they demanded to know what had happened an officer appeared.

'It's that guy, Pimiento,' Tamsy said. 'That's Cardenas by the cars.'

Pimiento halted in front of them, a slim hard-faced young man with a revolver in his hand. He gestured with the weapon. 'There's nothing here for you,' he snapped.

'What was the shooting?' Harley gestured at the group near the cars. 'And what's happening over there?'

Pimiento turned to glance behind him. 'There was a fight,' he said.

'What sort of fight?'

'They tried to rescue him. Madero's dead. He was killed. In the shooting. The vice-president too.'

Harley stared about him. There was no sign of any attackers. No wounded. No bodies lying at the street ends where he might have expected them. 'Who were they?' he demanded. 'The people who set up the rescue?'

Pimiento gestured. 'We don't know.'

'Can we go and look?'

Pimiento hesitated, glancing over his shoulder at the group round the cars as if for orders. In the end, Harley and the American pushed past. Pimiento made no attempt to stop them.

'Very well,' he said. 'It's all over now anyway.'

As they drew nearer the cars they saw two bodies lying on the ground. Then three men lifted one of them to place it inside the nearest vehicle.

'That's the vice-president,' the American newspaperman said.

Cardenas, the officer with the group, swung round. 'Who're you?'

They told him and he glanced at Pimiento, then repeated

the story. 'We were taking them to the prison,' he said, 'when we heard shots. I decided it must be an attempt to rescue the prisoners and ordered fire to be returned. The criminal Madero must have known an attempt would be made because he jumped up with his companion and started to run.'

'Surrounded by guards?'

Cardenas was not put off. 'In the confusion they managed to break clear. I think they must have run into the line of fire. The attackers finally fled and it was then we found them lying on the ground.'

'Where?'

Cardenas pointed. 'They didn't get far. We've just brought the bodies back.'

'Conveniently not merely wounded,' the American said grimly to Harley. 'But both goddam good and dead.'

Harley glanced at the second body as it was lifted. It was possible to recognize Madero only by his beard. Blood flowing from his mouth covered his face but his dead eyes were wide open and staring, and his hair was singed.

'Why didn't the rescuers put up a road block?' he asked. 'A quick rush would have rescued them before you could do a thing.'

Cardenas shrugged. 'They probably didn't have time.'

'And why fire on cars containing men they wanted to rescue? And why did they leap out and run? They must have been bent on suicide.'

Cardenas' face was expressionless. 'Who knows how a deposed president thinks?' he said.

'And,' Harley asked finally, 'why here?'

Cardenas' imperturbability slipped at last. 'Here?' he asked warily, as if afraid of something that hadn't occurred to him.

'Why *behind* the prison? If you were taking them to the prison what were you doing here?'

Cardenas frowned but he recovered. 'We approached from the north. We took a roundabout route from the palace because we were afraid just such an attempt might be made.'

'You went up the Avenida Argentina,' Harley snapped. 'And turned off into Granaditos and the Avenida del Trabajo. I followed you.'

Cardenas glanced at Pimiento but offered no explanation.

'And it's strange, isn't it, that there were no other casualties?'

Cardenas shrugged. 'That's the way it is, señor. Sometimes everybody is hurt. Sometimes only one or two.'

Harley's eyes were cold as the men of the escort slammed the car doors. 'Madero was shot in the back of the head,' he grated. 'At close range.'

'There'll be an enquiry,' Cardenas promised. 'The truth will emerge.'

He climbed with Pimiento into the cars. Soldiers cranked the engines and they began to move away, leaving a puff of blue smoke in the air. As they vanished Tamsy stepped from the shadows.

'Tell that to the Marines,' he said. 'The truth never emerges here.'

8

Madero had ruled for no more than fifteen months – fighting all the time against the army, established business interests, the American ambassador, and a press enjoying the very freedom he had given it.

Wild rumours were flying about the city. One version of his death was that he and his vice-president had been shot inside the palace and their bodies frogmarched to the cars which had been waiting in the patio, and that outside the prison a sham battle had taken place and the cars riddled with bullets.

Harley had been back with the *New York World* man to the prison and, watched all the time by an officer from the gateway, they had checked the surrounding buildings for bullet splashes on the plaster. Out of the line of the firing in the ten days battle between the Ciudadela and the Palace, they were unmarked and there was no sign of blood on the spot where Madero was supposed to have fallen in his rush for safety.

There was also no sign of the promised investigation and, as the autopsy on the bodies showed that Madero had been killed by a bullet to the brain, the rumours began to involve Huerta. It was impossible to pin anything on him but he had alienated many people in the city for not protecting Madero, and the hostile view of the little man began subtly to change so that once more, he was regarded as a martyred saint by those who not long before had been reviling him for his weakness.

By this time also Harley had been to the garage where the cars that had carried Madero and his vice-president to their deaths had been hired.

'Who paid for them?' Harley demanded.

The garage proprietor looked nervous. 'A friend of General Díaz put down the money,' he said.

'Who was it?'

'I don't know.'

'But Captain Cardenas conducted the transaction?'

'*Major* Cardenas, señor. He's been promoted.'

'For failing to keep Madero alive?'

The chauffeurs who had driven the cars had disappeared completely and their families were saying nothing, eyeing the newspapermen with large frightened eyes. Eventually, they learned that the two men had been shipped to Europe with enough funds to keep them out of Mexico for a long time.

The American ambassador was dismissing the murders as being without government knowledge but the press wasn't as easily convinced and Sproat cabled a demand for the outline for a leader. Harley found himself deeply affected by what he was writing and could only put it down to his Mexican blood crying out for justice.

Somehow his despatch fell into the hands of Ambassador Wilson and within twenty-four hours a sharp note arrived from him suggesting Harley was not doing his job properly and needed to have things in Mexico carefully explained. As he returned from Knowles' office to his flat, Harley's spirits were low.

Then he became aware of a man moving behind him and realized it was the policeman, Alemán. As he opened the door to his apartment, he half-expected the detective to follow him, but he didn't, and to his surprise Angelica was inside, waiting for him.

'The caretaker let me in,' she said. 'I had to come. That detective's been watching me.'

Harley smiled. 'He's been watching me, too.'

'He had one of the pamphlets. He wanted to know if I'd ever seen one before. I'd like to stay, Harley. In your apartment. I'll be no trouble. I'll keep out of the way, I promise.'

She was nervous but, despite her need, there was no sign

of warmth in her manner, no repeat of what she had shown only a few nights before. She even seemed to resent the fact that she needed his help, to be struggling as usual to maintain her independence.

'Help yourself,' he said. 'The place's yours. You know it is.'

He gave her a key and offered her a drink but she seemed angry at his casual attitude, as if she'd expected more.

'I'll go if you prefer,' she snapped. 'I know you couldn't care less.'

Harley sighed. Despite her hotheadedness, despite their bickering and their everlasting disagreements, a surprising rapport – fragile though it was and always likely to founder on her quick temper – had sprung up between them. He was deeply involved with her, her worries had become his worries, and he was ready to shoulder her problems. But at that moment he was tired. He felt a hundred years old, dispirited and in no mood to allow himself to be dragged into one of the interminable arguments about principle and duty that she loved so much. But he was also in no mood to quarrel. 'I could never be indifferent to you, Angelica,' he said with sincerity. 'Never.'

She stared at him strangely, struggling to control her emotions, then, as he turned to pour the drinks, he heard the door slam and found that she had gone.

The murdered men were buried the following day. Only the nearest relatives were permitted to attend. They were dressed in deepest black, something which in Mexico seemed blacker than anywhere else in the world. Immediately afterwards, Madero's widow left with members of her family for Cuba.

The pressmen gathered in a nearby café. As they sipped their drinks, Harley noticed Alemán had entered and was standing at the bar. When he left with Knowles, the detective turned and followed them outside.

He stayed at Knowles' apartment for some time and it was dark as he walked home. He felt depressed and the dingy streets didn't help. Many of the street lights had been knocked out in the recent shelling and people were still keeping their shutters closed for safety so that the pavements were deep in shadow.

There was a wind that wailed down the passages between the houses, and stirred the paper in the gutters. As he crossed the road to his apartment, he noticed a car following him. It was a big roadster and its lights were off as it cruised silently towards him, quickly closing the gap between them.

The driver must have caught the hasty glance he flung in his direction because the headlights came on in a yellow glare and he heard the engine roar. The beam swept across the damaged walls, momentarily catching the glowing eyes of a cat, then, as it fixed on him, he started to run.

The roaring increased to a thunder, drowning the sound of his heels on the pavement. Gasping, he flung himself into one of the dark cheerless passages, even as the screaming vehicle swerved and bounced with twanging springs on the pavement. There was a clang and the screech of metal, and sparks as a mudguard scraped the brickwork, and he was conscious of light flooding down the passage. Then the engine subsided and he heard a door slam.

Hearing voices, he began to run down the passage until he found himself in a garden wrecked during the shelling. A tree lay lopsided and a wall had been brought down. Scrambling over the broken brickwork, he found his way into the next garden and from there through the ruins of a burned-out house into a nearby street. As he emerged, he could still hear voices behind him but he seemed to have thrown his pursuers off and he started to run again.

When he reached his apartment, he saw a car waiting outside and for a moment thought that they had got ahead of him. Then he realized it was Johnny Cox, sitting in the dark smoking. He smelled of whisky and had been waiting for Harley for some time. In the darkened street he didn't notice that the knee of Harley's trousers was torn and that his hands were black from the sooty walls of the burned-out house.

'I've just come from taking pictures of Huerta leaving the National Palace,' he announced. 'Top hat and evening dress with the president's ribbon across his chest. Blanquet was with him – all gold lace and bicorne hat. The bastards looked set for a thousand years.' He lit a cigarette. 'I'm looking for Angelica. I heard she came here because she was scared.'

Harley could only assume she had but he gave nothing

away. 'Obviously she changed her mind,' he said. 'She's not here.'

'I'll come in for a nightcap.'

'Not tonight, Johnny. I'm going to bed.'

'Just one, Harl'. I'm leaving soon. Toral's after me for the cartoons. He's got a job in the government. Huerta's after me, too, I guess. Even Ambassador Wilson. He heard what I said about him at the reception. He's told me I'll get no further help from him and that I'd better quit. I guess I'll go back to Los Angeles.'

'Again?'

Cox grinned. 'Well, I might not make it that far. I thought Angelica might go with me. I tried to persuade her some time ago. She wouldn't. I guess she needs a shove. You sure I can't come in?'

Harley waited until the car drew away before he took out his key. Angelica was waiting behind the door. The place was in semi-darkness and as he appeared she jumped to her feet. She had a pistol in her hand.

'Who was that you were talking to?' she demanded.

'Johnny Cox. He thought you were here. I told him you weren't.'

She was silent for a second. 'He'll not believe you.'

'No. I don't think he will.' He indicated the pistol. 'What's this? I didn't think you hated me that much.'

She gave a helpless sort of gesture. 'That detective came again. Alemán. I thought I'd better stay here after all. They arrested those men who printed the pamphlets. They've been shot.' Tears came to her eyes and there was an agonized expression on her face. 'I didn't intend that.'

Harley shrugged. 'It's something you've got to live with, Angelica.'

'Nobody knew about the duplicating machine but me.'

'*I* knew, Angelica. Probably some of those women you had in the house knew, too.'

'They'd never say anything.'

'Faithful Fred? Was it him?'

'He wouldn't do that to me.'

'Mexicans are different, Angelica.' His mind was on the treacherous men he'd seen in the National Palace and the thought he had had about his own father, even about himself. 'You said so once yourself. Perhaps he prefers you out of the way.'

She was still pointing the pistol towards him and he gently took it from her.

'What'll I do, Harley?'

She looked so wretched, all his anger against her disappeared and he put his arms round her. 'I think you ought to disappear, Angelica. There's a feeling of anti-Americanism here since Wilson refused to save Madero's life. Until it blows over I think you'd better go to El Paso where they can't touch you.'

'They're watching the stations.'

'We'll find a way round that.'

'What about you?'

'I'm finished here, too. I suspect, in fact, that if I don't go soon, someone will probably find an opportunity to shoot me.'

For the first time she noticed the state of his clothes and hands, and her misery was forgotten in her anxiety for him. 'What happened?'

He told her and she stared at him in horror. 'Why, Harley? For God's sake, why?'

He shrugged. 'Because I knew of Huerta's meeting with Díaz's agent at the Globo. And because I was on the spot when Madero was murdered. Tamsy and I and the *New York World* man. Perhaps I showed I guessed too much. I've been followed ever since. One of these days I shall have an accident while cleaning a gun or be knocked down by an automobile.' He managed a smile. 'I could, of course, also be arrested and shot under the ley fuga while trying to escape. It's not hard to die in Mexico.'

Suddenly she was all concern. 'Harley, is it my fault?'

He shook his head. 'Not for a minute, Angelica. I got too close to the facts, that's all.'

'Will you be writing it all up, Harley? Will you tell what happened?'

'That's my job.'

'The truth? All of it?' She seemed to be recovering her courage and her words came more briskly. 'People should be told what happened.'

'Angelica!' Harley's voice was sharp and angry. 'For God's sake, stop organizing me!'

She seemed startled that he had turned on her. 'Okay, Harley,' she said meekly. 'I guess you're right.' She was silent for a moment, staring at her feet, then her head lifted.

'There's one who won't turn his back on Madero,'she said.

Harley laughed, caught as he always was by her never-failing enthusiasm. 'Villa?'

The old grin came, responding to his laugh. It transformed her. 'Who else?' she said. 'He's in El Paso, too. Will you be coming?'

Harley shrugged. 'Your ambassador has doubtless started the wheels turning already to have me made persona non grata.'

'He's not my ambassador! I'm Mexican!'

'Angelica.' Harley held her hands gently. 'Don't kid yourself. You're American. A good, big-hearted, God-fearing compassionate Irish-American who finds it hard to believe there's so much evil in the world. Your name wasn't even Ojarra. It was O'Hara.'

'Whatever it was – ' the words were a cry of unhappiness ' – I'm doing no goddam good here!'

When Tamsy appeared he was in a cheerful mood and had been in a bar celebrating the fact that he would no longer be spending his days driving between Mexico City and Querétaro.

'That train you put the despatches on, Tamsy,' Harley said. 'Better get the Stutz ready. We're going to meet it.'

Tamsy jaw dropped. 'I thought all that was finished.'

'We have a passenger to put aboard.'

'Who, Boss?'

'Dona Angelica. Me, too.' Harley explained what had happened. 'Perhaps even you, Tamsy. You were there when they shot Madero.'

Tamsy chewed his cigar. 'Okay, Boss. It don't matter none. I can sell the Stutz in Querétaro. I've had an offer.

All through that day they watched the street outside the apartment. A big roadster was waiting under the trees that surrounded a small park.

'They'll pick us up the minute we try to leave,' Angelica said.

Late in the afternoon, Angelica's Indian maid turned up. She had not been hurt in the fighting after all, only afraid to move from her home. As he let her in Harley noticed the car still waiting under the trees. While Angelica was questioning the girl, he drew Tamsy to one side.

'Can you have the Stutz ready at the back of the house after dark, Tamsy?' he asked.

'Sure can, Boss. Gassed up and everythin'.'

Reaching for the telephone, Harley contacted Knowles. As he outlined his idea, Knowles sounded startled but willing to help and, soon after dark, he arrived in a taxi which he kept waiting outside in the street as he entered. The startled maid, clutching a suitcase full of clothing and a fistful of money, and dressed in Angelica's familiar green dress, coat and hat, was waiting in the hall. As Knowles appeared, Angelica hugged her.

'Dona Angelica,' the girl wailed, 'I can't take all your fine clothes!'

'Yes, you can. They're a gift to you. Think how smart you'll look when you go to Mass on Sunday. And don't worry. No one can harm you. You're only being taken home in a taxi because the streets are dark.'

'Our Lady of Guadalupe go with you.' The girl could hardly speak through her tears.

As she hurried out and climbed into the taxi, Harley, watching from the window, saw hurried movement round the roadster down the road. As the taxi drove off, the watching men climbed into it and followed slowly, the headlights dimmed.

'Right,' Harley said. 'Come on, Angelica. Time to go.'

As the big roadster disappeared, the Stutz appeared, creeping quietly round the corner to roll to a stop in front of the house. Tamsy had a revolver that looked as big as a howitzer stuck in his belt.

With Angelica crouching under a blanket in the rear seat, they got away from the city without being stopped. For a while a large car followed them but eventually it swung off the road. There was no further sign of pursuit and Angelica came out of her hiding place, putting on a large hat with a veil and a shawl which she kept up to her face.

As they halted near Tepozotlán at dawn, a strong wind was coming down off the northern plains and the Stutz was filled with gritty dust. At San Juan del Rio, just to the south of Querétaro, a man was waiting with a roll of notes to take the Stutz from Tamsy; and nobody questioned them as they climbed aboard the northbound train out of the sweeping dust clouds and headed for the private compartment Tamsy had reserved. To Harley's surprise, Johnny Cox was in the restaurant car drinking a beer. He looked drunk.

'The cartoons,' he said. 'The police came. I got out in a rush. Is Angelica with you?'

'Why should she be?'

'Thought mebbe she might suddenly have decided to up and leave. Scared mebbe.'

He left the train at Juárez with nothing more than a wave of the hand. 'See you,' he said to Harley. He didn't look back.

They took a cab over the International Bridge and directed it to Angelica's house. As Harley left, Angelica kissed him.

'Goodbye, Harley Marquis,' she said. 'You're a good man. What are you going to do now?'

'I'm going to find Villa.'

'I thought you were finished with Mexico.'

He smiled. 'I find I'm not as finished as I thought I was.'

Villa had changed his quarters for safety because he was under constant surveillance. He had moved deeper into Little Chihuahua, where he had found a room, bare, low-ceilinged and square, with a damp dirt floor. A kerosene lamp on a pile of saddles and boxes gave the only light there was. The fly screen at the window was wadded with a pair of old socks. Villa had a copy of the *El Paso Times* and had clearly heard of the events in Mexico City because his face was puffed and his eyes were red with weeping. Jauregui was with him, his face anxious.

'He was too forgiving,' Villa said wildly. 'He didn't heed what I had to say because I was stupid and dirty and poor, and when he made me a captain I put on too many airs and graces. He must have laughed at me when I wasn't looking.'

The blame, he felt, was his, not Madero's. 'It's impossible that men could be so cruel! I have shed the bitterest tears of my life! What happened to all the things we did? How did they do it, Inglés?'

Harley told him what he knew and Villa hammered with his fist in savage frustration against the wall until there was blood on his knuckles. 'I warned him there were vultures!' he said. 'But they won't have it all their own way! There's a storm blowing up in Sonora and Coahuila. Carranza's already come out against Huerta. He's been joined by Alvaro Obregón. I don't know him but they say he's good.' He flailed the air with his powerful arms. 'Those Judases in the capital don't know what they've stirred up! We beat them once! Those perfumed chocolateros were no match for us! The people – *our* people, mi amigo, yours and mine! – beat them at their own game because, while *they* were thinking of what they were going to get out of it, the people thought only of freedom! Of Mexico for Mexicans, of the right to possess their own strip of land. They fought with their hearts! Now it's all got to be done all over again! I'm going back!'

'How, mi jefe?' Jauregui asked. 'There are always men watching us. And you've got no army.'

Villa looked up. There was a difference in him. Living with the Americans, he had learned a lot. He was still a peasant, crude and often ignorant, but he had become more worldly-wise.

'I can raise an army,' he said. 'I can raise it out of the soil. Out of the mountains and the deserts. They know me here in the north. I can raise men from Chihuahua and Durango. From Zacatecas and round San Luís Potosí. The políticos took my gente away from me but I can go back to their roots. And this time I'll trust nobody." He looked at Harley. 'I've been in touch with Ochoa, Saavedra, Silva, Avila, Tómas Urbana. I tried Governor González who first recruited me but he's been replaced by one of Huerta's bootlickers. We just need a little time. We have weapons. Not many yet, but we shall get them as we always got them. From the enemy. When you want eggs you go to the hen house.'

During the next few days, Harley made no attempt to catch the train north for New York and a ship to England. In his heart of hearts, he realized, he didn't fancy facing Sproat and he knew that Isobel would be waiting for him, all smiles, convinced he had returned because of her. It was something he found he could not face and he took to haunting the Mexican area of the city with its shabby dusty streets, its smell a mixture of urine, horse dung and frying food. By this time it was as familiar to him as his own breathing. And he knew things were stirring and the need to be part of them stirred in him, too.

Messages had gone across the border to Villa's old comrades ordering meat to be dried and maize to be ground. Rifles and ammunition, hidden when Madero had demobilized his guerillas, were to be brought from their hiding places in the roofs and under the floors. But Harley deliberately ignored Villa because there were always men watching and he had heard that German agents, still promising to back Villa to embarrass the Americans with another revolution, had been seeing him again. They offered troops, money, armaments and propaganda, in return – when Villa was successful – for ports where German ships and submarines could put in. Where the stories came from nobody knew, but it was clear they were common knowledge because Johnny Cox turned up again, his grin as wide as ever, his face as innocent as a choirboy's.

'They tell me this is where the action's gonna be,' he said. 'North Mexico.' His grin widened. 'I also heard Angelica's around.'

The following day, the *El Paso Times* carried the news of a new outrage. Aware that Chihuahua would always be a trouble spot for his régime, Huerta had arrested Abraham González, Villa's old mentor, and while being transferred by train to prison, he had been thrown under the wheels and his remains buried alongside the track.

'If nothing else,' Cox said, 'that'll bring Villa out.'

It did. A few nights later, a telephone call arrived at Harley's hotel. The voice was quiet but it sounded like Jauregui's.

'Tonight,' it said. "The patch of sand in the Río Grande to the west of the town. It's known as Yselta. It divides the river into two fords.'

The night was moonless and there was mist along the

water's edge. Waiting in the trees, Harley held his horse by the bridle, his hand over its nose to discourage it from snorting. Tamsy was with him, grumbling softly to himself, his eyes watchful.

'I'd rather be in the Stutz,' he kept saying. 'I'm better behind the wheel of an automobile than in the saddle.'

As they talked they heard the soft thud of hooves in the dust and a horseman appeared through the darkness. It was Jauregui.

'Señor Maŕquez? Follow me.'

Villa was standing under a little group of eucalyptus trees with two other men. His face was grim.

'You have your story, compadre,' he growled. 'Tell the world I'm taking the field against Madero's murderers. The American agents think I'm still in El Paso.' He gestured at the two shadowy figures behind him. 'What do you think of my army?'

'It's not a very big one, Don Pancho.'

'I have five more.' As Villa whistled softly more horses appeared from the darkness. 'It's bigger now, amigo,' he said. 'Nine of us. With nine horses – "borrowed" from a hire stable in El Paso, to be paid for when I've raised the money. We can commandeer more as we find them. We also have nine rifles, five hundred rounds of ammunition, two pounds of coffee, two of sugar, one of salt, a pair of wire cutters, and a war chest of thirty-five pesos and a silver watch.'

'It's not much, Don Pancho.'

'It will soon increase.' Villa gestured. 'Over there's Terrazas land and Don Luís Terrazas supported Díaz and set Orozco against Madero. His cattle sell well north of the border and before Madero recruited me I was good at rustling. In a fortnight the war chest will be thirty-five thousand pesos and it'll go to pay for the Winchester 30-30s I've ordered.' He gave Harley an affectionate abrazo. 'I'll see you in Mexico City, mi amigo.'

Swinging to the saddle, he raised his arm and, turning his horse, splashed into the shallows, moving chest-high towards the opposite shore. His tiny army followed, the spray they threw up glinting faintly in the darkness. At the other side, they grouped together, dim figures in the shadows, then, as they reached Mexican soil, they broke into a racing gallop and disappeared from sight.

For a long time Harley sat in the saddle, busy with his thoughts, aware that he was more deeply involved with Mexico than he had planned, even than he ought to be.

'He's gone!'

The voice made him swing round. Angelica had appeared from the trees, leading a horse.

'What are you doing here?'

'Same as you. Those men of Villa's have girl friends and they talked."

Harley was silent for a moment. 'I'm going with him,' he said.

'I thought you had to go back to England.'

Harley remembered Sproat's words – 'You're too much of a Mexican' – and he knew he was.

'He's going to go through it all again,' he said. 'I'm going with him.'

'To tell the world why?'

He smiled. 'It might be more than that. I've been a soldier, too.'

She was still with him as he moved towards the river.

"Go back, Angelica," he said.

'No.' She was smiling and he was aware of her warm approval for what he was doing. 'Villa's just begun his personal invasion of Mexico. You're going with him. I'm coming with *you*.'

MAX HENNESSY is the pseudonym of John Harris, author of many acclaimed historical novels including *The Sea Shall Not Have Them* and *Covenant with Death*. Ex-newspaperman, ex-sailor, ex-airman, ex-travel courier, ex-history teacher, he went to sea in the Merchant Navy before the war and during the war served with two air forces and two navies. He returned to newspapers as a cartoonist after the war, but has been a full-time writer for over thirty years. He lives by the sea and kept up his interest in flying until his late fifties. He has recently been on an extended tour of Mexico researching into the history of the Revolution.